John Doran

## In an about Drury Lane

and other papers, reprinted from the pages of the 'Temple bar' magazine - Vol. 1

John Doran

**In an about Drury Lane**
*and other papers, reprinted from the pages of the 'Temple bar' magazine - Vol. 1*

ISBN/EAN: 9783337250744

Printed in Europe, USA, Canada, Australia, Japan

Cover: Foto ©Andreas Hilbeck / pixelio.de

More available books at **www.hansebooks.com**

# DRURY LANE

VOL. I

LONDON: PRINTED BY
SPOTTISWOODE AND CO., NEW-STREET SQUARE
AND PARLIAMENT STREET

# IN AND ABOUT

# DRURY LANE

## *AND OTHER PAPERS*

REPRINTED FROM THE PAGES OF THE 'TEMPLE BAR' MAGAZINE

BY

## D<sup>R</sup> DORAN

AUTHOR OF 'TABLE TRAITS AND SOMETHING ON THEM' 'JACOBITE LONDON'
'QUEENS OF ENGLAND OF THE HOUSE OF HANOVER'

IN TWO VOLUMES

VOL. I.

LONDON

RICHARD BENTLEY & SON, NEW BURLINGTON STREET

Publishers in Ordinary to Her Majesty the Queen

1881

# PREFATORY REMARKS.

THE REPUBLICATION of papers which have originally appeared in a Magazine frequently requires justification.

In the present instance this justification, it is thought, may be found in the special knowledge which Dr. DORAN had of all matters pertaining to the stage; in his intimacy with the literature which treats of manners and customs, English and foreign; and in his memory, which retained and retailed a great amount of anecdote, told with a sprightly wit.

These volumes, reprinted with one or two exceptions from the pages of the 'Temple Bar' Magazine, will, it is believed, be found to contain many good stories, and much information unostentatiously conveyed. It is hoped, therefore, that the public will endorse the opinion of the writer of this Preface, and consider that the plea of justification has been made out.

G. B.

# CONTENTS

OF

## THE FIRST VOLUME.

In the afternoon of 'Boxing-day,' 1865, I had to pass through Drury Lane, and some of the worst of the 'slums' which find vent therein. There was a general movement in the place, and the effect was not savoury. There was a going to-and-fro of groups of people, and there was nothing picturesque in them; assemblings of children, but alas! nothing lovable in them. It was a universal holiday, yet its aspect was hideous.

Arrived at the stage-door of Drury Lane Theatre, I found my way on to the stage itself, where the last rehearsal of the pantomime, to be played for the first time that evening, was progressing.

The change from the external pandemonium to the hive of humming industry in which I then stood, was striking and singular. Outside were blasphemy and drunkenness. Inside, boundless activity, order, hard work, and cheerful hearts. There was very much to do, but every man had his especial work assigned him, every girl her allotted task. An unaccustomed person might have pronounced as mere confusion, that shifting of scenes, that forming, unforming, and reforming of groups, that unintelligible dumb show, that collecting, scattering, and gathering together of 'young ladies' in sober-coloured dresses and business-like faces, who were to be so resplendent in the evening as fairies, all gold, glitter, lustrous eyes, and virtuous intentions. There was Mr. Beverley—perhaps the greatest magician there—not only to see that nothing should mar the beauty he had created, but to take care that the colours of the costumes should not be in antagonism with the scenes before which they were to be worn. There was that Michael Angelo of pantomimic mask inventors, Mr. Keene, anxiously looking to the expressions of the masks, of which he is the prince of designers. Then, if you think those graceful and varied figures of the *ballet* as easy to invent, or to trace, as they seem, and are, at last, easily performed, you should witness the trouble taken to invent, and the patience taken to bring to perfection—the figures and the figurantes—on the part of the artistic ballet-master, Mr. Cormack. But, responsible for the good result of all, there stands Mr. Roxby, stern as Rhadamanthus, just as Aristides, inflexible as determination can make him, and good-natured as a happy child, he is one of the most efficient of stage-managers, for he is both loved and feared. No defect escapes his eye, and no well-directed zeal goes without his word of approval. Messrs. Falconer and Chatterton are meanwhile busy with a thousand details, but they wisely leave the management of the stage to their lieutenant-general, who has the honour of Old Drury at heart.

When a spectator takes his seat in front of the curtain, he is hardly aware that he is about to address himself to an entertainment, for the production of which nearly nine hundred persons—from the foremost man down to the charwoman—are constantly employed and liberally remunerated. Touching this 'remuneration,' let me here notice that I have some doubt as to the story of Quin ever receiving 50*l.* a night. By the courtesy of Mr. ——, the gentleman at the head of the Drury Lane treasury, and by the favour of the proprietors, I have looked through many of the well-kept account-books of bygone years. These, indeed, do not, at least as far as I have seen, go back to the days of Quin, but there are traces of the greater actor Garrick, who certainly never received so rich an *honorarium.* His actual income it is not easy to ascertain, as his profits as proprietor were mixed up with his salary as actor. It has often been said that Garrick was never to be met with in a tavern (always, I suppose, excepting the 'Turk's Head'), but he appears to have drawn refreshment during the Drury Lane seasons, as there is unfailing entry in his weekly account of 'the Ben Jonson's Head bill,' the total of which varies between sixteen and five-and-twenty shillings.

At Drury Lane, John Kemble does not appear to have ever received above 2*l.* a night, exclusive of his salary as a manager. Nor did his sister's salary for some years exceed that sum. When Edmund Kean raised the fallen fortunes of old Drury, he only slowly began to mend his own. From January 1814, to April 1815, during the time the house was open, Kean's salary was 3*l.* 8*s.* 8*d.* nightly. If the theatre was open every night in the week, that sum was the actor's nightly stipend, whether he performed or not. If there were only four performances weekly, as in Lent, he and all other actors were only paid for those four nights. Within the period I have named, Elliston received a higher salary than Kean, namely 5*l.* per night, or 30*l.* per week, if the house was open for six consecutive nights. The salary of Dowton and Munden, during the same period, was equal to that of Kean. They received at the rate of 3*l.* 8*s.* 8*d.* nightly, or 20*l.* weekly, if there were six performances, irrespective as to their being employed in them or not. That great actor Bannister, according to these Drury Lane account-books, at this period received 4*s.* per night less than Kean, Dowton, and Munden; while Jack Johnstone's salary was only 2*l.* 10*s.* nightly, and that was 6*s.* 8*d. less* than was paid to the handsome, rather than *good* player, Rae.

It was not till April 1815, when Kean was turning the tide of Pactolus into the treasury, that his salary was advanced to 4*l.* 3*s.* 8*d.* per night. This was still below the sum received by Elliston. Kean had run through the most brilliant part of his career, before his salary equalled that of Elliston. In 1820, it was raised to 30*l.* per week if six nights; but Elliston's stipend at that time had fallen to 20*l.*, and at the close of the season that of Kean was further raised to 40*l.* for every six nights that the house was open. That sum is occasionally entered in the books as being for ' seven days' pay,' but the meaning is manifestly ' for the acting week of six days.'

At this time Mrs. Glover was at the head of the Drury Lane actresses, and that eminent and great-hearted woman never drew from the Drury Lane treasury more than 7*l.* 13*s.* 4*d.* weekly. From these details, it will be seen that the most brilliant actors were not very brilliantly paid. The humbler yet very useful players were, of course, remunerated in proportion..

There was a Mr. Marshall who made a successful *début* on the same night with Incledon in 1790, in the ' Poor Soldier,' the sweet ballad-singer, as Dermot; Marshall, as Bagatelli. The latter soon passed to Drury Lane, where he remained till 1820. The highest salary he ever attained was 10*s.* per night; yet with this, in his prettily-furnished apartments in Crown Court, where he lived and died, Mr. Marshall presided, like a gentleman, at a hospitable table, and in entertaining his friends never exceeded his income. You might have taken him in the street for one of those enviable old gentlemen who have very nice balances at their bankers.

The difference between the actor's salaries of the last century and of this, is as great in France as in England. One of the greatest French tragedians, Lekain, earned only a couple of thousand livres, yearly, from his Paris engagement. When Gabrielli demanded 500 ducats yearly, for singing in the Imperial Theatre at St. Petersburg, this took the Czarina's breath away. 'I only pay my field-marshals at that rate,' said Catherine.

'Very well,' replied Gabrielli, 'your Majesty had better make your field-marshals sing.'

With higher salaries, all other expenses have increased. Take the mere item of advertisements, including bill-sticking and posters at railway stations, formerly, the expense of advertising never exceeded 4*l.* per week; now it is never under 100*l.* Of bill-stickers and board-carriers, upwards of one hundred are generally employed. In the early part of the last century, the proprietors of a newspaper thought it a privilege to insert theatrical announcements gratis, and proprietors of theatres forbade the insertion of their advertisements in papers not duly authorised !

Dryden **was** the first dramatic author who wrote a programme of his piece ('The **Indian** Emperor'), and distributed **it** at the playhouse door. Barton Booth, the original ' Cato,' drew 50*l.* a year for writing **out** the daily bills for the printer. **In still** earlier days, theatrical announcements were made by sound of drum. **The absence of the names of** actors in old play-books, **perhaps,** arose from a feeling which animated French actors as late **as 1789, when those of Paris** entreated the *maire* not to **compel them to have** their names in the ' Affiche,' as it might prove detrimental to their interests. Some of our earliest announcements only name the piece, and state that it will be acted by ' all the best members of the company, now in town.' There **was** a fashion, which only expired about a score or so **of years** ago, as the curtain was descending at **the close** of the five-act piece, which **was always played first, an actor stepped forward,** and **when the curtain separated him from his fel-** lows, he gave out the next evening's performance, and retired, bowing, through one of the doors which **always** then stood, with brass knockers on them, upon the stage.

The average expenses of Drury Lane Theatre

at Christmas-tide, when there are extra performances, amount to nearly 1,500*l.* per week. The rent paid is reckoned at 4,500*l.* for two hundred nights of acting, and only 5*l.* per night for all performances beyond that number. About 160*l.* must be in the house before the lessees can begin to reckon on any profit. In old times, the presence of royalty made a great difference in the receipts. On February 12, 1777, I find from the books that the 'Jealous Wife,' and 'Neck or Nothing,' were played. An entry is added that 'the king and queen were present,' and the result is registered under the form, 'receipts 245*l.* 9*s.* 6*d.*, a hundred pounds more than the previous night.'

The number of children engaged in a pantomime at Drury Lane generally exceeds two hundred. The girls are more numerous than the boys. It is a curious fact that in engaging these children the manager prefers the quiet and dull to the smart and lively. Your smart lad and girl are given to 'larking' and thinking of their own cleverness. The quiet and dull are more 'teachable,' and can be made to seem lively without flinging off discipline. These little creatures are thus kept from the streets ; many of them are sons and daughters of persons employed in the house, and their shilling a night and a good washing tells pleasantly in many a humble household, to which, on Saturday nights, they contribute their wages and clean faces. It was for a clever body of children of this sort that *benefits* were first established in France in 1747. In England they date from Elizabeth Barry, on whose behalf the first was given, by order of James the Second.

Then there are the indispensable, but not easily procured, 'ladies of the ballet.' They number about five dozen; two dozen principals, the rest in training to become so. Their salary is not so low as is generally supposed—twenty-five, and occasionally thirty shillings a week. They are 're-spectable.' I have seen three or four dozen of them together in their green-room, where they conducted themselves as 'properly' as any number of well-trained young ladies could at the most fashionable of finishing establishments.

There was a scene in the 'Sergeant's Wife' which was always played with a terrible power by Miss Kelly; and yet the audience, during the most exciting portion of the scene, saw only the back of the actress. Miss Kelly represented the wife, who, footsore and ignorant of her way, had found rude hospitality and rough sleeping quarters in a wretched hut. Unable to sleep, something tempts her to look through the interstices of the planks which divide her room from the adjoining one. While looking, she is witness of the commission of a murder. Spell-bound, she gazes on, in terror almost mute, save a few broken words.

During this incident the actress had her back turned to the audience; nevertheless, she conveyed to the enthralled house an expression of overwhelming and indescribable horror as faithfully as if they had seen it in her features or heard it in her voice. Every spectator confessed her irresistible power, but none could even guess at the secret by which she exercised it.

The mystery was, in fact, none at all. Miss Kelly's acting in this scene was wonderfully impressive, simply because she kept strictly to nature. She knew that not to the face alone belongs all power of interpretation of passion or feeling. This knowledge gave to Rich his marvellous power as Harlequin. In the old days, when harlequinades had an intelligible plot in which the spectators took interest, it was the office of Harlequin to guard the glittering lady of his love from the malice of their respective enemies. There always occurred an incident in which Columbine was carried off from her despairing lord, and it was on this occasion that Rich, all power of conveying facial expression being cut off by his mask, used to move the house to sympathy, and sometimes, it is said, to tears, by the pathos of his mute and tragic action. As he gazed up the stage at the forced departure of Columbine every limb told unmistakably that the poor fellow's heart was breaking within him. When she was restored the whole house broke forth into a thunder of exultation, as if the whole scene had been a reality.

I cannot tell how this was effected, but I *can* tell a story that is not unconnected with the terrible pantomime of suffering nature.

Some years ago an unfortunate man, who had made war against society, and had to suffer death for it in front of the old Debtors' door, Newgate, took leave of his wife and daughters not many hours before execution, in presence of the 'Reverend Ordinary,' Mr. Cotton, and a young officer in the prison, who has since attained to eminence and corresponding responsibility in the gloomy service to which he is devoted. The scene of separation was heartrending to all but the doomed man, who was calm, and even smiled once or twice, in order to cheer, if he could, the poor creatures whom he had rendered cheerless for ever. When the ordinary and the prison officer were left alone, the reverend gentleman remarked—' Well, H——, what do you think of the way in which the prisoner went through *that?*'

'Wonderfully, sir,' answered H——, 'considering the circumstances.'

'Wonderfully!' replied Mr. Cotton, 'yes; but not in your sense, my friend.'

'In what sense, then, sir?' asked H——.

'You said "wonderfully." I know very well, wherefore—because you saw him smile; and because he smiled, you thought he did not feel his condition as his wife and daughters did.'

'I confess that is the case,' said the young officer.

'Ah! H——,' exclaimed Mr. Cotton, 'you are new to this sort of thing. You looked in the man's face, and thought he was bold. I had my eye on his back, and I saw that it gave his face the lie. It showed that he was suffering mortal agony.'

H—— looked inquiringly at the chaplain, who answered the look by saying, ' Listen to me, H——. You are young. Some day you will rise to a post that will require you to sit in the dock, behind the prisoners who are tried on capital charges. On one of those occasions, you will see what is common enough—a prisoner who is saucy and defiant, and who laughs in the judge's face as he puts on the black cap, and while he is condemning him. Well, H——, if you want to know what that prisoner really feels, don't look at his face—look at his back. All along and about the spine, you will find it boiling, heaving, surging, like volcanic matter. Keep your eye upon it, H—— ; and when you see the irrepressible emotion in the back suddenly subsiding, open wide your arms, my boy, for the seemingly saucy fellow is about to tumble into them, in a dead faint. All the " sauce," Mr. H——, will be out of him at once, and perhaps for ever, unless he be exceptionally constituted.'

A little party of visitors was gathered round the narrator of this, the other day, in that dreadful room where Calcraft keeps his ' traps and things.' I had my hand on the new coil already prepared and in order for the next criminal who may deserve it; another was looking at Jack Sheppard's irons, which were never able to confine him ; and others, with a sort of unwilling gaze at things in a half-open cupboard, which looked like the furniture of a saddle-room, but which were instruments of other purposes. We all turned to the speaker, as he ceased, and inquired if his experience corroborated Mr. Cotton's description. H—— answered in the affirmative, and he went into particulars to which we listened with the air of men who were curious yet not sympathizing ; but I felt, at the same time, under the influences of the place, and of being suddenly told that I was standing where Calcraft stands on particular occasions, a hot and irrepressible motion adown the back, which satisfied me that the Cottonian theory had something in it, and that Miss Kelly, without knowing it, was acting in strict accordance with nature, when she made her back interpret to an audience all the anguish she was supposed to feel at the sorry sight on which her face was turned.

By way of parenthesis, let me add that Mr. Cotton himself was a most accomplished actor on his own unstable boards. When he grew somewhat a-weary of his labour—it was a heavy labour when Monday mornings were hanging mornings, and wretches went to the beam in leashes—when Mr. Cotton was tired of this, he thought of a good opportunity for retiring. 'I have now,' he said, 'accompanied just three hundred and sixty-five poor fellows to the gallows. That's one for every day in the year. I may retire after seeing such a round number die with *cotton in their ears.'* Whether the reverend gentleman was the author of this ingenious comparison for getting hanged, or whether he playfully adopted the phrase which was soon so popularly accepted as a definition, cannot now be determined.

While on this subject, let me notice that, with the exception of one Matthew Coppinger, a sub-altern player in the Stuart days, no English actor has ever suffered death on the scaffold. Mat's offence was not worse than the mad Prince's on Gad's Hill, and it must be confessed that one or two other gentlemen of the King's or Duke's company 'took to the road' of an evening, and perhaps deserved hanging, though the royal grace saved them. Neither in England nor France has an actor ever appeared on the scaffold under heavy weight of crime. As for taking to the highway, baronets' sons have gone that road on their fathers' horses; and society construed lightly the offences of highwaymen who met travellers face to face and set life fairly against life.  In England, Coppinger alone went to Tyburn.  In France, I can recall but two out of the many thousands of actors who have trodden its very numerous stages,—not including an occasional player who suffered for political reasons during the French Revolution.  One of the two was Barrières, a Gascon, who, after studying for the church and the law, turning dramatic poet and mathematician, and finally enlisting in the army, obtained leave of absence, and profited thereby by repairing to Paris, and appearing at the Théâtre Français, in 1729, as Mithridate.  His Gascon extravagance and eccentricity caused at first much amusement, but he speedily established himself as an excellent general actor, and forgot all about his military leave of absence.  Not so his colonel, who had no difficulty in laying his hand on the Gascon recruit, who was playing in his own name in Paris, and under authority of a furlough, the period of which he had probably exceeded—the document itself he had unfortunately lost.  Barrières was tried, condemned, and shot, in spite of all the endeavours made to save him.

Sixty years later it went as hardly with Bordier, an actor of the Variétés, of whom I have heard old French players speak with great regard and admiration.  He was on a provincial tour, when he talked so plainly at *tables d'hôte* of the misery of the times and the prospects of the poor, that he was seized and tried at Rouen under a charge of fomenting insurrection in order to lower the price of corn.   Just before his seizure he had played the principal part (L'Olive) in 'Trick against Trick' (*Ruses contre Ruses*), in which he had to exclaim gaily : 'You will see that to settle this affair, I shall have to be hanged !'   And Bordier *was* hanged, unjustly, at Rouen.   He suffered with dignity, and a touch of stage humour.   He had been used to play in Pompigny's 'Prince turned Sweep' (*Ramoneur Prince*)—a piece in which Sloman used to keep the Coburg audience in a roar of delight.   In the course of the piece, standing at the foot of a ladder, and doubtful as to whether he should ascend or not, he had to say : 'Shall I go up or not ?'   So, when he came to the foot of the lofty ladder leaning against the gigantic gallows in the market-place at Rouen, Bordier turned with a sad smile to the hangman and said : 'Shall I go up or not ?'   The hangman smiled too, but pointed the way that Bordier should go ; and the wits of Rouen were soon singing of him in the spirit of the wits of Covent Garden singing of Coppinger :

> Mat did not go dead, like a sluggard to bed,
> But boldly, in his shoes, died of a noose
> That he found under Tyburn tree.

To return to more general statistics, it may be stated that, in busy times, four dozen persons are engaged in perfecting the wardrobes of the ladies and gentlemen. Only to attire these and the children, forty-five dressers are required; and the various *coiffures* you behold have busily employed half a dozen hairdressers. If it should occur to you that you are sitting over or near a gasometer, you may find confidence in knowing that it is being watched by seventeen gasmen; and that even the young ladies who glitter and look so happy as they float in the air in transformation scenes, could not be roasted alive, provided they are released in time from the iron rods to which they are bound. These ineffably exquisite nymphs, however, suffer more or less from the trials they have to undergo for our amusement. Seldom a night passes without one or two of them fainting; and I remember, on once assisting several of them to alight, as they neared the ground, and they were screened from the public gaze, that their hands were cold and clammy, like clay. The blood had left the surface and rushed to the heart, and the spangled nymphs who seemed to rule destiny and the elements, were under a nervous tremor; but, almost as soon as they had touched the ground, they shook their spangles, laughed their light laugh, and tripped away in the direction of the stately housekeeper of Drury,

Mrs. Lush, with dignity enough not to care to claim kinship with her namesake, the judge ; for she was once of the household of Queen Adelaide, and now has the keeping of 'the national theatre,' with nine servants to obey her behests.

To those who would compare the season of 1865—1866 at Drury Lane with that of 1765—1766, it is only necessary to say that a hundred years ago Mrs. Pritchard was playing a character of which she was the original representative in 1761, namely, Mrs. Oakley, in Coleman's 'Jealous Wife,' a part which has been well played this year by Mrs. Vezin to the excellent Mr. Oakley of Mr. Phelps. The Drury Lane company, a hundred years ago, included Garrick, Powell, Holland, King, Palmer, Parsons, Bensley, Dodd, Yates, Moody, Baddeley, all men of great but various merit. Among the ladies were Mrs. Cibber, Mrs. Yates, Mrs. Clive, Mrs. Abington, Mrs. Pritchard, Miss Pope, Mrs. Baddeley, and some others—a galaxy the like of which, in any one company, could nowhere be found in these later days. In that season of a hundred years ago, a new actress, Mrs. Fitzhenry, very nearly gained a seat upon the tragic throne. In the same season Melpomene lost her noblest daughter, albeit the last character her name was attached to in the bills was Lady Brute. I allude to Mrs. Cibber. 'Mrs. Cibber dead !' was Garrick's cry ; 'then tragedy has died with her.'

Since that season of a century since, there has been no such Ophelia as hers, the touching charm of which used to melt a whole house to tears. It was the season in which Garrick abolished the candles in brass sockets, fixed in chandeliers, which hung on the stage; in place of which he introduced the footlights, which were then supplied by oil, and long retained the significant name of 'floats.' In that season, the first benefit was given for the Drury Lane Theatrical Fund, 'for the relief of those who, from infirmities, shall be obliged to retire from the stage.' On this occasion Garrick acted *Kitely*, in 'Every Man in his Humour.' Lastly, in that season was produced, for the first time, the ever-lively comedy, 'The Clandestine Marriage,' in which King, as Lord Ogleby, won such renown that Garrick never ceased to repent of his having declined the character. After he left the stage he did not seem to be sorry for the course he had taken. 'You all think,' he used to say, 'that no one can excel, or even equal King, in Lord Ogleby. It had great merit, but it was not MY Lord Ogleby; and if I could appear again, that is the only character in which I should care to play.' And, no doubt, Roscius would have delighted his audience, though his new reading might not have induced them to forget the original representation.

## ABOUT MASTER BETTY.

IN a valley at the foot of the Slieve Croob mountains, in County Antrim, there is a pretty village called Ballynahinch. The head of the river Lagan, which flows by Belfast into the lough, is to be found in that valley. Near the town is a ' spa,' with a couple of wells, and a delicious air, sufficient in itself to cure all travellers from Dublin who have narrowly escaped being poisoned by the Liffey, in whose murderous stinks the metropolitan authorities seem to think the chief attraction to draw strangers to Dublin is now to be found.

To the flax-cultivating Ballynahinch, in the last quarter of the last century, a gentleman named Betty brought (after a brief sojourn at Lisburn) his young English wife and their only child, a boy. This married couple were of very good blood. The lady was of the Stantons, of Hopton Court. Mr. Betty's father was a physician of some celebrity, at Lisburn, where, and in the neighbourhood, he practised to such good purpose that he left a handsome fortune to his son. That son invested a portion of his inheritance in a farm, and in the manu-

facture of linen at Ballynahinch. Whence the
Bettys originally came it would be hard to say.
A good many Huguenots lie in the churchyard at
Lisburn, and the Bettys may have originally sprung
from a kindred source. In the reign of George
the Second there was a Rev. Joseph Betty, who
created a great sensation by a sermon which he
preached at Oxford. Whether the Betty of Oxford
was an ancestor of him of Ballynahinch is a question which may be left to Mr. Forster, the pedigree
hunter.

I have said that with his young wife Mr. Betty
took to Ireland their son. Their boy was, and
remained, their only child. He was born at
Shrewsbury, which place is also proud of having
given birth to famous Admiral Benbow, also to Orton, the eminent Nonconformist. Master Betty was
English born and Irish bred ; half-bred, however ;
for his English mother was his nurse, his companion, his friend—in other words, his true mother.
Such an only child used to be called ' a parlour
child,' to denote that there was more intercourse
between child and parent than exists in a ' nur-
sery child,' to whom the nurse seems his natural
guide and ruler.

The English lady happened to be a lady well
endowed as to her mind, her tastes, and her ac-
complishments. She was exactly the mother for
such a boy. She was not only excessively fond of

reading the best poets, but of reading passages aloud, or reciting them from memory. Her audience was her boy. His tastes were in sympathy with his mother's, and he was never more delighted than when he sat listening to her reading or reciting, except when he was reciting passages to her. It was a peculiar training ; it really shaped the boy's life—and it was no ill shape which the life took. The father had his share, however, in clearing the path for the bright, though brief, career. One day the father, whose intellectual tastes responded to his wife's, repeated to his son the speech of Cardinal Wolsey, beginning, ' Farewell, a long farewell, to all my greatness.' In doing this, he suited the action to the word. Young Betty had never seen this before, and he asked the meaning of it. ' It is what is called acting,' said the father. The boy thought over it, tried by himself action and motion with elocution, and he spoke and acted the cardinal's soliloquy before his mother with an effect that excited in her the greatest surprise and admiration.

Not the faintest idea of the stage had, at this time, entered the minds of any of the family. The eager young lad himself was satisfied with reading plays, learning passages from them, and reciting speeches from ' Douglas ' and ' Zara,' from ' Pizarro ' and the ' Stranger.' He also repeated the episodical tales from Thomson's ' Seasons.'

Only the above trace of his learning anything
from Shakespeare is to be found, but he listened to
readings from the national poet by one or other
of his parents. This course had its natural results.
By degrees the boy took to rude attempts, from
domestic materials, of dress. 'Properties' were
created out of anything that could be turned to
the purpose; a screen was adopted for scenery;
audiences of ones and twos were pressed by the
stage-struck youth to tarry and see him act; and
finally his father, well qualified, taught him fencing,
the son proving an apt pupil, and becoming a
swordsman as perfect and graceful as Edmund
Kean himself.

His reputation spread beyond home into distant branches of the family. Those branches shook
with disgust. The parents were warned that if
they did not take care the boy would come to the
evil end of being a play-actor! They were alarmed.
The domestic stage was suppressed; silence reigned
where the echoes of the dramatic poets once
pleasantly rang, and the heir of Hopton Court and
Hopton Wafers was ignominiously packed off to
school. When I say 'the heir,' it is because Master
Betty was so called; but it really seems as if his
claim resembled that of the Irish gentleman who
was kept out of his property by the rightful owner.

There is no record of Master Betty's school life.
We only know that it did not suppress his taste

for dramatic poetry and dramatic action. At this time, 1802, Mrs. Siddons, who had been acting with her brother, John Kemble, to empty houses at Drury Lane, left England, in disgust at the so-called 'Drury treasury,' for Ireland. It was the journey on which she set out with such morbid feelings of despair, as if she were assured of the trip ending by some catastrophe. It was, in fact, all triumph, and in the course of her triumphant career she arrived in Belfast, where, with other parts, she acted Elvira in 'Pizarro.' She had not thought much of the part of the camp-follower when she was first cast for it, and Sheridan was so dilatory that she had to learn the last portion of the character after the curtain had risen for the first acting of the piece. But Sarah Siddons was a true artist. She ever made the best of the very worst materials; she invested Elvira with dignity, and it became by far the most popular of the characters of which she was the original representative. Young Betty entered a theatre for the first time to see Sheridan's 'Pizarro' acted at the Belfast theatre, and Mrs. Siddons as Elvira. The boy's tastes were in the right direction. He had neither eyes, nor ears, nor senses, but for her. He was, so to speak, 'stricken' by her majestic march, her awful brow, her graceful action, and her incomparable delivery. He drank at a fresh fountain he beheld a new guiding light; he went home in a trance; he now knew what was meant by 'the stage,' what acting was, what appropriate speech meant, what it was to be an actor, and what a delicious reward there was for an inspired artist in the music of tumultuous applause. When Master Betty awoke from his dream it was to announce to his parents that he should certainly die if he were not allowed to be a play-actor!

He was only eleven years old, and those parents did not wish to lose him. They at first humoured his bent, and listened smilingly to his rehearsal of the whole part of Elvira. They had to listen to other parts, and still had to hear his impressive iteration of his resolution to die if he were thwarted in his views. At length they yielded. The father addressed himself to Mr. Atkins, the proprietor and manager of the Belfast theatre, who consented that the boy should give him a taste of his quality. When this was done, Atkins was sufficiently struck by its novelty not to know exactly what to make of it. He called into council Hough, the prompter, who was warm in his approval. 'You are my guardian angel!' exclaimed the excited boy to the old prompter. Atkins, with full faith in Hough's verdict, observed, when the lad had left, 'I never expected to see another Garrick, but I have seen an infant Garrick in Master Betty!'

After some preliminary bargaining, Atkins would not go further than engage the promising 'infant' for four nights. The terms were that, after deducting *twelve pounds* for the expenses of the house, the rest was to be divided between the manager and the *débutant*. The tragedy of 'Zara' was accordingly announced for August 16, 1803, 'Osman (Sultan of Jerusalem) by a Young Gentleman.' Now, that year (and several before and after it) was a troubled year, part of a perilous time, for Ireland. Sedition was abroad, and everybody, true man or not, was required to be at home early. The manager could not have got his tragedy and farce ended and his audience dismissed to their homes within the legal time but for the order which he obtained from the military commander of the district that (as printed in the bill), 'At the request of the manager the drums have been ordered to beat an hour later at night.' The performance was further advertised 'to begin precisely at six o'clock, that the theatre may be closed by nine.' The prices were reckoned by the Irish equivalent of English shillings—'Boxes, 3*s.* 3*d.* ; Pit, 2*s.* 2*d.* : Gallery, 1*s.* 1*d.*' In return for the military courtesy, if not as a regular manifestation of loyalty, it was also stated in the bill, 'GOD SAVE THE KING' (in capital letters!) 'will be played at the end of the second act, and RULE BRITANNIA at the end of the play.'

Belfast was, as it is, an intellectual town. The audience assembled were not likely to be carried away by a mere phenomenon. They listened, became interested, then deeply stirred, and at last enthusiastic. The next day the whole town was talking of the almost perfection with which this boy represented the rage, jealousy, and despair of Osman. In truth, there was something more than cleverness in this representation. Let anyone, if he can, read Aaron Hill's adaptation of Voltaire's 'Zaire' through. He will see of what dry bones it is made. Those heavy lines, long speeches, dull movement of dull plot, stirred now and then by a rant or a roar, require a great deal more than cleverness to make them endurable. No human being could live out five acts of such stuff if genius did not uphold the stuff itself. It was exquisite Mrs. Cibber who gave 'Zara' life when she made her *début* on the stage, when the tragedy was first played in 1736. Spranger Barry added fresh vigour to that life when he acted Osman in 1751. Garrick's genius in Lusignan galvanised the dead heap into living beauty, never more so than in his last performance in 1776 ; but the great genius was Mrs. Cibber; neither Mrs. Bellamy, nor Mrs. Barry, nor Miss Younge, equalled her. Mrs. Siddons, after them, made Zara live again, and was nearly equal to Mrs. Cibber. Since her time there has been neither a Zara, nor Lusignan, nor grown-up Osman, of any note ; and nothing short of genius could make the dry bones live. Voltaire's 'Zaire'

is as dull as Hill's, but it has revived, and been
played at the Théâtre Français. But every character is well played, from Mounet Sully, who acts
Orosmane, to Dupont Vernon, in Corasmin. The
accomplished Berton plays Nerestan ; and it is a
lesson to actors only to hear Maubant deliver the
famous lines beginning with 'Mon Dieu, j'ai com-
battu.'

Mdlle. Sarah Bernhardt is the Zaïre, and I can
fancy her a French Cibber. She dies, however, on
the stage too much in the horrible fashion of the
'Sphinx'; but what attracts French audience is,
that the piece abounds in passages which such
audiences may hail in ecstasy or denounce in disgust. The passages are political, religious, and
cunningly framed free-thinking passages. For these
the audience waits, and signalises their coming by
an enthusiasm of delight or an excess of displeasure.

At Belfast there was only the eleven-years-old
Osman to enthral an audience. The rest were
respectable players. It is not to be believed that
such an audience would have been stirred as they
were on that August night had there not been
some mind behind the voice of the young *débutant*.
He had never been on a stage before, had only once
seen a play acted, had received only a few hints
from the old prompter, yet he seemed to be the
very part he represented. There were many
doubters and disbelievers in Belfast, but they, for

the most part, went to the theatre and were convinced. The three other parts he played were
Douglas, Rolla, and, for his benefit on August 29,
Romeo. From that moment he was 'renowned,'
and his career certain of success.

While this boy snatched a triumph, there was
another eagerly, painfully, yet hopefully and
determinedly, struggling for one. *This* boy scarcely
knew by what name to pass, for his mother was a
certain Nance Carey, and his reputed father was
one of two brothers, he did not know which, named
Kean. This boy claimed in after years to be an
illegitimate son of the Duke of Norfolk, and he
referred, in a way, to this claim when he called his
first child Howard. For Nance Carey the boy had
no love. There was but one woman who was kind
to him in his childhood, Miss Tidswell, of Drury
Lane Theatre, and Edmund Kean used to say, ' If
she was not my mother, why was she kind to me ? '
When I pass Orange Court, Leicester Square, I
look with curiosity at the hole where he got a
month's schooling.

Born and dragged up, the young life experiences of Edmund Kean were exactly opposite to
those of William Henry West Betty. He had
indeed, because of his childish beauty, been
allowed at three years old to stand or lie as Cupid
in one of Noverre's ballets; and he had, as an
unlucky imp in the witches' scene of ' Macbeth,'

been rebuked by the offended John Kemble. Since then he had rolled or been kicked about the world. When Master Betty, at the age of eleven, or nearly twelve, was laying the foundations of his fortune at Belfast, Edmund Kean was fifteen, and had often laid himself to sleep on the lee side of a haystack, for want of wherewith to pay for a better lodging. He had danced and tumbled at fairs, and had sung in taverns; he had tramped about the country, carrying Nance Carey's box of *falbalas* for sale; he had been over sea and land; he had joined Richardson's booth company, and, at Windsor, it is said that George III. had heard him recite, and had expressed his approbation in the shape of two guineas, which Miss Carey took from him.

It was for the benefit of a mother so different from Master Betty's mother that he recited in private families. It is a matter of history that by one of these recitations he inspired another boy, two years older than himself, with a taste for the stage and a determination to gain thereon an honourable position. This third boy was Charles Young. His son and biographer has told us, that as Charles was one evening at Christmas time descending the stairs of his father's house full dressed for *dessert* —his father, a London surgeon, lived in rather high style—he saw a slatternly woman seated on one of the chairs in the hall, with a boy standing by her side dressed in fantastic garb, with the blackest and most penetrating eyes he had ever beheld in human head. His first impression was that the two were strolling gipsies who had come for medical advice. Charles Young, we are told, ' was soon undeceived, for he had no sooner taken his place by his father's side than, to his surprise, the master, instead of manifesting displeasure, smirked and smiled, and, with an air of self-complacent patronage, desired his butler to bring in the boy. On his entry he was taken by the hand, patted on the head, and requested to favour the company with a specimen of his histrionic ability. With a self-possession marvellous in one so young he stood forth, knitted his brows, hunched up one shoulder-blade, and with sardonic grin and husky voice spouted forth Gloster's opening soliloquy in "Richard the Third." He then recited selections from some of our minor British poets, both grave and gay ; danced a hornpipe ; sang songs, both comic and pathetic ; and, for fully an hour, displayed such versatility as to elicit vociferous applause from his auditory and substantial evidence of its sincerity by a shower of crown pieces and shillings, a napkin having been opened and spread upon the floor for their reception. The accumulated treasury having been poured into the gaping pockets of the lad's trousers, with a smile of gratified vanity and grateful acknowledgment he withdrew, rejoined his tatterdemalion friend in the hall,

and left the house rejoicing. The door was no
sooner closed than the guests desired to know the
name of the youthful prodigy who had so astonished
them. The host replied that this was not the first
time he had had him to amuse his friends ; that he
knew nothing of the lad's history or antecedents,
but that his name was Edmund Kean, and that of
the woman who seemed to have charge of him and
was his supposititious mother, Carey.' This pretty
scene, described by the Rev. Julian Young, had a
supplement to it of which he was not aware. ' She
took all from me,' was Edmund Kean's cry when
he used to tell similar incidents of his hard youthful
times.

While Edmund was thus struggling, Master
Betty had leaped into fame. Irish managers were
ready to fight duels for the possession of him.
When the announcement went forth that Mr.
Frederick Jones, of the Crow Street Theatre, Dublin, was the possessor of the youthful phenomenon
for nine nights, there was a rush of multitudes to
secure places, with twenty times more applicants
than places. There was ferocious fighting for what
could be secured, and much spoliation, with peril
of life and damage to limb, and an atmosphere filled
with thunder and lightning, delightful to the Dublin
mind.

On November 29, 1803, Master Betty, not in
his own name, but simply as a ' young gentleman,

only twelve years of age,' made his *début* in Dublin
as Douglas. The play-bill, indeed, did add, 'his
admirable talents have procured him the deserved
appellation of the INFANT ROSCIUS.' As there were
sensitive people in Dublin who remembered that
Dublin itself was in what would now be called a
state of siege, and that it was unlawful to be out
after a certain hour in the evening, these were won
over by this delicious announcement : ' The public
are respectfully informed that no person coming
from the theatre will be stopped till after eleven
o'clock.' This was the time, too, when travellers
were induced to trust themselves to mail and stage-
coaches by the assurance that the vehicles were
made proof against shot. There was no certainty
the travellers would not be fired at, but the comfort
was that if the bullets did not go through the window and kill the travellers, they could not much
injure the vehicle itself !

There was the unheard-of sum of four hundred
pounds in that old Crow Street Theatre on that
November night. The university students in the
gallery, who generally made it rattle with their
wit, were silent as soon as the curtain rose. The
Dublin audience was by no means an audience easy
to please, or one that would befool itself by passing
mediocrity with the stamp of genius upon it.
' Douglas,' too, is a tragedy that must be atten-
tively listened to, to be enjoyed, and enjoyment is

out of the question if the poetry of the piece be a
lost beauty to the deliverer of the lines.  On this
night, Dublin ratified the Belfast verdict.  The
graceful boy excited the utmost enthusiasm, and
the manager offered him an engagement at an
increasing salary, for any number of years.  The
offer was wisely declined by Master Betty's father,
and the 'Infant Roscius' went on his bright career.
He played one other part, admirably suited to him
in every respect, Prince Arthur, in 'King John,'
and he fairly drowned the house in tears with it.
Frederick, in 'Lovers' Vows,' and Romeo, were
only a trifle beyond his age, not at all beyond his
grasp, though love-making was the circumstance
which he could the least satisfactorily portray.  A
boy sighing like furnace to young beauty must
have seemed as ridiculous as a Juliet of fifty, looking older than the Nurse, and who, one would
think, ought to be ashamed of herself to be out in
a balcony at that time of night, talking nonsense
with that young fellow with a feather in his cap
and a sword on his thigh!  Dublin wits made fun
of Master Betty's wooing, and were epigrammatic
upon it in the style of Martial, and saucy actresses
seized the same theme to air their saucy wit.  These
casters of stones from the roadside could not im-
pede the boy's triumph.  He produced immense
effect, even in Thomson's dreary 'Tancred,' but I
am sorry to find it asserted that he acted Hamlet,

after learning the part in three days. The great
Betterton, greatest of the great masters of their art,
used to say that he had acted Hamlet and studied
it for fifty years, and had not got to the bottom of
its philosophy even then. However, the boy's remarkable gifts made his Hamlet successful. There
was a rare comedian who played with him, Richard
Jones, with a cast in one eye. Accomplished Dick,
whose only serious fault was excess in peppermint
lozenges, acted Osric, Count Cassel, and Mercutio,
in three of the pieces in which Master Betty played
the principal characters. What a glorious true
comedian was Dick ! After delighting a whole
generation with his comedy, Jones retired. He
taught clergymen to read the Lord's Prayer as if
they were in earnest, and to deliver the messages
of the Gospel as if they believed in them ; and
in this way Dick Jones did as much for the church
as any of the bishops or archbishops of his time.

It is to be noted here that Master Betty's first
appearance in Dublin in 1803 was a more triumphant matter than John Kemble's in 1781. This
was in the older Smock Alley Theatre. The alley
was so called from the Sallys who most did con-
gregate there. He played high comedy as well
as tragedy ; but, says Mr. Gilbert, in his ' History
of Dublin,' ' his negligent delivery and heaviness
of deportment impeded his progress until these
defects were removed by the instruction of his

friend, Captain Jephson.'    Is not this delicious?
Fancy John Kemble being made an actor by a
half-pay captain who had written a tragedy!  This
tragedy was called the 'Count of Narbonne,' and
therein, says Gilbert, 'Kemble's reputation was
first established.'  It was not on a very firm basis,
for John was engaged only on the modest salary of
5*l.* a week!

Master Betty's progress through the other parts
of Ireland was as completely successful as at Dublin and Belfast.   Mrs. Pero engaged him for six
nights at Cork.   His terms here were one-fourth
of the receipts and one clear benefit, that is to say,
the whole of the receipts free of expense.  As the
receipts rarely exceeded ten pounds, the prospects
were not brilliant.   But, with Master Betty, the
'houses' reached one hundred pounds.   The
smaller receipts may have arisen from a circumstance sufficient to keep an audience away.   There
was a Cork tailor hanged for robbery; but, after
he was cut down, a Cork actor, named Glover,
succeeded, by friction and other means, in bringing
him to life again!   On the same night, and for
many nights, the tailor, drunk and unhanged,
*would* go to the theatre and publicly acknowledge
the service of Mr. Glover in bringing him to life
again!   And it *is* said that he was the third tailor
who had outlived hanging during ten years!

There was no ghastly interruption of the performance of the Roscius.  The engagement was extended to nine nights, and the one which followed at Waterford was equally successful.  As he proceeded, Master Betty studied and extended his *répertoire*.  He added to his list Octavian, and on his benefit nights he played in the farce, on one occasion Don Carlos in 'Lovers' Quarrels,' on another Captain Flash in 'Miss in her Teens.'  Subsequently, in Londonderry, the flood of success still increasing, the pit could only be entered at box prices.  Master Betty played in Londonderry long before the time when a Mr. MacTaggart, an old citizen, used to be called upon between the acts to give his unbiassed critical opinions on the performances.  It was the rarest fun for the house, and the most painful wholesomeness for the actors, Frank Connor and his father, Villars, Fitzsimons, Cunningham, O'Callaghan, and clever Miss M'Keevor (with her pretty voice and sparkling one eye), to hear the stern and salubrious criticism of Mr. MacTaggart, at the end of which there was a cry for the tune of 'No Surrender!'  Not to wound certain susceptibilities, and yet be national, the key-bugle gentleman, who was half the orchestra, generally played 'Norah Creena,' and thus the play proceeded merrily.

Master Betty played Zanga at Londonderry, and he passed thence to Glasgow, where for fourteen nights he attracted crowded audiences, and

added to his other parts Richard the Third, which
he must have learnt as he sailed from Belfast up
the Clyde.    Jackson, the manager, went all but
mad with delight and full houses.  He wrote an
account of his new treasure in terms more transcendent than ' the transcendent boy ' himself could
accept.  Had Young Roscius been a divinity descended upon earth, the rhapsody could not have
been more highly pitched ; but it was fully en-
dorsed by nine-tenths of the Glasgow people, and
when a bold fellow ventured to write a satirical
philippic against the divine idol of the hour, he
was driven out of the city as guilty of something
like sacrilege, profanation, and general unutterable
wickedness.

On May 21, 1804, the transcendental Mr. Jackson was walking on the High Bridge, Edinburgh,
when he met an old gentleman of some celebrity,
the Rev. Mr. Home.  ' Sir,' said Jackson, ' your play,
" Douglas," is to be acted to-night with a new and
wonderful actor.  I hope you will come down to
the house.'   Forty-eight years before (1756) Home
had gone joyously down to the Edinburgh Theatre
to see his ' Douglas ' represented for the first time.
West Digges (not **Henry West Betty**) was the Norval, and the house was half full of ministers of the
Kirk, who got into a sea of troubles for presuming
to see acted a play written by a fellow in the
ministry.

The Lady Randolph was Mrs. Ward, daughter
of a player of the Betterton period, and mother, I
think, of Mrs. Roger Kemble.  On that night one
enthusiastic Scotsman was so delighted that at the
end of the fourth act he arose and roared aloud,
' Where's Wully Shakespeare noo?'  Home had
also seen Spranger Barry in the hero (he was the
original Norval (Douglas) on the play being first
acted in 1757 in London).  Home was an aged
man in 1804, and lived in retirement.  He did
not know his ' Douglas ' was to be played, nor
had he ever heard of Master Betty !  Never heard
of him whom Jackson said he had been presented to Earth by Heaven and Nature !  'The
pleasing movements of his perfect and divine nature,' said Jackson, ' were incorporated in his person previous to his birth.'  Home could not refuse
to go and see this phenomenon.  He stipulated to
have his old place at the wing, that is, behind the
stage door, partially opened, so that he could see
up the stage.  The old man was entirely overcome.
Digges and Barry, he declared, were leather and
prunella compared with this inspired child who
acted his Norval as he the author had conceived
it.  Home's enthusiasm was so excited that, when
Master Betty was summoned by the ' thunders '
of applause and the ' hurricane ' of approbation
to appear before the audience, Home tottered forward also, tears streaming from his eyes, and rap-

ture beaming on his venerable countenance. The triumph was complete. The most impartial critics especially praised the boy's conception of the poet, and it was the highest praise they could give. Between June 28 and August 9 he acted fifteen times, often under the most august patronage that could be found in Edinburgh. For the first time he played Selim (Achmet) in 'Barbarossa' during this engagement, and with such effect as to make him more the 'darling' than ever of duchesses and ladies in general. Four days after the later date named above, the marvellous boy stood before a Birmingham audience, whither he had gone covered with kisses from Scottish beauties, and laden with the approval, counsel, and blessing of Lords of Session.

Mr. Macready, father of the lately deceased actor, bargained for the Roscius, and overreached himself. He thought 10*l.* a night too much! He proposed that he should deduct 60*l.* from each night's receipts, and that Master Betty should take half of what remained. The result was that Roscius got 50*l.* nightly instead of 10*l.* The first four nights were not overcrowded, but the boy grew on the town, and at last upon the whole country. Stage-coaches were advertised specially to carry parties from various distances to the Birmingham Theatre. The highest receipt was 266*l.* to his Richard. Selim was the next,

261*l.* The lowest receipt was also to his Richard.
On the first night he played it there was only
80*l.* in the house. He left Birmingham with the
assurance of a local poet that he was Cooke,
Kemble, Holman, Garrick, all in one.' Sheffield
was delighted to have him at raised prices of admission. He made his first appearance to deliver a
rhymed deprecatory address, in reference to wide-
cast ridicule on his being a mere boy, in which
were these lines :

> When at our Shakespeare's shrine my swelling heart
> Bursts forth and claims some kindred tear to start,
> Frown not, if I avow that falling tear
> Inspires my soul and bids me persevere.

His Hamlet drew the highest sum at Sheffield,
140*l.* ; his Selim the lowest, 60*l.*, which was just
doubled when he played the same part for his
own benefit. London had caught curiosity, if not
enthusiasm, to see him ; the Sheffield hotels became crowded with London families, and ' Six-
inside coaches to see the Young Roscius ' plied
at Doncaster to carry people from the races.
At Liverpool there were riots and spoliation at
the box-office. At Chester wild delight. At Man-
chester tickets were put up to lottery. At Stock-
port he played morning and evening, and travelled
after it all night to play at Leicester, where he
also acted on some occasions twice in one day !
and where every lady who could write occasional

verses showered upon him a very deluge of rhyme.

November had now been reached. In that month John Kemble, who is supposed to have protested against the dignity of the stage being lowered by a speaking puppet, wrote a letter to Mr. Betty. In this letter John said: ' I could not deny myself the satisfaction I feel in knowing I shall soon have the happiness of welcoming you and Master Betty to Covent Garden Theatre. Give me leave to say how heartily I congratulate the stage on the ornament and support it is, by the judgment of all the world, to receive from Master Betty's extraordinary talents and exertions.' After this we may dismiss as nonsense the lofty talk about the Kemble feeling as to the dignity of the stage being wounded. Mr. Kemble and Mrs. Siddons would not play in the same piece with Master Betty, as Jones, Charles Young, Miss Smith (Mrs. Bartley), and others had done in the country, but Mr. Kemble (as manager) was delighted that the Covent Garden treasury should profit by the extraordinary talents of a boy whom the Kemble followers continually depreciated.

On Saturday, December 1, 1804, Master Betty appeared at Covent Garden in the character of Selim. Soon after mid-day the old theatre—the one which Rich had built and to which he transferred his company from Lincoln's Inn Fields—was beset by a crowd which swelled into a multitude, not one in ten of whom succeeded in fighting his way into the house when the doors were opened.  Such a struggle—sometimes for life—had never been known.  Even in the house strong men fainted like delicate girls; an hour passed before the shrieks of the suffering subsided, and we are even told that 'the ladies in one or two boxes were employed almost the whole night in fanning the gentlemen who were behind them in the pit!'  The only wonder is that the excited multitude, faint for want of air, irritable by being overcrowded, and fierce in struggling for space which no victor in the struggle could obtain, ever was subdued to a condition of calm sufficient to enable them to enjoy the 'rare delight' within reach.  However, in the second act Master Betty appeared—modest, self-possessed, and not at all moved out of his assumed character by the tempest of welcome which greeted him.  From first to last, he 'electrified' the audience.  He never failed, we are told, whenever he aimed at making a point.  His attention to the business of the stage was that of a careful and conscientious veteran.  His acting denoted study.  His genius won applause—not his age, and youthful grace.  There was 'conception,' rather than 'instruction' to be seen in all he did and said.  His undertones could be heard at the very back of the galleries.  The pathos, the joy, the exultation of a part (once

so favourite a part with young actors), enchanted
the audience.  That they felt all these things sincerely is proved by the fact that—as one newspaper critic writes—' the audience could not lower
their minds to attend to the farce, which was not
suffered to be concluded.'

The theatrical career of his ' Young Roscius '
period amounted to this.  He played at both houses
in London from December 1804 to April 1805, in a
wide range of characters, and supported by some
of the first actors of the day.  He then played in
every town of importance throughout England and
Scotland.  He returned to London for the season
1805–6, and acted twenty-four nights at each
theatre, at fifty guineas a night.  Subsequently he
acted in the country ; and finally, he took leave of
the stage at Bath in March 1808.  Altogether, London possessed him but a few months.  The madness which prevailed about him was ' midsummer
madness,' though it was but a short fit.  That he
himself did not go mad is the great wonder.
Princes of the blood called on him, the Lord Chancellor invited him, nobles had him day after day
to dinner, and the King presented him to the
Queen and Princesses in the room behind the Royal
box.  Ladies carried him off to the Park as those
of Charles II.'s time did with Kynaston.  When he
was ill the sympathetic town rushed to read his
bulletins with tremulous eagerness.  Portraits of

him abounded, presents were poured in upon him, poets and poetasters deafened the ear about him, misses patted his beautiful hair and asked ' locks ' from him. The future King of France and Navarre, Count d'Artois, afterwards Charles X., witnessed his performance, in French, of ' Zaphna,' at Lady Percival's; Gentleman Smith presented him with Garrick relics; Cambridge University gave ' Roscius ' as the subject for the Brown Prize Medal, and the House of Commons adjourned, at the request of Pitt, in order to witness his ' Hamlet.' At the Westminster Latin Play (the ' Adelphi ' of Terence) he was present in a sort of royal state, and the Archbishop of York all but publicly blest him. Some carping persons remarked that the boy was too ignorant to understand a word of the play that was acted in his presence. When it is remembered how Latin was and is pronounced at Westminster, it is not too much to say that Terence (had he been there) would not have understood much more of his own play than Master Betty did.

The boy reigned triumphantly through his little day, and the professional critics generally praised to the skies his mental capacity as well as his bodily endowments. They discovered beauty in both, and it is to the boy's credit that their praise did not render him conceited. He studied new parts, and his attention to business, his modesty, his boyish spirits in the green room, his docility, and the respect he paid to older artists, were among the items of the professional critic's praise.

Let us pass from the professional critics to the judgment of private individuals of undoubted ability to form and give one (we have only to premise that Master Betty played alternately at Covent Garden and Drury Lane). And first, Lord Henley. Writing to Lord Auckland, on December 7, 1804, he says, ' I went to see the Young Roscius with an unprejudiced mind, or rather, perhaps, with the opinion you seem to have formed of him, and left the theatre in the highest admiration of his wonderful talents. As I scarcely remember Garrick, I may say (though there be, doubtless, room for improvement) that I never saw such fine acting, and yet the poor boy's voice was that night a good deal affected by a cold. I would willingly pay a guinea for a place on every night of his appearing in a new character.'

Even Fox, intent as he was on public business, and absorbed by questions of magnitude concerning his country, and of importance touching himself, was caught by the general enthusiasm. There is a letter of his, dated December 17, 1804, addressed to his ' Dear Young One,' Lord Holland, who was then about thirty years old. The writer urges his nephew to hasten from Spain to England, on account of the serious parliamentary struggle

likely to occur ; adding, ' there is always a chance
of questions in which the Prince of Wales is
particularly concerned ; ' and subjoining the sa-
gacious statesmanlike remark : ' It is very desir-
able that the power, strength, and union of the
Opposition should appear considerable while out
of office, in order that if ever they should come
in it may be plain that they have an existence
of their own, and are not the mere creatures of
the Crown.' But Fox breaks suddenly away from
subjects of crafty statesmanship, with this sentence : ' Everybody here is mad about this Boy
Actor, even Uncle Dick is full of astonishment
and admiration. We go to town to-morrow to
see him, and from what I have heard, I own I
shall be disappointed if he is not a prodigy.'

On the same day Fox wrote a letter from St.
Anne's Hill to the Hon. C. Grey (the Lord Grey
of the Reform Bill). It is bristling with ' politicks,'
but between reference to party battles and remarks
on Burke, the statesman says : ' Everybody is mad
about this Young Roscius, and we go to town to-
morrow to see him. The accounts of him seem
incredible ; but the opinion of him is nearly
unanimous, and Fitzpatrick, who went strongly
prepossessed against him, was perfectly astonished
and full of admiration.'

We do not find any letter of Fox's extant to
tell us his opinion of the ' tenth wonder.' We

can go with him to the play, nevertheless. ' While young Betty was in all his glory,' says Samuel Rogers, in his ' Table Talk,' ' I went with Fox and Mrs. Fox, after dining with them in Arlington Street, to see him act Hamlet ; and, during the play scene, Fox, to my infinite surprise, said, " This is finer than Garrick ! " ' Fox would not have said so if he had not thought so. He did not say as much to Master Betty, but he best proved his sympathy by sitting with and reading to him passages from the great dramatists, mingled with excellent counsel.

Windham, the famous statesman, who as much loved to see a pugilistic fight as Fox did to throw double sixes, and to whom a stroll in Leicester Fields was as agreeable as an hour with an Italian poet was to Fox—Windham hurried through the Fields to Covent Garden. His diary for the year 1804 is lost ; but in that for 1805 we come upon his opinion of the attractive player, after visits in both years. On January 31, 1805, there is this entry in his diary ;—' Went, according to arrangement, with Elliot and Grenville to play ; Master Betty in Frederick ' (' Lovers' Vows '). ' Lord Spencer, who had been shooting at Osterley, came afterwards. Liked Master B. better than before, but still inclined to my former opinion ; his action certainly very graceful, except now and then that he is a little tottering on his legs, and his recitation just, but his countenance not expressive ; his voice neither powerful nor pleasing.'

The criticisms of actors were generally less favourable. Kemble was ' riveted,' we are told, by the acting of Master Betty ; but he was contemptuously silent. Mrs. Siddons, according to Campbell, ' never concealed her disgust at the popular infatuation.' At the end of the play Lord Abercorn came into her box and told her that that boy, Betty, would eclipse everything which had been called acting, in England. ' My Lord,' she answered, ' he is a very clever, pretty boy ; but nothing more.' Mrs. Siddons, however, was meanly jealous of all that stood between her and the public. When Mrs. Siddons was young, she was jealous of grand old Mrs. Crawford. When Mrs. Siddons was old, and had retired, she was jealous of young Miss O'Neill. She querulously said that the public were fond of setting up new idols in order to annoy their former favourites. George Frederick Cooke who had played Glenalvon to Master Betty's Norval— played it finely too, at his very best—and could not crush the boy, after whom everybody was repeating the line he made so famous,

The blood of Douglas can protect itself!

—Cooke alluded to him in his diary, for 1811, thus : ' I was visited by Master Payne, the American Young Roscius; I thought him a polite, sensible youth, and the reverse of our Young Roscius.' This was an ebullition of irritability. Even those who could not praise Roscius as a tenth wonder, acknowledged his courtesy and were struck by his good common sense. Boaden, who makes the singular remark that 'all the favouritism, and more than the innocence, of former patronesses was lavished on him,' also tells us more intelligibly, that Master Betty 'never lost the genuine modesty of his carriage ; and his temper, at least, was as steady as his diligence.' One actor said, 'Among clever boys he would have been a Triton among minnows;' but Mrs. Inchbald remarked, 'Had I never seen boys act, I might have thought him extraordinary.' 'Baby-faced child!' said Campbell. 'Handsome face! graceful figure! marvellous power!' is the testimony of Mrs. Mathews. The most unbiassed judgment I can find is Miss Seward's, who wrote thus of him in 1804, after seeing him as Osman in 'Zara': 'It could not have been conceived or represented with more grace, sensibility, and fire, though he is veritably an effeminate boy of thirteen; but his features are cast in a diminutive mould, particularly his nose and mouth. This circumstance must at every period of life be injurious to stage effect; nor do I think his ear for blank verse faultless. Like Cooke, he never fails to give the

passions their whole force, by gesture and action
natural and just; but he does not do equal justice
to the harmony.   It is, I think, superfluous to
look forward to the mature fruit of this luxuriant
blossom.'   Miss Seward was right; but she was
less correct in her prophecy, ' He will not live
to bear it.   Energies various and violent will blast
in no short time the vital powers, evidently
delicate.'   He survived this prophecy just seventy
years!   One other opinion of him I cannot forbear
adding.   It is Elliston's, and it is in the very
loftiest of Robert William's manner, who was born
a little more than one hundred years ago !   'Sir,
my opinion of the young gentleman's talents will
never transpire during my life.   I have written
my convictions down.   They have been attested
by competent witnesses, and sealed and deposited
in the iron safe at my banker's, to be drawn forth
and opened, with other important documents, at
my death.   The world will then know what Mr.
Elliston thought of Master Betty !'

The Young Roscius withdrew from the stage
and entered Christ's College, Cambridge.   He there
enjoyed quiet study and luxurious seclusion.
Meanwhile that once boy with the flashing eyes,
Edmund Kean, had got a modest post at the Haymarket, where he played Rosencrantz to Mr. Rae's
Hamlet.   He had also struggled his way to Belfast,
and had acted Osman to Mrs. Siddons' Zara.   'He

plays well, very well,' said the lady : ' but there is too little of him to make a great actor.'　Edmund, too, had married ' Mary Chambers,' at Stroud, and Mr. Beverley had turned the young couple out of his company, ' to teach them not to do it again ! ' In 1812, ' Mr. Betty,' come to man's estate, returned to the stage, at Bath.　A few months previously Mr. and Mrs. Kean were wandering from town to town.　In rooms, to which the public were invited by written bills, in Kean's hand, they recited scenes from plays and sang duets; and *he* trilled songs, spoke soliloquies, danced hornpipes, and gave imitations !—and starved, and hoped— and would by no means despair.

Mr. Betty's second career lasted from 1812 to 1824, when he made his last bow at Southampton, as the Earl of Warwick.　Within the above period he acted at Covent Garden, in 1812 and 1813. He proved to be a highly ' respectable ' actor; but the phenomenon no longer existed.　His last performance in London was in June 1813, when he played ' Richard III. ' and ' Tristram Fickle ' for his benefit.　In the following January Edmund Kean, three years his senior, took the town by storm in Shylock, and made his conquest good by his incomparable Richard.　The genius of Mr. Betty left him with his youth.　Edmund Kean drowned his genius in wine and rioting before his manhood was matured.　Forty-eight years have

elapsed since he was carried to his grave in Richmond churchyard.  Honoured and regretted, all
that was mortal of the once highly-gifted boy, who
lived to be a venerable and much-loved old man,
'fourscore years and upwards,' was borne to his
last resting-place in the cemetery at Highgate.
*Requiescat in pace!*

## CHARLES YOUNG AND HIS TIMES.

CHARLES MAYNE YOUNG, one of the last of the school of noble actors, has found a biographer in his son, the Rev. Julian Young, Rector of Ilmington. Here we have stage and pulpit in happy and not unusual propinquity. There was a time when the clergy had the drama entirely to themselves; they were actors, authors, and managers. The earliest of them all retired to the monastery of St. Alban, after his theatre at Dunstable had been burnt down, at the close of a squib-and-rocket sort of drama on the subject of St. Theresa. At the Reformation the stage became secularised, the old moralities died out, and the new men and pieces were denounced as wicked by the ' unco righteous ' among their dramatic clerical predecessors. Nevertheless, the oldest comedy of worldly manners we possess—' Ralph Roister Doister '—was the work of the Rev. Dr. Nicholas Udall, in 1540. During the three centuries and nearly a half which have elapsed since that time, clergymen have ranked among the best writers for the stage. The two most successful tragedies of the last century were the Rev. Dr. Young's 'Revenge,' and the Rev. J. Home's 'Douglas.' In the present century few comedies have made such a sensation as the Rev. Dr. Croly's 'Pride shall have a Fall,' but the sensation was temporary, the comedy only illustrating local and contemporary incidents.

A dozen other 'Reverends' might be cited who have more or less adorned dramatic literature, and there are many instances of dramatic artists whose sons or less near kinsmen having taken orders in the Church. When Sutton, in the pulpit of St. Mary Overy, A.D. 1616, denounced the stage, Nathaniel Field, the eminent actor, published a letter to the preacher, in which Field said that in the player's trade there were corruptions as there were in all others ; he implied, as Overbury implied, that the actor was not to be judged by the dross of the craft, but by the purer metal. Field anticipated Fielding's Newgate Chaplain, who upheld 'Punch' on the same ground that the comedian upheld the stage—that it was nowhere spoken against in Scripture! The year 1616 was the year in which Shakespeare died. It is commonly said that the players of Shakespeare's time were of inferior birth and culture, but Shakespeare himself was of a well-conditioned family, and this Nathaniel Field who stood up for the honour of the stage against the censure of the pulpit, had for brother that Rev. Theophilus Field who was successively Bishop of Llandaff, St. David's, and Hereford.  Charles Young was not the only actor of his day who gave a son to the Church.  His old stage-manager at Bath, Mr. Charlton, saw not only his son but his grandsons usefully employed in the more serious vocation.  As for sons of actors at the universities, they have seldom been wanting, from William Hemming (son of John Hemming, the actor, and joint-editor with Condell of the folio edition of Shakespeare's Works), who took his degree at Oxford in 1628, down to Julian Charles Young, son of the great tragedian, who took his degree in the same university two centuries later; or, to be precise, A.D. 1827.

Charles Mayne Young, who owed his second name to the circumstance of his descent from the regicide who was so called, was born in Fenchurch Street, in 1777.  His father was an able surgeon and a reckless spendthrift.  Before the household fell into ruin, Charles Young had passed a holiday year, partly at the Court of Copenhagen.  He had seen a boy with flashing eyes play bits from Shakespeare before the guests at his father's table—a strolling, fantastically-dressed, intellectual boy, whose name was Edmund Kean.  Further, Charles Young saw and appreciated, at the age of twelve, Mrs. Siddons as the mother of Coriolanus.  He also passed through Eton and Merchant Taylors'. When the surgeon's household was broken up, and

Young and his two brothers took their ill-used mother to their own keeping, they adopted various courses for her and their own support, and all of them succeeded. Charles Young, after passing a restless novitiate in a merchant's office (the more restless, probably, as he thought of two personages—the bright, gipsy-looking boy who had acted in his father's dining-room, and the Volumnia of Mrs. Siddons, as she triumphed in the tragedy of Coriolanus), went upon the stage, triumphed in his turn, and assumed the sole guardianship and support of the mother he loved.

Young's father was a remarkably detestable person. He never seems to have forgiven his sons for the affection which they manifested towards their mother. After the separation of the parents, George Young, the eldest son, was in a stage-coach going to Hackney; on the road, a stranger got in, took the only vacant seat, and, on seeing George Young opposite to him, struck him a violent blow in the face. George quietly called to the coachman to stop, and without exchanging a word with the stranger, got out, to the amazement of the other passengers. But, as he closed the door, he looked in and simply said, ' Ladies and gentlemen, that is my father!' In 1807, when Charles Young made his first appearance in London, at the Haymarket, as Hamlet, his father sat ensconced in a corner of the house, and hissed him! Neither the blow nor the hiss did more than momentarily wound the feelings of the sons.

Before Young came up to London, he had seen some of the sunshine and some of the bitterness of life. He married the young, beautiful, and noble woman and actress, Julia Grimani. They had a brief, joyous, married time of little more than a year, when the birth of a son was the death of the mother. For the half-century that Young survived her no blandishment of woman ever led him to be untrue to her memory. To look with tears on her miniature-portrait, to touch tenderly some clustered locks of her hair, to murmur some affectionate word of praise, and, finally, to thank God that he should soon be with her, showed how young heart-feelings had survived in old heart-memories.

Charles Young adorned the English stage from 1807 to 1832. Because he acted with the Kembles he is sometimes described as being of the Kemble school. In a great theatre the leading player is often imitated throughout the house. There was a time when everybody employed at Drury Lane seemed a double of Mr. Macready. Charles Young, however, was an original actor. It took him but five years to show that he was equal in some characters to John Kemble himself. This was seen in 1812, in his Cassius to Kemble's Brutus.

On that occasion Terry is said to have been the
Casca—a part which was really played by Fawcett.
About ten years later, Young left the Covent Garden
company and 25*l.* a week, for Drury Lane and 50*l.*
a night, to play in the same pieces with Kean. The
salary proved that the manager thought him equal
in attractiveness to Kean ; and Kean was, undoubtedly, somewhat afraid of him. Young's se-
cession was as great a loss to the company he had
been acting with, as Compton's has been to the
Haymarket company. In both cases, a perfect
artist withdrew from the brotherhood.

Young was fifteen years upon the London stage
before he could free himself from nervousness—
nervousness, not merely like that of Mrs. Siddons,
before going on, but when fairly in face of the
audience. In 1826, he told Moore, at a dinner of
the Anacreontics, that any close observer of his
acting must have been conscious of a great improvement therein, dating from the previous four
years. That is to say, dating from the time when
he first played in the same piece with Edmund
Kean. The encounter with that great master of
his art seems to have braced Young's nerves. Kean
could not extinguish him as he extinguished Booth
when those two acted together in the same play.
Edmund, who spoke of Macready as ' a player,'
acknowledged Young to be ' an actor.' Kean confessed Young's superiority in Iago, and he could

not bear to think of playing either that character
or Pierre after him. Edmund believed in the
greater merit of his own Othello. Young allowed
that Kean had genius, but he was not enthusiastic
in his praise ; and Edmund, whose voice in tender
passages was exquisite music, referred to the
d——d musical voice of Young; and in his irritable moments spake of him as ' that Jesuit!'

The greatest of Young's original characters was
his Rienzi. In Miss Mitford's tragedy, Young pronounced 'Rome' *Room*. Many old play-goers can
recollect how ill the word fell from his musical
lips. John Kemble would never allow an actor in
his company to give other utterance to the mono-
syllable. It was a part of the vicious and fantastic
utterances of the Kemble family. Leigh Hunt has
furnished a long list of them. Shakespeare, indeed,
has ' Now it is Rome indeed, and room enough,' as
Cassius says. But in 'Henry VI.,' when Beaufort
exclaims, ' Rome shall remedy this!' Warwick
replies, ' *Roam* thither, then!' The latter jingle
is far more common than the former. We agree
with Genest, ' Let the advocates for *Room* be consistent. If the city is *Room*, the citizens are
certainly *Roomans*.' They who would have any
idea how John Kemble mutilated the pronunciation of the English language on the stage, have
only to consult the appendix to Leigh Hunt's
' Critical Essays on the Performers of the London

Theatres.' Such pronunciation seems now more appropriate to burlesque than to Shakespeare.

When the idea was first started of raising a statue in honour of Kemble, Talma wrote to 'mon cher Young,' expressing his wish to be among the subscribers. 'In that idea I recognise your countrymen,' said Talma. 'I shall be too fortunate here if the priests leave me a grave in my own garden.' The Comte de Soligny, or the author who wrote under that name, justly said in his 'Letters on England,' that Young was unlike any actor on the stage. His ornamental style had neither model nor imitators. 'I cannot help thinking,' writes the Count, ' what a sensation Young would have created had he belonged to the French instead of the English stage. With a voice almost as rich, powerful, and sonorous as that of Talma—action more free, flowing, graceful, and various; a more expressive face, and a better person—he would have been hardly second in favour and attraction to that grandest of living actors. As it is, he admirably fills up that place on the English stage which would have been a blank without him.' This is well and truly said, and it is applicable to 'Gentleman Young' throughout his whole career—a period during which he played a vast variety of characters, from Hamlet to Captain Macheath. He was not one of those players who were always in character. Between the scenes of his most serious parts he would keep the green-room merry with his stories, and be serious again as soon as his part required him.   Young's modest farewell to the stage reminds us of Garrick's.   The latter took place on June 10, 1776.   The play was 'The Wonder,' Don Felix by Garrick; with 'The Waterman.'   The bill is simply headed, 'The last time of the company's performing this season,' and it concludes with these words: 'The profits of this night being appropriated to the benefit of the Theatrical Fund, the Usual Address upon that Occasion Will be spoken by Mr. Garrick before the Play.'   The bill is now before us, and not a word in it refers to the circumstance that it was the last night that Garrick would ever act, and that he would take final leave after the play.   All the world was supposed to know it.   The only intimation that something unusual was on foot is contained in the words, 'Ladies are desired to send their servants a little after 5, to keep places, to prevent confusion.'   Garrick's farewell speech is stereotyped in all dramatic memories.   His letter to Clutterbuck in the previous January is not so familiar.   He says, 'I have at last slipt my theatrical shell, and shall be as fine and free a gentleman as you should wish to see upon the South or North Parade of Bath.   I have sold my moiety of patent, &c., for 35,000*l*., to Messrs. Dr. Ford, Ewart, Sheridan, and Linley. . . . I grow somewhat older,

though I never played better in all my life, and am
resolved not to remain upon the stage to be pitied
instead of applauded!' Garrick was sixty years
of age when he left the stage. Young was five
years less. In his modest farewell speech, after
the curtain had descended on his Hamlet, he said,
'It has been asked why I retire from the stage
while still in possession of whatever qualifications
I could ever pretend to unimpaired. I will give
you my *motives*, although I do not know you will
accept them as *reasons*—but reason and feeling are
not always cater-cousins. I feel then the toil and
excitement of my calling weigh more heavily upon
me than formerly; and, if my qualifications are
unimpaired, so I would have them remain in your
estimate. . . . I am loth to remain before my
patrons until I have nothing better to present
them than tarnished metal.' Among Young's after-
enjoyments was that of music. We well remember
his always early presence in the front row of the
pit at the old Opera House, and the friendly greet-
ings that used to be exchanged between him and
Mori, Nicholson, Linley, Dragonetti, and other
great instrumentalists, as they made their appearance in the orchestra.

*Some* theatrical impulses never abandoned him.
During his retirement at Brighton, he was a con-
stant attendant on the ministry of Mr. Sortain.
'Mr. Bernal Osborne told me he was one day shown

into the same pew with my father, whom he knew. He was struck with his devotional manner during the prayers and by his rapt attention during the sermon. But he found himself unable to maintain his gravity when, as the preacher paused to take breath after a long and eloquent outburst, the habits of the actor's former life betrayed themselves, and he uttered in a deep undertone, the old familiar " *Bravo !* "'  As a sample of his cheerfulness of character, we may quote what Mr. Cole says of Young, in the life of Charles Kean :—' Not long before he left London for his final residence at Brighton, he called, with one of his grandsons, to see the writer of these pages, who had long enjoyed his personal friendship, and who happened at the moment to be at dinner with his family. " Tell them," he said to the servant, " not to hurry ; but when they are at leisure, there are two little boys waiting to see them."'

A quiet humour seems to have been among the characteristics of a life which generally was marked by unobtrusive simplicity and moral purity. A man who, when a boy, had been at Eton and Merchant Taylors' could not have been ignorant of such a fact as the Punic War, though he may have forgotten the date. He was once turned to by a lady at table (she had been discussing history with the guest on her other side), and she suddenly asked Young to tell her the date of the Second Punic War.

Young frankly replied in one of his most tragic tones; 'Madam, I don't know anything about the Punic War, and what is more, I never did! My inability to answer your question has wrung from me the same confession which I once heard made by a Lancashire farmer, with an air of great pride, when appealed to by a party of his friends in a commercial room, "I tell you what, in spite of all your bragging, I'll wedger (wager) I'm th' igno-rantest man in t' coompany!"' There can be little doubt that many of the stories of mistakes made by actors may be traced to him. Among them, perhaps, that of the player who, invariably, for 'poisoned cup,' said 'coisoned pup;' and who, once pronouncing it correctly, was hissed for his pains. Thence too perhaps came the tale of him who, instead of saying,

> How sharper than a serpent's tooth it is,
> To have a thankless child,

exclaimed :

> How sharper than a serpent's *thanks* it is,
> To have a *toothless* child.

Whatever may be the source of such stories, it is certain that Young's criticisms of others were always clear and generous. A few words tell us of Mrs. Siddons' Rosalind, that 'it wanted neither playfulness nor feminine softness; but it was totally without archness, not because she did not properly conceive it—but how could such a countenance be arch ?' Some one has said more irreverently of her Rosalind, that it was like Gog in petticoats! Young looked back to the periods during which he had what he called 'the good fortune to act with her, as the happiest of his own professional recollections.' When he was a boy of twelve years of age (1789), he saw Mrs. Siddons in Volumnia (Coriolanus). Long after, he described her bearing in the triumphal procession in honour of her son in this wise: 'She came alone marching and beating time to the music, rolling from side to side, swelling with the triumph of her son. Such was the intoxication of joy which flashed from her eye and lit up her whole face, that the effect was irresistible. She seemed to me to reap all the glory of that procession to herself. I could not take my eye from her. Coriolanus' banner and pageant, all went for nothing to me, after she had walked to her place.'

We have spoken of the unobtrusive simplicity and the moral purity of this great actor's life. Temptations sprang up about him. Young first appeared on the stage when the old drinking days had not yet come to an end. His name, however, never occurs among the annals of the fast and furious revelries. John Kemble belonged to the old school and followed its practices. He was not indeed fast and furious in his cups. He was

solemnly drunken as became an earnest tragedian.
It is somewhere told of him that he once went to
Dicky Peake's house half-cocked, at half-past nine
P.M.; Sheridan, he said, had appointed to meet him
there, and he would not neglect being in time for
the world. Peake sat him down to wine with Dunn
the treasurer: the three got exceedingly drunk,
and all fell asleep, Kemble occupying the carpet.
The tragedian was the first to wake. He arose,
opened the window shutters, and dazzled by the
morning sun-light roused his two companions, and
wondered as to the time of day. They soon heard
eight strike. 'Eight!' exclaimed Kemble; 'this is
too provoking of Sheridan; he is always late in
keeping his appointments; I don't suppose he will
come at all now. If he *should*, tell him, my dear
Dick, how long I waited for him!' Therewith,
*exit* John Philip, in a dreamy condition—leaving,
at all events, *some* incidents out of which imaginative
Dunn built this illustrative story.

Great writers in their own houses, like prophets
among their own people, proverbially lack much of
the consideration they find abroad. Mrs. Douglas
Jerrold always wondered what it was people found
in her husband's jokes to laugh at. It is *said* that
many years had passed over the head of Burns's
son before the young man knew that his father was
famous as a poet. It is certain that Walter Scott's
eldest son had arrived at more than manhood before

he had the curiosity to read one of his sire's novels.
He thought little of it when he had read it.  This
want of appreciation the son derived from his
mother.    Once, when Young was admiring the
fashion of the ceiling, in Scott's drawing-room at
Abbotsford, Lady Scott exclaimed in her droll
Guernsey accent, ' Ah ! Mr. Young, you may look
up at the bosses in the ceiling, as long as you like,
but you must not look down at my poor carpet, for
I am ashamed of it. I must get Scott to write some
more of his nonsense books and buy me a new one !'
To those who remember the charm of Young's
musical voice, Lady Dacre's lines on his reciting
' Tam o' Shanter ' to the other guests at Abbotsford,
will present themselves without any thought of
differing from their conclusion, thus neatly put :—

> And Tam o' Shanter roaring fou,
> By thee embodied to our view,
> The rustic bard would own sae true,
>     He scant could tell
> Wha 'twas the livin' picture drew,
>     Thou or himsel' !

It is a curious fact that Scott, harmonious poet
as he was, had no ear for music, unless it were that
of a ballad, and he would repeat that horribly out
of tune.  He was, however, in tune with all humanity ; as much so with a king as with the
humblest of his subjects.  When he went on board
the royal yacht which had arrived near Leith, with

George IV., amid such rain as only falls in Scotland, Scott, in an off-hand, yet respectful way, told the king that the weather reminded him of the stormy day of his own arrival in the Western Highlands, weather which so disgusted the landlord of the inn, who was used to the very worst, that he apologised for it. 'Gude guide us! this is just awfu'! Siccan a downpour, was ever the like! I really beg your pardon! I'm sure it's nae faut o' mine. I canna think how it should happen to rain this way just as you o' a' men i' the warld should come to see us! It looks amaist personal! I can only say, for my part, I'm just ashamed o' the weather!' Having thus spoken to the king, Scott added; 'I do not know, sire, that I can improve upon the language of the honest innkeeper. I canna think how it should rain this way, just as your majesty, of all men in the world, should have condescended to come and see us. I can only say in the name of my countrymen, I'm just ashamed o' the weather!' It was at Scott's petition that the royal landing was deferred till the next day, which brought all the sunshine that was considered necessary for the occasion.

It is singular to find Charles Mathews, senior, writing of himself; 'I only perform for one rank of persons. The lower orders hate and avoid me, and the middle classes cannot comprehend me.' He used to get fun enough out of his own man-servant,

whose awe and pride at seeing a titled personage at
his master's house were amply stimulated by friends
of Mathews who visited him under assumed dig-
nities.  Charles Kemble was always announced as
the Persian Ambassador, Fawcett as Sir Francis
Burdett, and Young as the Duke of Wellington.
One day, a real Lord—Lord Ranelagh—called and
sent in a message expressive of his desire to see
Mathews.   Mathews, supposing the visitor was a
fellow-player passing as a peer, sent a reply that he
was just then busy with Lord Vauxhall.  When
Mr. Julian Young once told Mathews he was going
to Lord Dacres at the Hoo, the actor replied, *Who?*
and thinking Bob Acres was raised to the peerage,
begged to be remembered to Sir Lucius O'Trigger !

One of the most flattering kindnesses ever paid
to the elder Mathews was when he was once standing among the crowd in, a Court of Assize, where
Judge Alan Park was presiding.  His lordship sent
a note down to him, requesting him to come and
take a seat on the bench.  The actor obeyed, and
the judge was courteously attentive to him.
Mathews was subsequently the guest of his old
friend Mr. Rolls, at whose house in Monmouthshire
the judge had previously been staying.  The player
asked if his lordship had alluded to him.  ' Yes,'
said Rolls, who proceeded to relate how Judge
Park had been startled at seeing in court a fellow
who was in the habit of imitating the voice and

manners of the judges on the stage. Indeed, his imitation of Lord Ellenborough, in 'Love, Law, and Physic,' had well nigh brought the imitator to grief. Park said the presence of Mathews so troubled him that he invited the mimic to sit near him, and behaved so kindly that he hoped the actor, out of simple gratitude, would not include him in his Legal Portraits in comedy or farce.

Appreciation of the drama is neither strong nor clear in at least one part of the vicinity of Shakespeare's native town. After the busy time of the ' Tercentenary,' Mr. Julian Young sent his servants to the theatre in Stratford. They had never been in a playhouse before. The piece represented was ' Othello.' On the following morning, wishing to know the effect of the drama on his servants' minds, Mr. Julian Young questioned them in their several departments. The butler was impressed to this effect : ' Thank you, sir, for the treat. The performers performed the performance which they had to perform excellent well—especially the female performers—in the performance.' The more impulsive coachman, in the harness-room, exclaimed, ' 'Twas really beautiful, sir ; I liked it onaccountable !' But when he was asked what the play was about he frankly confessed he didn't exactly know ; but that it was very pretty, and was upon sweethearting ! On a former occasion, when the gardener and his wife had been treated to the Bristol

Theatre, their master, on the next day, asked,
'Well, Robert, what did you see last night?'   The
bewildered fellow replied, after a pause, 'Well, sir,
I saw what you sent me to see!'  'What was that?'
'Why, the play, in course.'   'Was it a tragedy or
a comedy?'   'I don't know what you mane.   I
can't say no more than I have said, nor no fairer!
All I know is there was a precious lot on 'em on
the theayter stage ; and there they was, in and out,
and out and in again!'   The wife had more defi-
nite ideas.   She was all for the second piece, she
said, 'The pantrymine, and what I liked best in it
was where the fool fellar stooped down and grinned
at we through his legs!'   Good creature! after
all, her taste was in tune with that of King
George III., who thought Garrick fidgety, and
who laughed himself into fits at the clown who
could get a whole bunch of carrots into his mouth,
and apparently swallow them, with supplementary
turnips to make them go down!   The gardener's
wife, therefore, need not be ashamed.   She is not
half so much called upon to blush as the wife of
the treasurer of Drury Lane Theatre, who was one
of a score of professional ladies and gentlemen
dining together some forty years ago.   The lady
hearing 'Venice Preserved' named, made the remark that she believed 'it was one of Shakespeare's
plays, was it not?'   We have ourselves a bill of
Drury Lane, not ten years old, in which 'Othello'

is announced as Bulwer's tragedy, &c.; but that, of course, was a misprint. On our showing it in the green-room, however, not one of the per- formers saw the error!

Let us now look at some of the other personages who figured in the bygone period; and first, of kings. Poor old George III. cannot be said at any time to have been 'every inch a king.' He was certainly not, by nature, a cruel man. Yet he betrayed something akin to cruelty when, on the night of the Lord George Gordon riots, an officer who had been actively employed in suppressing the rioters waited on the king to make his report. George III. hurried forward to meet him, crying out with screaming iteration, 'Well! well! well! I hope you peppered them well! peppered them well! peppered them well!' There may, however, have been nothing more in this than there was in Wellington's injunction to his officers on the day that London was threatened with a Chartist revo- lution, 'Remember, gentlemen, there must be no little war.' In such cases humanity to revolution- ists is lack of mercy to the friends of order.

It is well known that George III. had an insu- perable aversion to Dr. John Willis, who had at- tended him when the King was labouring under his early intermitting attacks of insanity. Willis was induced to take temporary charge of the King, on Pitt's promise to make him a baronet and give him a pension of 1,500*l.* a year—pleasant things which never came to pass. Queen Charlotte hated Willis even more than the King did. The physician earned that guerdon by putting George III. in a strait waistcoat whenever he thought the royal violence required it. The doctor took this step on his own responsibility. The Queen never forgave him, and the King, as long as he had memory, never forgot it. In 1811, when the fatal relapse occurred, brought on, Willis thought, by Pitt's persistent pressure of the Roman Catholic claims on the King's mind, the Chancellor and the Prince of Wales had some difficulty in inducing the doctor to take charge of the sovereign. When Willis entered that part of Windsor Castle which was in-habited by the King he heard the monarch hum-ming a favourite song in his room. A moment after George III. crossed the threshold on to the landing-place. He was in Windsor uniform as to his coat, blue, with scarlet cuffs and collar, a star on the breast. A waistcoat of buff chamois leather, buskin breeches and top-boots, with the familiar three-cornered hat, completed the costume. He came forth as a bridegroom from his chamber, full of hope and joy, like Cymon, ' whistling as he went for want of thought,' and switching his boot with his whip as he went. Suddenly, as his eye fell on Willis, he reeled back as if he had been shot. He shrieked out the hated name, called on

God, and fell to the ground. It was long before the unhappy sovereign could be calmed. In his own room the King wept like a child. Every now and then he broke into heartrending exclamations of ' What can I do without doing wrong ? They forget my coronation oath ; but I don't ! Oh, my oath ! my oath ! my oath !' The King's excitement on seeing Willis was partly caused by his remembering the Queen's promise that Willis should never be called in again in case of the King's illness. Willis on that occasion consented to stay with the King after a fearful scene had taken place with the Queen, her doctors, and council. When Mr. Julian Young knew Willis, from whom he had the above details, the doctor was above eighty years of age, upright and active. He was still a mighty hunter ; and, unless Mr. Young was misinformed, on the very day before his death he shot two or three brace of snipes in the morning, and danced at the Lincoln ball at night. Willis did not reach his hundredth year, as Dr. Routh, of Magdalen College, Oxford, did. Just before the death of the latter, Lord Campbell visited and had a long conversation with him. At parting the centenarian remarked : ' I hope it will not be many years before we meet again.' ' Did he think,' said Lord Campbell afterwards, ' that he and I were going to live for ever ?'

Monarchs, who have to submit to many tyran-

nies by which monarchs alone can suffer, must have
an especial dread of levees and presentations. The
monotony must be killing; at the very best, irri-
tating. George IV. had the stately dreariness very
much relieved. On one occasion, when a nervous
gentleman was bowing and passing before him, a
lord-in-waiting kindly whispered to him, 'Kiss
hands!' The nervous gentleman accordingly
moved on to the door, turned round, and there
kissed his hands airily to the King by way of
kindly farewell! George IV. laughed almost as
heartily as his brother, King William, did at an
unlucky alderman who was at Court on the only
day Mr. Julian Young ever felt himself constrained
to go into the royal presence. The alderman's
dress-sword got between his legs as he was backing
from that presence, whereby he was tripped up
and fell backwards on the floor. King William
cared not a fig for dignity. He remarked with
great glee to those who stood near: 'By Jove!
the fellow has cut a crab!' and the kingly laughter was, as it were, poured point blank into the
floundering alderman. This was not encouraging
to Mr. Young, who had to follow. As newly-
appointed royal chaplain in Hampton Court Palace
Chapel, King William had expressed a wish to see
him at a levee, and obedience was a duty. The
chaplain had been told by Sir Horace Seymour
that he had nothing to do but follow the example

of the gentleman who might happen to be before him. The principal directions to the neophyte were: 'Bow very low, and do not turn your back on the King!' The instant the chaplain had kissed the King's hand, however, he turned his back upon his sovereign, and hurried off. Sir Horace Seymour afterwards consoled him for this breach of etiquette by stating that a Surrey baronet who had followed him made a wider breach in court observance. The unlucky baronet, seeing the royal hand outstretched, instead of reverently putting his lips to it, caught hold of it and wrung it heartily! The King, who loved a joke, probably enjoyed levees, the usual monotony of which was relieved by such screaming-farce incidents as these.

Those royal brothers, sons of George III., were remarkably outspoken. They were not witty themselves, but they were now and then the cause of wit in others. It must have been the Duke of Cumberland who (on listening to Mr. Nightingale's story of having been run away with when driving, and that at a critical moment he jumped out of the carriage) blandly exclaimed: 'Fool! fool!' 'Now,' said Nightingale, on telling the incident to Horace Smith, 'it's all very well for him to call me a fool; but I can't conceive why he should. Can you?' 'No,' rejoined Horace, 'I can't, because he could not suppose you ignorant of the fact!'

Among the most unhappy lords of themselves who lived in a past generation, there was not one who might have been so happy, had he pleased, as the author of 'Vathek.' It is very well said of Beckford that there has seldom existed a man who, inheriting so much, did so little for his fellow-creatures. There was a grim humour in some of his actions. In illustration of this we may state that when Beckford was living in gorgeous seclusion at Fonthill, two gentlemen, who were the more curious to spy into the glories of the place because strangers were forbidden, climbed the park walls at dusk, and on alighting within the prohibited enclosure, found themselves in presence of the lord of the place. Beckford awed them by his proud condescension. He politely dragged them through all the splendours of his palace, and then, with cruel courtesy, made them dine with him. When the night was advanced, he took his involuntary guests into the park, bidding them adieu with the remark, that as they had found their way in they might find their way out. It was as bad as bandaging a man's eyes on Salisbury Plain, and bidding him find his way to Bath. At sunrise the weary guests, who had pursued a fruit-less voyage of discovery all night, were guided to a point of egress, and they never thought of calling on their host again.

Ready wit in women (now passed away); wit,

too, combined with courage, is by no means rare.
During the ruro-diabolical reign of 'Swing,' that
incarnation of ruffianism, in the person of the most
hideous blackguard in the district, with a mob of
thieves and murderers at his back, attacked Fifield,
the old family residence of two elderly maiden
ladies, named Penruddock.  When the mob were
on the point of resorting to extreme violence, Miss
Betty Penruddock expressed her astonishment to
the ugly leader of the band that ' such a good-
looking man as he should be captain of such an
ill-favoured band of robbers.  Never again will I
trust to good looks!' cried the old lady, whose
flattery so touched the vanity of 'Swing' that he
prevailed on his followers to desist.  ' Only give us
some beer,' he said, ' and we won't touch a hair of
your head !'  ' You can't,' retorted the plucky old
lady, ' for I wear a wig !'  On the other hand, the
vanity of young ladies was once effectually checked
at Hampton Court Chapel.  A youthful beauty
once fainted, and the handsome Sir Horace Seymour carried her out.  On successive Sundays
successive youthful beauties fainted, and the handsome Sir Horace carried them successively out, till
he grew tired of bearing such sweet burdens.  A
report that in future all swooning nymphs would
be carried out of the chapel by *the dustman* cured
the epidemic.

We are much disposed to think that there is

at least as much ready wit and terseness of expression among the humbler classes as among those who are higher born and better taught. Much has been said of the ladies of Llangollen, Lady Eleanor Butler and Miss Ponsonby. We question if in all that has been written of those pseudo-recluses, they have been half so well hit-off as by Mrs. Morris, a lodging-house keeper in the neighbourhood. 'I must say, sir, after all,' observed Mrs. Morris, 'that they were very charitable and cantankerous. They did a deal of good, and never forgave an injury!' There is something of the ring of Mrs. Poyser in this pithily-rendered judgment. Quite as sharp a passage turns up in the person of an eccentric toll-keeper, Old Jeffreys, who was nearly destitute of mental training, and whom Mr. Julian Young was anxious to draw to church service. The old man was ready for him. 'Yes, sir, it be a pity, bain't it? We pike-keepers, and shepherds, and carters, and monthly nusses has got souls as well as them that goes to church and chapel. But what can us do? "Why," I says, says I, to the last parson as preached to me, "don't catechism say summat or other about doing our duty in that state of life in which we be?" So, after all, when I be taking toll o' Sundays, I'm not far wrong, am I?' The rector proposed to find a paid substitute for him while he attended church. Jeffreys was ready with his reply. 'That 'ud never do, sir,' he said. 'What! leave my post to a stranger? What would master say to me if he heard on't.' Mr. Julian Young, pointing with pleasure to a Bible on old Jeffreys' shelf, expressed a hope that he often read it. 'Can't say as how I do, sir,' was the candid rejoinder; 'I allus gets so poorus over it!' When the rector alluded to a certain wench as 'disreputable,' Jeffreys protested in the very spirit of chivalry. 'Don't do that! Do as I do! I allus praises her. Charity hides a deal o' sin, master! ain't that Scripture? If it are, am I to be lectured at for sticking up and saying a good word for she?' When it was urged that this light-o'-love queen ought to be married, Samaritan Jeffreys stept in with his sympathetic balsam. 'Poor thing!' he exclaimed, ' *she ain't no turn to it!* ' The apology was worthy of my Uncle Toby!

There are other stories quite worthy of him who invented Uncle Toby; but, *basta!* we have been, as it were, metaphorically dining with Mr. Julian Young—dining so well that we cannot recall to mind half the anecdotes told at his table in illustration of Charles Young and his times.

## WILLIAM CHARLES MACREADY.

In the year 1793, a gentleman who was a member of the Covent Garden company, in the department of 'utilities,' might be seen, any day during the season, punctually on his way to the theatre, for rehearsal or for public performance. At the above date he had been seven years on the London boards, having first appeared at the 'Garden' in 1786, as Flutter in 'The Belle's Stratagem.' His name was William Macready, father of *the* Macready, and his *début* on the English stage was owing to the influence of Macklin, whom the young fellow had gratified by playing Egerton to the veteran's Sir Pertinax, exactly according to the elaborate instructions he had patiently received from Macklin himself at rehearsal.

William Macready had left the vocation of his father in Dublin—that of an upholsterer—for the uncertain glories of the stage. The father was a common councilman, and was respectably connected—or, rather, his richer relatives were respectably connected in having him for a kinsman. In Ireland there is a beggarly pride which looks down upon trade as a mean thing.  Mr. Macready, the flourishing Dublin upholsterer, took to that sound mean thing, and found his account in so doing.  His prouder kinsmen may have better respected their blood, but they had not half so good a book at their banker's.

The upholsterer's son took his kinsmen's view of trade, and deserted it accordingly.  He could hardly, however, have gratified them by turning player; but he followed the bent of his inclinations, addressed himself to sock and buskin, toiled in country theatres, was tolerated rather than patronised in his native city, and, as before said, got a footing on the Covent Garden stage in 1786.

William Macready's position there in 1793 was much the same that it was when he first appeared. Perhaps he had a little improved it, by the popular farce of which he was the author, 'The Irishman in London,' which was first acted at Covent Garden in 1792.  In 1793 he was held good enough to act Cassio to Middleton's Othello, and was held cheap enough to be cast for Fag in the 'Rivals.'  On his benefit night—he was in a position to share the house with Hull—the two partners played such walking gentlemen's characters as Cranmer and Surrey (the latter by Macready) to the Wolsey and Queen Catharine of Mr. and Mrs. Pope; but Macready, in the afterpiece, soared to vivacious comedy, and acted Figaro to the Almaviva of mercurial Lewis. If he ever played an Irish part, it was only when Jack Johnstone was indisposed— which was not his custom of an afternoon.

The best of these actors, and others better than the best named above, received but very moderate salaries. Mr. Macready's was probably not more than three or four pounds per week. Upon certainly some such salary the worthy actor maintained a quiet home in Mary Street, Tottenham Court (or Hampstead) Road. At the head of the little family that gathered round the table in Mary Street was one of the best of mothers ; and chief among the children—the one at least who became the most famous—was William Charles Macready, whom so many still remember as a foremost actor, and in whom some even recognised a great master of his art.

Among the earliest remembrances of this eminent player, he has noticed in his most interesting ' Reminiscences,' that ' the *res angustæ domi* called into active duty all the economical resources and active management of a mother ' (whose memory, he says, is enshrined in his heart's fondest gratitude) ' to supply the various wants ' of himself and an elder sister, who only lived long enough to make him ' sensible of her angelic nature.' Macready was the fifth child of this family, but his sister, Olivia, was the only one (then born) who lived long enough for him to remember. She was older than he by a year and a half, and she survived only till he was just in his sixth year ; ' but she lives,' he says, ' like a dim and far-off dream, to my memory, of a spirit of meekness, love, and truth, interposing itself between my infant will and the evil it purposed. It is like a vision of an angelic influence upon a most violent and self-willed disposition.'

It may be added here that Macready had a younger brother, Edward, who distinguished himself as a gallant officer in the army, and two younger sisters, Letitia and Ellen, to whom he was an affectionate brother and friend. Meanwhile Macready passed creditably through a school at Birmingham, and thence to Rugby. At the latter place, where one of his kinsmen was a master, the student laid the ground of all the classical knowledge he possessed, took part in private plays, and was hurt at the thought that he had any inclination to be a professional actor. At Rugby, too, he showed, but with some reason, the fiery quality of his temper. He was unjustly sent up for punishment, and was flogged accordingly. ' Returning,' he says, ' to my form, smarting with choking rage and indignation, where I had to encounter the compassion of some and the envious jeers of others, my passion broke out in the exclamation, " D——n old Birch ! I wish he was in Hell ! " '

Macready's excellent mother, of whom he never speaks without dropping, as it were, a flower to honour her memory, died before he reached home from Rugby, so that the world was, for a time, without sun to him, for the sire was not a very amiable person. The younger Macready resorted to the best possible cure for sorrow, steady and active work, and plenty of both. At last, with no very cheerful encouragement from his father and with doubt and fear on his own part, he, in June 1811, made his *début*, in Birmingham, in 'Romeo and Juliet,' 'the part of Romeo by a Young Gentleman, being his first appearance on any stage.' He, who was afterwards so very cool and self-possessed, nearly marred all by what is called 'stage-fright.' A mist fell on his eyes; the very applause, as he came forward, bewildered him; and he describes himself as being for some time like an automaton, moving in certain defined limits. 'I went mechanically,' he says, 'through the variations in which I had drilled myself;' but he gradually gained courage and power over himself. The audience stimulated the first and rewarded the second by their applause. 'Thenceforward,' says Macready, 'I trod on air, became another being or a happier self, and when the curtain fell and the intimate friends and performers crowded on the stage to raise up the *Juliet* and myself, shaking my hands with fervent congratulations, a lady asked

me, ' Well, sir, how do you feel now?' my boyish
answer was without disguise, ' I feel as if I should
like to act it all over again!'

Between this and his first appearance in London
Macready acted in most of the theatres of every
degree in the three kingdoms.  Often this practice
was rendered the more valuable by his having to
perform with the most perfect actors and actresses
who were starring in the country.  But, whether
with them or without, whether with audiences or
with a mere two or three, he did his best.  Like
Barton Booth, he would play to a man in the pit.
' It was always my rule,' he says, ' to make the
best out of a bad house, and before the most
meagre audiences ever assembled it has been my
invariable practice to strive my best, using the opportunity as a lesson; and I am conscious of having derived great benefit from the rule.  I used to
call it acting to myself.'  Macready had another
rule which is worth mentioning.  Some of the old
French tragedy queens used to keep themselves all
day in the temper of the characters they were to
represent in the evening.  So that, at home or on
the boards, they swept to and fro in towering rage.
So, Macready was convinced of the necessity of
keeping, on the day of exhibition, the mind as intent as possible on the subject of the actor's portraiture, even to the very moment of his entrance
on the scene.  With the observance of this rule,

Macready must have made 64 Frith Street, Soho,
re-echo with joyous feelings and ebullitions of fury,
to suit the temper of the night, when in 1816 he
made his bow to a London audience as Orestes in
the ' Distressed Mother,' and when the curtain
rose grasped Abbot almost convulsively by the
hand, and dashed upon the stage, exclaiming as in
a transport of the highest joy, ' Oh, Pylades ! what's
life without a friend ? '   The Orestes was a success ;
but it was never a favourite character with the
public, as Talma's was with the French.   The career
thus begun (at ten, fifteen, and at last eighteen
pounds per week for five years) came to a close in
1851.   Five-and-thirty years out of the fifty-eight
Macready had then reached.   We need not trace
this progressive career, beginning with Ambrose
Phillips and ending with Shakespeare (' Macbeth ').
During that career he created that one great
character in which no player could come near him,
namely, Virginius, in 1820.   Macready, however,
was not the original representative of Virginius.
That character in Knowles's most successful play
was first acted by John Cooper in Glasgow ; but
Macready really created the part in London.
Further, Macready did his best to raise the drama,
actors, and audiences to a dignity never before
known, and gained nothing but honour by his two
ventures at management.   He was the first to put
a play upon the stage with an almost lavish per-

fection  In this way he was never equalled.  Mr. Charles Kean imitated him in this artist-like proceeding ; but that highly respectable actor and man was as far behind Macready in magnificence of stage management as he was distant from his own father in genius.

If Macready, on his *début* as a boy, was scared, he was deeply moved when, within a stone's throw of sixty, he was to act for the last time, and then go home for ever. This was upwards of thirty years ago; so rapidly does time fly — the 28th of February, 1851.  His emotion was not in the acting, but in the taking leave of it, and of those who came to see it for the last time.  He says himself of his Macbeth that he never played it better than on that night.  There was a reality, with a vigour, truth, and dignity, which he thought he had never before thrown into that favourite character.  'I rose with the play, and the last scene was a real climax.'  On his first entrance, indeed, at the beginning of his part, 'the thought occurred to me of the presence of my children, and that for a minute overcame me ; but I soon recovered myself into self-possession.'  Still more deeply moved at the 'farewell' to a house bursting into a wild enthusiasm of applause, he 'faltered for a moment at the fervent, unbounded expression of attachment from all before me ; but preserved my self-possession.'  Those of his ten children who

had survived and were present on that occasion had
ample reason to be proud of their father. For
many years he would not sanction their being present at his public exhibitions. This was really to
doubt the dignity and usefulness of his art, to feel
a false shame, and to authorise in others that contempt for the ' playactor ' which, entertaining it,
as he did thoroughly, for many of his fellows, he
neither felt for himself nor for those whom he
could recognise as being great and worthy masters
in that art. When his children were allowed the
new delight of witnessing how nobly he could
interpret the noblest of the poets, the homage of
their reverential admiration must have been added
to that of their unreserved affection. That he was
not popular at any time with inferior or subordi-
nate players is undoubtedly true. Such persons
thought that only want of luck and opportunity
placed them lower in the scale than Macready. It
would be as reasonable for the house-painters to
account in the same way for their not being Van-
dycks and Raffaelles.

Sensitive to criticism he was, and yet scarcely
believed himself to be so. He belabours critics
pretty roughly; but we observe that theatrical
critics dined with him occasionally, and we mark
that he praises the good sense and discrimination
of one of these critics—whose criticism was very
much in the actor's favour. Vanity he also had,

certainly. We should have come to this conclusion, had we nothing more to justify the assertion than what we find in his own record. We see his vanity in the superabundant excess of his modesty; but we think none the worse of him for it. An artist who is not somewhat vain of his powers has, probably, no ground for a little wholesome pride. It was in Macready tempered with that sort of fear that a vain man may feel, lest in the exercise of his art he should fall in the slightest degree short of his self-estimation, or of that in which he believed himself to be held by the public. He never, on entering a town, saw his name on a bill, without feeling a flutter of the heart, made up of this mingled fear and pride. So, Mrs. Siddons never went on the stage at any time without something of the same sensation. We should think little of any actor or actress who should avow that they ever 'went on,' in a great part, without some hesitation lest the attempt might fall short of what it was their determination to achieve, and what they felt themselves qualified to accomplish. Vanity and timidity? All true artists are conscious of both—ought to possess both; just as they ought to possess not only impulse but judgment; not only head, but heart; heart to flash the impulses, head to control them.

Macready carried to the stage his genuine piety. It is, perhaps, a little too much aired in his 'Diary,'

but it is not the less to be believed in.  He went
by a good old-fashioned rule, to do his duty in that
state of life to which it had pleased God to call
him—as the Catechism teaches, or used to teach,
all of us.  In his pious fervour, in his prayers that
what he is going to act may be for good, that what
in the management he has undertaken may be to
the increase of the general happiness rather than
to that of his banking account; in these and a
score of other instances we are reminded of those
French and Italian saints of the stage who, as
they stood at the wing, crossed themselves at the
sound of sacred names in the play; or, who
counted their beads in the green-room ; kept their
fasts ; mortified themselves, and never missed a
mass.  Nay, the religious feeling was as sponta-
neous in Macready as it was in the Italian actors
whom he himself saw, and who, at the sound of
the ' Angelus ' in the street, stopped the action of
the play, fell on their knees, gently tapped their
breasts, and were imitated in these actions by the
sympathising majority of the audience.

We fully endorse the judgment of a critic who
has said that with the worst of tempers Macready
had the best of hearts.  Some of the tenderest of
his actions are not registered in the volumes of his
life, but they are recorded in grateful bosoms.
There were married actresses in his company,
when he managed the ' Garden,' and afterwards

the 'Lane,' whom he would rate hashly enough for inattention; but there were certain times when he was prompted to tell them that their proper place, for a while, was home; and that till they recovered health and strength their salary would be continued, and then run on as usual. The sternest moralist will forgive him for knocking down Mr. Bunn, when he remembers this tender part in the heart of Macready.

Towards women that heart may be said to have been sympathetically inclined. His early life led him into many temptations; he had, as he confesses, many loves in his time, real and imaginary; but the first true and ever-abiding one was that which ended in his marriage with a young actress, Miss Atkins. The whole story is touchingly told. We feel the joys and the sorrows of the April time of that love. We share in the triumph of the lovers; and throughout the record of their union Macready inspires us with as much respectful affection for that true wife as in other pages he stirs us to honour the memory of his mother. He was singularly happy in the women whom it was his good fortune to know. Early in life, after his mother's death, he found wise friends in some of them, whose wisdom 'kept him straight,' as the phrase goes, when crooked but charming ways opened before him. At his latest in life, the inestimable good of woman's best companionship was vouchsafed to him; and further than this it would be impertinent to speak.

The dignity of the departed actor was his attribute, which in his busy days atoned for such faults as cannot be erased from his record. How he supported the dignity of the drama, and, we may say, of its patrons, may be seen in the registry of the noble dramas he produced, and in his purification of the audience side of the house. No person born since his time can have any idea of the horrible uncleanness that presented itself in the two patent theatres in the days before Macready's management commenced. When he found that he was bound by the terms of his lease to provide accommodation and refreshment for women who had no charm of womanhood left in them, Macready assigned a dingy garret and a rush-light or two for that purpose, and the daughters of joy fled from it, never to return.

It is a strange and repulsive thing to look back at the sarcasm flung at him by the vile part of the press at that time, for his enabling honest-minded women to visit a theatre without feeling ashamed at their being there, in company with those who had no honest-mindedness. In this, as in many other circumstances, he was worth all the Lord Chamberlains—silly, intruding, inconsistent, unreasonable beings—that have ever existed.

The career of the actor—we may say, of the

actor and of the private gentleman—was a long
one. Among the great dramatic personages whom
Macready saw in the course of that career, were
' a glimpse of King dressed as Lord Ogilvy,' his
original character, 'and distinguished for its performance in Garrick's day ; ' Lewis, whose face he
never forgot, but he never saw that restless, ever-
smiling actor on the stage. Macready was struck
with the beauty and deportment of Mrs. Siddons,
long before he acted with her ; and he was enthralled by Mrs. Billington, though he could in
after years only recall the figure of a very lusty
woman, and the excitement of the audience when
the orchestra struck up the symphony of Arne's
rattling bravura, ' The Soldier Tired,' in the opera
of ' Artaxerxes.' One of the most remarkable of
these illustrious persons was seen by him at the
Birmingham Theatre, 1808. The afterpiece was
' Alonzo the Brave and the Fair Imogene,' a ballet
pantomime. The lady fair was acted by the
manager's wife, Mrs. Watson—ungainly, tawdry,
and as fat as a porpoise, an enormous hill of flesh.
Alonzo the Brave was represented by ' a little
mean-looking man in a shabby green satin dress
. . . the only impression I carried away was that
the hero and heroine were the worst in the piece '
(a ballet of action, without words). Macready
adds that he neither knew nor guessed that ' under
that shabby green satin dress was hidden one of

the most extraordinary theatrical geniuses that have ever illustrated the dramatic poetry of England!'  In half a dozen years more, what was Macready's astonishment to find this little, insignificant Alonzo the Brave had burst out into the grandly impassioned personator of Othello, Richard, and Shylock—Edmund Kean!

Macready's testimony to Kean's marvellous powers is nearly always highly favourable.  Macready saw the great master act Richard III. at Drury Lane in his first season, 1814.  'When,' he tells us, ' a little keenly-visaged man rapidly bustled across the stage, I felt there was meaning in the alertness of his manner and the quickness of his step.'  The progress of the play increased the admiration of the young actor in his box, who was studying the other young actor on the stage.  He found mind of no common order in Edmund Kean. ' In his angry complaining of Nature's injustice to his bodily imperfections, as he uttered the line, " To shrink my arm up like a withered shrub," Kean remained looking on the limb for some moments with a sort of bitter discontent, and then struck it back in angry disgust.'  To his father's whisper, ' It's very poor,' the son replied readily, ' Oh, no ! it is no common thing.'  Macready praises the scene with Lady Anne, and that in which Richard tempts Buckingham to the murder of the young princes.  In the latter, he found

Kean's interpretation ‘consistent with his conception, proposing their death as a political necessity,
and sharply requiring it as a business to be done.’
Cooke interpreted the scene in another way. In
Cooke's Richard, ‘ the source of the crime was apparent in the gloomy hesitation with which he
gave reluctant utterance to the deed of blood.’  If
Cooke was more effective than Kean on one or two
solitary points, Kean was superior in the general
portraiture.  As Macready remarks, Kean ‘ hurried
you along in his resolute course with a spirit that
brooked no delay.  In inflexibility of will and
sudden grasp of expedients he suggested the idea
of a feudal Napoleon.’

With respect to the characters enacted by the
greatest actor of the present century, Macready's
testimony of Kean is that in none of Kean's per-
sonations did he display more masterly elocution
than in the third act of ‘ Richard III.’  In Sir
Edward Mortimer, Kean was unapproachable, and
Master Betty (whom Macready praises highly) next
to him, though far off.  In Sir Edward, Kean
‘ subjected his style to the restraint of the severest
taste.  Throughout the play the actor held absolute sway over his hearers ; and there is no
survivor of those hearers who will not enjoy a
description which enables them to live over
again moments of a bygone delight which the
present stage cannot afford  There are, perhaps,

not so few who remember Kean's Sir Edward
Mortimer as of those who remember his 'Oroonoko.' Those who do will endorse all that Macready says of that masterly representation of the
African Prince in slavery, where Kean, with a
calm submission to his fate, still preserved all
his princely demeanour. There was one passage
which was 'never to be forgotten'—the prayer
for his Imoinda. After replying to Blandford,
'No, there is nothing to be done for me,' he remained, says Macready, 'for a few moments in
apparent abstraction; then, with a concentration
of feeling that gave emphasis to every word, clasp-
ing his hands together, in tones most tender,
distinct, and melodious, he poured out, as if from
the very depths of his heart, his earnest suppli-
cation :—

> Thou God ador'd, thou ever-glorious Sun!
> If she be yet on earth, send me a beam
> Of thy all-seeing power to light me to her!
> Or if thy sister-goddess has preferr'd
> Her beauty to the skies, to be a star,
> Oh, tell me where she shines, that I may stand
> Whole nights, and gaze upon her!'

We may refer to another passage, in 'Othello,'
in which the tenderness, distinctness, and mournful
melodiousness of Edmund Kean's voice used to
affect the whole house to hushed and rapt admiration; namely, the passage beginning with, 'Fare-

well, the plumed troop!' and ending with, 'Othello's occupation's gone!' It was like some magic instrument, which laid all hearts submissive to its irresistible enchantment.

While Macready allows that flashes of genius were rarely wanting in Kean's least successful performances, he does not forget to note that when he played Iago to Kean's Othello, he observed that the latter was playing not at all like to his old self. It is to be remembered that this was in 1832, when Kean was on the brink of the grave, broken in constitution, and with no power to answer to his will. But Macready justly recognised the power when it existed, and set the world mad with a new delight. Others were not so just, nor so generous. 'Many of the Kemble school,' he says, 'resisted conviction of Kean's merits, but the fact that he made me feel was an argument to enrol me with the majority on the indisputable genius he displayed.' Some of the Kemble family were as reluctant to be convinced as many of the Kemble school were, but we must except the lady whom we all prefer to call 'Fanny Kemble.' She, in her 'Journal,' speaks without bias, not always accurately, but still justly and generously. To her, the great master was apparent, and she truly says that when Kean died there died with him Richard, Shylock, and Othello.

Before quitting Kean for the Kembles, we must

permit ourselves to extract the account given by Macready of a supper after Richard III. had been played :—

We retired to the hotel as soon as the curtain fell, and were soon joined by Kean, accompanied, or rather attended, by Pope. I need not say with what intense scrutiny I regarded him as we shook hands on our mutual introduction. The mild and modest expression of his Italian features, and his unassuming manner, which I might perhaps justly describe as partaking in some degree of shyness, took me by surprise, and I remarked with special interest the indifference with which he endured the fulsome flatteries of Pope. He was very sparing of words during, and for some time after, supper; but about one o'clock, when the glass had circulated pretty freely, he became animated, fluent, and communicative. His anecdotes were related with a lively sense of the ridiculous; in the melodies he sang there was a touching grace, and his powers of mimicry were most humorously or happily exerted in an admirable imitation of Braham; and in a story of Incledon acting Steady the Quaker at Rochester without any rehearsal, where, in singing the favourite air, ‘When the lads of the village so merrily, oh!’ he heard himself to his dismay and consternation accompanied by a single bassoon; the music of his voice, his perplexity at each recurring sound of the bassoon, his undertone maledictions on the self-satisfied musician, the peculiarity of his habits, all were hit off with a humour and an exactness that equalled the best display Mathews ever made, and almost convulsed us with laughter. It was a memorable evening, the first and last I ever spent in private with this extraordinary man.

Macready's estimation of Kemble and the

Kemble school is not at all highly pitched, save in the case of Mrs. Siddons ; but he notes how she outlived her powers, and returned a few times to the stage when her figure had enlarged and her genius had diminished. When John Kemble took leave of the Dublin stage, in 1816, Macready was present ; he records that ' the house was about half full.' Kemble acted Othello (which, at that time, Kean had made his own). ' A more august presence could hardly be imagined.' He was received with hearty applause, ' but the slight bow with which he acknowledged the compliment spoke rather dissatisfaction at the occasional vacant spaces before him than recognition of the respectful feeling manifested by those present. I must suppose he was out of humour, for, to my exceeding regret, he literally walked through the part.' The London audiences, as Kemble's career was drawing to a close, were not more sympathetic. At Kemble's Cato, ' The house was moderately filled ; there was sitting room in the pit, and the dress circle was not at all crowded.' To the dignity of the representation Macready renders homage of admiration ; but he says that Cato was not in strict Roman attire, and that with only one effort, the ' I am satisfied,' when he heard that Marcius ' greatly fell,' Kemble's husky voice and laboured articulation could not enliven the monotony of a tragedy which was felt to be a tax on the patience of the audience.  The want of variety and relief rendered it uninteresting, and  those at least who were not classical antiquaries found the whole thing uncommonly tedious.

It is unquestionably among the unaccountable things connected with ' the stage ' that Kemble's farewell performances in London, 1817, were as a whole unproductive.  Those closing nights, not answering the manager's expectations of their attraction, were given for benefits to those performers who chose to pay the extra price.  Macready was not present on the closing night of all, when Kemble nobly played his peerless Coriolanus ; but he witnessed several other representations, and he dwells especially on the last performance of ' Macbeth,' when Mrs. Siddons acted the Lady to her brother's Macbeth.  Macready was disappointed with both.  Mrs. Siddons was no longer the enchantress of old : ' years had done their work, and those who had seen in her impersonations the highest glories of her art, now felt regret that she had been prevailed on to leave her honoured retirement, and force a comparison between the grandeur of the past and the feeble present.  It was not a performance, but a mere repetition of the poet's text ; no flash, no sign of her pristine, all-subduing genius.'  Kemble, as Macbeth, was ' correct, tame, and ineffective,' through the first four acts of the play, which moved heavily on ;

but he was roused to action in the fifth act. With
action there was pathos ; and ' all at once, he
seemed carried away by the genius of the scene.'
Macready brings the scene itself before his readers,
ending with the words : ' His shrinking from
Macduff, when the charm on which his life hung
was broken, by the declaration that his antagonist
" was not of woman born," was a masterly stroke
of art. His subsequent defiance was most heroic ;
and, at his death, Charles Kemble received him in
his arms and laid him gently on the ground, his
physical powers being unequal to further effort.'

Of persons non-dramatic, many pass before the
mind's eye of the reader. Lord Nelson visited the
Birmingham Theatre, and Macready noted his pale
and interesting face, and listened so eagerly to all
he uttered that for months after he used to be
called upon to repeat ' what Lord Nelson said to
your father,' which was to the effect that the esteem
in which the elder Macready was held by the town
made it ' a pleasure and a duty' for Lord Nelson
to visit the theatre. With the placid and mourn-
ful-looking Admiral was Lady Hamilton, who
laughed loud and long, clapped her uplifted hands
with all her heart, and kicked her heels against the
foot-board of her seat, as some verses were sung in
honour of her and England's hero.

There was a time when Macklin ceased to belong to the drama, when he was out of the world,

in his old age, and his old Covent Garden house. One of the most characteristic of incidents is one told of Macklin in his dotage, when prejudice had survived all sense. Macready's father called on the aged actor with lack-lustre eye, who was seated in an arm-chair, unconscious of anyone being present. Mrs. Macklin drew his attention to the visitor: 'My dear, here is Mr. Macready come to see you.' 'Who?' 'Mr. Macready, my dear.' 'Ah! who is he?' 'Mr. Macready, you know, who went to Dublin, to play for your benefit.' 'Ha! my benefit! what was it? what did he act?' 'I acted Egerton, sir,' replied Mr. Macready, 'in your own play.' 'Ha! my play! what was it?' 'The "Man of the World," sir.' 'Ha! "Man of the World!" devilish good title! who wrote it?' 'You did, sir.' 'Did I? well, what was it about?' 'Why, sir, there was a Scotchman' —— 'Ah! damn them!' Macklin's hatred of the Scotch was vigorous after all other feeling was dead within him.

Equally good as a bit of character-painting is the full length of Mrs. Piozzi, whom William Charles Macready met at Bath, in the house of Dr. Gibbs. She struck the actor as something like one of Reynolds's portraits walking out of its frame: 'a little old lady dressed *point derise* in black satin, with dark glossy ringlets under her neat black hat, highly rouged, not the end of a ribbon or lace out of its place,' and entering the room with unfaltering step. She was the idol of the hour, and Macready, specially introduced to her, was charmed with her vivacity and good humour. The little old lady read, by request, some passages from Milton, a task she delighted in, and for doing which effectively she considered herself well qualified. She chose the description of the lazar-house, from the 11th Book of 'Paradise Lost,' and dwelt with emphatic distinctness on the various ills to which mortality is exposed. 'The finger on the dial-plate of the *pendule* was just approaching the hour of ten, when, with a Cinderella-like abruptness, she rose and took her leave, evidently as much gratified by contributing to our entertainment as we were by the opportunity of making her acquaintance.' According to Dr. Gibbs, the vivacious old Cinderella never stayed after ten was about to strike. Circumstances might indeed prompt the sensitive lady to depart earlier. Mr. Macready subsequently met the lively little lioness at the Twisses. The company was mixed, old and young; the conversation was general, or people talked the young with the young, the old among themselves. Mrs. Piozzi was not the oracle on whose out-speakings all hearers reverentially waited. Consequently, 'long before her accustomed hour, Mrs. Piozzi started up, and coldly wishing Mr. and Mrs. Twiss 'good night,' she left the room. To the general inquiries, by look or word, the hostess simply remarked,

'She is very much displeased.' The really gifted old lady's vanity was wounded ; lack of homage sent her home in a huff. Some of the best sketches in the book are of scenes of Macready's holiday travel. On one occasion, in a corner of an Italian garden, near a church, he caught a priest kissing a young girl whom he had just confessed. Nothing could be merrier or better-humoured than Macready's description of this pretty incident. The young Father, or brother, was quite in order ; Rome claims absolute rule over faith—and morals.

We close this chronicle of so many varied hues with reluctance. That which belongs to the retired life of the actor is fully as interesting as the detail of the times when he was in harness. Indeed, in the closing letters addressed to the present Lady Pollock, there are circumstances of his early career not previously recorded. The record of the home-life is full of interest, and we sympathise with the old actor, who, as the fire of temperament died out, appeared purified and chastened by the process.

Macready, throughout his long life, had no 'flexibility of spine' for men of wealth or title, but he had, if he describes himself truly, perfect reverence for true genius, wheresoever found. He was oppressed with his own comparative littleness and his seeming inability to cope with men better endowed, intellectually, than himself. And yet, we find him, when he must have felt that he was great, was assured he was so by his most intimate admirers, and counted amongst them some of the foremost literary men and critics of the day—we find him, we say, moodily complaining that he was not sought for by 'society,' and not invited into it. There was no real ground for the complaint. He who made it was an honour to the society of which he was a part. Every page of this record, not least so those inscribed with confession of his faults, will raise him in the esteem of all its readers. He went to his rest in 1873, and he is fortunate in the friend to whom he confided the task of writing his life. The work, edited with modesty and judgment, is a permanent addition to our dramatic literature.

## PRIVATE THEATRICALS.

As in Greece a man suffered no disparagement by being an actor there was no disposition to do in private what was not forbidden in public. The whole profession was ennobled when an actor so accomplished as Aristodemus was honoured with the office of ambassador.

In Rome a man was dishonoured by being a player. Accordingly noble Roman youths loved to act in private, excusing themselves on the ground that no professional actor polluted their private stage. Roman youths, however, had imperial example and noble justification when a Roman emperor made his first appearance on the public stage, and succeeded, as a matter of course.

Nero and Louis XIV. were the two sublime monarchs who were most addicted to private theatricals; but the Roman outdid the Frenchman. We know that persons of the Senatorial and Equestrian orders, and of both sexes, played the parts, but we do not know how they liked or disliked what they dared not decline. One can fancy, however, the figure and feelings of the Roman knight when he began to practise riding on an elephant that trotted swiftly along a rope. What strong expletives he must have muttered to himself!—any one of which, uttered audibly, would have cost him his head as a fine levied by his imperial manager. As to Nero's riding, and racing, and wrestling, and charioteering, as an amateur, among professionals who always took care to be beaten by him, these things were nothing compared with his ardour as a private player, and especially as what would now be called an opera singer. After all, Nero was more like an amateur actor who plays in public occasionally than an actor in strictly private theatricals. There is no doubt of his having been fond of music; he was well instructed in the art and a skilful proficient. His first great enjoyment after becoming emperor was in sitting up night after night playing with or listening to Terpnus the harper. Nero practised the harp as if his livelihood depended on it; and he went through a discipline of diet, medicine, exercise, and rest, for the benefit of his voice and its preservation, such as, it is to be hoped, no vocalist of the present day would submit himself to. Nero's first appearance on any stage was made at Naples. The *débutant* was not at all nervous, for, though an earthquake made the house shake while he was singing, he never ceased till he had finished his song. Had any of the audience fled at the earthquake, they probably would have been massacred for attending more to the natural than the imperial phenomenon. But we can fancy that, when some terrified Drusus got home and his Drusilla asked him about the voice of the *illustrissimo* Signor Nerone, Drusus looked at her and answered, 'Never heard such a shake in all my life!'

What an affable fellow that otherwise terrible personage was! How gracious he must have seemed as he dined in the theatre and told those who reverently looked on that by-and-by he would sing clearer and deeper! Our respect for this august actor is a little diminished by the fact that he not only invented the *claque*, but taught his hired applauders how they were to manifest approbation. He divided them into three classes, constituting several hundreds of individuals. The *bombi* had to hum approval, the more noisy *imbrices* were to shower applause like heavy rain upon the tiles, and the *testas* were to culminate the effect by clapping as if their hands were a couple of bricks. And, with reputation thus curiously made at Naples, he reached Rome to find the city mad to hear him. As the army added their sweet voices of urgency, Nero modestly yielded. He enrolled his name on the list of public singers, but so far kept his imperial identity as to have his harp carried for him by the captain of his Prætorian Guard, and to be half surrounded by friends and followers—the not too exemplary Colonel Jacks and Lord Toms of that early time.

Just as Bottom the weaver would have played, not only Pyramus, but Thisbe and the Lion to boot, so Nero had appetite for every part, and made the most of whatever he had. Suetonius says that, when Nero sang the story of Niobe, 'he held it out till the tenth hour of the day;' but Suetonius omits to tell us at what hour the imperial actor first opened his mouth. 'The Emperor did not scruple,' says a quaint translation of Suetonius's 'Lives of the Twelve Cæsars,' 'done into English by several hands, A.D. 1692,' 'in private Spectacles to Act his Part among the Common Players, and to accept of a present of a Million of Sesterces from one of the Prætors. He also sang several tragedies in disguise, the Visors and Masks of the Heroes and the Gods, as also of the Heroesses and the Goddesses, being so shap'd as to represent his own Countenance or the Ladies for whom he had the most Affection. Among other things he sang " Canace in Travail," " Orestes killing his Mother," " Œdipus struck blind," and " Hercules raging mad." At what time it is reported that a young Soldier, being placed sentinel at the Door, seeing him drest up and bound, as the Subject of the Play required, ran in to his Assistance as if the thing had been done in good earnest.' (Here we have the origin of all those soldiers who have stood at the wings of French and English stages, and who have interfered with the action of the play, or even have fainted away in order to flatter some particular player). Nero certainly had his amateur-actor weaknesses. He provided beforehand all the bouquets that were to be spontaneously flung to him, or awarded as prizes in the shape of garlands. French actresses are said to do the same thing, and this pretty weakness is satirised in the duet between Hortense, the actress, and Brillant, the fine gentleman, in the pretty vaudeville of 'Le Juif' (by A. Rousseau, Désaugiers, and Mesnard), brought out at the Porte St.-Martin fifty odd years ago. Hortense is about to appear at Orleans, and she says, or sings:

> Je suis l'idole dont on raffole.
> Après demain mon triomphe est certain !

'Oui,' rejoins Brillant,

> Oui ! de tous les points de la salle,
> Je prédis que sur votre front,
> Trente couronnes tomberont.

And Hortense replies confidentially :

> Elles sont dans ma malle !

This is a custom, therefore, which French actresses derive from no less a person than Nero. This gentleman, moreover, invariably spoke well of every other actor to that actor's face, but never at any other time. If this custom has survived—

which is, of course, hardly possible—he who practises it can justify himself, if he pleases, by this
Neronic example.

Although it was death to leave the theatre
before the imperial amateur had finished his part,
there were some people who could not 'stand it,'
but who must have handsomely tipped the incorruptible Roman guard to be allowed to vanish
from the scene. There were others who insisted
on being on the point of death, but it is not to be
supposed that they were carried home without
being munificently profuse in their recompense.
There was no shamming on the part of the indefatigable Roman ladies, who, it is said, sometimes
added a unit to the audience and a new member to
the roll of Roman citizens, before they could be
got away. And, when a man ran from the theatre,
dropped from the walls of the town, and took to
his heels across country, he must have been even
more disgusted with the great amateur than you
are, my dear reader, with, let us say, your favourite
worst actor on any stage. *Exit Nero, histrio et
imperator.*

Some one has said that the Italians had not the
necessary genius for acting. Ristori has wiped out
that reproach. Private theatricals may be said to
have been much followed by them. Plays were
acted before popes just as they used to be (and on
Sundays too) before our bishops. It is on record

that the holiest of Holy Fathers have held their sides as they laughed at the ' imitations ' of English archbishops given to the life by English bishops on mission to Rome ; and, on the other hand, there is no comedy so rich as that to be seen and heard in private, acted by a clever, joyous Irish priest, imitating the voice, matter, and manner of the street preachers in Italy. Poliziano's ' Orfeo,' which inaugurated Italian tragedy, was first played in private before Lorenzo the Magnificent. Italian monks used to act Plautus and Terence, and the nuns of Venice were once famous for the perfection with which they acted tragedy in private to select audiences.

Altogether, it seems absurd for anyone to have said that the Italians had not the genius for acting. Groto, the poet—' the blind man of Adria '—played Œdipus, in Palladio's theatre at Vicenza, in the most impressive style. Salvator Rosa, the grandest of painters, was the most laughable of low comedians ; and probably no Italian has played Saul better than Alfieri, who wrote the tragedy which bears that name.

In France, private theatricals may be said to date from the seventeenth century ; but there, as in England, were to be found, long before, especial ' troops ' in the service of princes and nobles. We are pleased to make record of the fact that Richard III., so early as the time when he was the young Duke of Gloucester, was the first English prince who maintained his own private company of actors, of whom he was the appreciating and generous master. No doubt, after listening to them in the hall of his London mansion, he occasionally gave them an 'outing' on his manor at Notting Hill. We have more respect for Duke, or King, Richard, as patron of actors, than we have for Louis XIV. turning amateur player himself, and not only 'spouting' verses, but acting parts, singing in operas, and even dancing in the ballets of Benserade and the *divertissements* of Molière. Quite another type of the amateur actor is to be found in Voltaire. On the famous private stage of the Duchess of Maine, Voltaire acted (in 'Rome sauvée') Cicero to the Lentulus of the professional actor, Lekain. If we may believe the illustrious actor himself, nothing could be more truthful, more pathetic, more Roman, than the poet, in the character of the great author.

Voltaire prepared at least one comedy for private representation on the Duchess's stage, or on that of some other of his noble friends. A very curious story is connected with this piece. It bore the title of 'Le Comte de Boursoufle.' After being acted by amateurs, in various noble houses, it gave way to other pieces, the manuscript was put by, and the play was forgotten. Eleven years ago, however, the manuscript of the comedy,

in Voltaire's handwriting, was discovered, and ' Le
Comte de Boursoufle ' was produced at the Odéon.
M. Jules Janin and all the French theatrical critics
were in a flutter of convulsive delight at the
recovery of this comedy. Some persons there
were who asked if there was any doubt on the
matter, or was the piece by any other clever
Frenchman. They were laughed to scorn. The
comedy was so full of wit and satire that it could
only be the work of the wittiest and most satirical
of Frenchmen. ' If it is not Voltaire's,' it was
asked, ' whose could it possibly be ? ' This
question was answered immediately by the critics
in this country, who pointed out that ' Le Comte
de Boursoufle,' which Voltaire had prepared for a
company of private actors, was neither more nor
less than an exact translation of Sir John Van-
brugh's ' Relapse.'

Private theatricals in France became a sort of
institution. They not only formed a part, often a
very magnificent part, of the noble mansions of
princes, dukes, marquesses, *et tout ça,* but the
theatre was the most exquisite and luxurious
portion of the residences of the most celebrated
and prodigal actresses. Mademoiselle Guimard, to
surpass her contemporaries, possessed two ; one in
her magnificent house in the Chaussée d'Antin, the
other in her villa at Pantin. The one in Paris was
such a scene of taste, splendour, extravagance, and

scandal, that private boxes, so private that nobody
could be seen behind the gilded gratings, were
invented for the use and enjoyment of very great
ladies. These, wishing to be witnesses of what
was being acted on and before the stage, without
being supposed to be present themselves, were
admitted by a private door, and after seeing all
they came to see, and much more, perhaps, than
they expected, these high and virtuous dames,
wrapped their goodly lace mantles about them,
glided down the private staircase to their carriages,
and thought La Guimard was the most amiable
hussey on or off the stage.

Voltaire's private theatre, at Monrepos, near
Lausanne, has been for ever attached to history by
the dignified pen of Gibbon. The great historian's
chief gratification, when he lived at Lausanne, was
in hearing Voltaire in the Frenchman's own
tragedies on his own stage. The 'ladies and
gentlemen' of the company were not geniuses,
for Gibbon says of them in his 'Life,' that 'some
of them were not destitute of talents.' The
theatre is described as 'decent.' The costumes
were 'provided at the expense of the actors,' and
we may guess how the stage was stringently
managed, when we learn that 'the author directed the rehearsals with the zeal and attention
of paternal love.' In his own tragedies, Voltaire represented Lusignan, Alvarez, Benassur,

Euphemon, &c. 'His declamation,' says Gibbon, 'was fashioned to the pomp and cadence of the old stage; and he expressed the enthusiasm of poetry rather than the feelings of nature.' This sing-song style, by which diversified dramas, stilted rather than heroic, horribly dull rather than elevated and stirring, had an effect on Gibbon such as we should never have expected in him, or in any Englishman, we may say on any created being with common sense, in any part of the civilised world. His taste for the French theatre became fortified, and he tells us, 'that taste has perhaps abated my idolatry for the gigantic genius of Skakespeare, which is inculcated in our infancy as the first duty of Englishmen.' This is wonderful to read, and almost impossible to believe. We may give more credit to the assertion that 'the wit and philosophy of Voltaire, his table and theatre, refined in a visible degree the manners of Lausanne.' It is worthy of note that a tragedy of Voltaire's is now rarely, if ever, acted. We question if one of his most popular pieces, 'Adelaïde Du Guesclin,' has ever been played since it was given at the Théâtre Français (spectacle gratis), 1822, on occasion of the baptism of the Duc de Bordeaux, whom we now better know as the Comte de Chambord, and who knows himself only as 'Henry V., Roi de France et de Navarre.'

One of Voltaire's favourite stage pupils was an

actor named Paulin, who played a tyrant in the Lausanne company. Voltaire had great hopes of him, and he especially hoped to make much of him as Polifonte, in Voltaire's tragedy ' Mérope.' At the rehearsals, Voltaire, as was customary with him, overwhelmed the performers with his corrections. He sat up one night, to re-write portions of the character of the tyrant Polifonte, and at three in the morning he aroused his servant and bade him carry the new manuscript to Paulin. ' Sir,' said the man, ' at such an unseasonable hour as this M. Paulin will be fast asleep, and there will be no getting into his house.' ' Go! run!' exclaimed Voltaire, in tragic tones. ' Know that tyrants never sleep!'

Some of the French private theatres of the last century were singular in their construction. We know that the theatre of Pompey was so constructed that, by ingenious mechanism, it could form two amphitheatres side by side or could meet in one extensive circus. On a smaller scale, the *salon* of the celebrated dancer D'Auberval could be instantaneously turned into a private theatre, complete in all its parts. Perhaps the most perfect, as regards the ability of the actors, as well as the splendour of the house, audience and stage, were the two private theatres at Saint-Assise and Bagnolet, of the Duke of Orleans and Madame de Montesson. None but highly-gifted amateurs trod those boards. The Duke himself was admirable in peasants and in characters abounding in sympathies with nature. Madame de Montesson was fond of playing shepherdesses and young ladies under the pleasures, pains, or perplexities of love ; but, with much talent, the lady was far too stout for such parts. It might be said of her, as Rachel said of her very fat sister, whom she saw dressed in the costume of a shepherdess ; 'Bergère! tu as l'air d'une bergère qui a mangé ses brebis !'

Out of the multitude of French private theatres there issued but one great actress, by profession, the celebrated Adrienne Lecouvreur ; and *she* belonged, not to the gorgeous temple of Thespis in the palaces of nobles, but to a modest stage behind the shop of her father, the hatter ; and latterly, to one of more artistic pretensions in the courtyard attached to the mansion of a great lawyer whose lady had heard of Adrienne's marvellous talent, and, to encourage it, got up a theatre for her and her equally young comrades, in the *cour* of her own mansion. The acting of the hatter's daughter, especially as Pauline, in Corneille's 'Polyeucte,' made such a sensation that the jealous Comédie Française cried ' *Privilège* !' and this private theatre was closed, according to law.

We have less interest in recalling the figure of Madame de Pompadour, playing and warbling the chief parts in the sparkling little operettas on the stage of her private theatre at Bellevue, than we have in recalling the figure of the young Dauphine, Marie-Antoinette, with the counts of Provence and Artois (afterwards Louis XVIII. and Charles X.), with their wives, and clever friends, playing comedy especially, with a grace and perfection which were not always to be found in the professional actor. But what the old king Louis XV. had encouraged in the Pompadour he and his rather gloomy daughters discouraged in Marie-Antoinette. It was not till she was queen, and had profited by the lessons of the singer Dugazon, that the last royal private theatre in France commenced its career of short-lived glory, at Choisy and the Trianon. Louis XVI. never took kindly to these representations. He went to them occasionally, but he disliked seeing the queen on the stage. It is even said that he once directed a solitary hiss at her, as she entered dressed as a peasant. It is further stated that the royal actress stepped forward, and with a demure smile informed the house that the dissatisfied individual might have his money returned by applying at the door. It is a pretty story, but it is quite out of character with the place and the personages, and it may be safely assigned to that greatest of story-tellers, Il Signor Ben Trovato.

Adverse critics have said of Marie-Antoinette's Rosine, that it was '*royalement mal jouée.*' Perhaps they opposed the whole system of private acting.   This amusement had the advocacy of Montaigne, who was himself a good amateur actor. Of course, the thing may be abused.   It was not exemplary for French bishops to go to hear Collé's gross pieces in private.   There was more dignity in Louis XIV. and Madame de Maintenon listening to 'Esther' and 'Athalie,' acted by the young ladies of Saint-Cyr; and there was less folly in the princes and nobles who began the French Revolution by acting the 'Mariage de Figaro' in private, than there was in the Comte d'Artois (afterwards Charles X.) learning to dance on the tight rope, with a view of giving amateur performances to his admiring friends.

Mercier, in his 'Tableau de Paris,' under the head 'Théâtre bourgeois,' states that in the last quarter of the last century there was a perfect rage for private theatricals in France, and that it extended from the crown to the humblest citizen. He thought that the practice had its uses, but its abuses also; and he counselled simple country-townsmen to leave acting to the amateurs in large cities, where people were not too nice upon morals; where lovers gave additional fire to Orosmane, and the timidest young ladies found audacity enough to play Nanine. Mercier had seen the private theatricals at Chantilly, and he praises the care, taste, and simple grace which distinguished the

acting of the Prince of Condé and the Duchess of
Bourbon. It is very clear that if they had not
been cast for the genteelest comedy in the drama
of life, they would have got on very well in the
world as players. So the Duke of Orleans, at his
private theatre at Saint-Assise, pleased Mercier by
the care and completeness of his acting. 'The
Queen of France,' he adds, ' has private theatricals,
in her own apartments, at Versailles. Not having
had the honour to see her I can say nothing on the
subject.'

With these players of lofty social quality,
Mercier contrasts the amateurs in humble society.
These were given to act tragedy—or nothing. He
cites, from ' Le Babillard,' the case of a shoemaker,
renowned for his skill in gracefully fitting the
most gracefully small feet of the beauties of the
day. On Sundays, Crispin drew on his own legs
the buskins which he himself or his journeymen
had made ; and he acted, in his own house, the
lofty tragedy then in vogue. It happened once
that his manager, with whom he had quarrelled,
had to provide a dagger to be deposited on an altar,
for the amateur player's suicidal use. Out of
spite, the fellow placed there the shoemaker's
professional cutting-knife. The amateur, in the
fury of his acting, and not perceiving the trick,
snatched up the weapon, and gave himself the
happy despatch with the instrument which helped

him to live. This stage business excited roars of laughter, which brought the tragedy to an end as merrily as if it had been a burlesque. The shoemaker could find nothing to say, by which he might turn the laughter from himself. He was not as witty as the English shoemaker's apprentice whom his master seized, about this time, on the private stage in Berwick Street, acting no less a character than Richard III., in a very dilapidated pair of buskins. As the angry master pointed to them in scorn, the witty lad sustained his royal quality in his reply : ' Oh ! shoes are things we kings don't stand upon ! '

In England, private theatricals are to be traced back to an early date. We go far enough in that direction, however, by referring to Mary Tudor, the solemn little daughter of Henry VIII., who, with other children, acted before her royal sire, in Greenwich Palace, to the intense delight of her father and an admiring court. Henrietta Maria, Queen of Charles I., is remembered in court and theatrical annals for the grace with which she played in pretty pastoral French pieces, assisted by her ladies, on the private stages at Whitehall and Hampton Court. The private theatricals of the Puritan days were only those which took place surreptitiously, and at the risk of the performers being arrested and punished. Holland House, Kensington, was occasionally the place where the players found refuge and gave a taste of their quality. The 'good time' came again; and that greatest of actors, Betterton, with his good and clever wife, taught the daughters of James II. all that was necessary to make those ladies what they both were, excellent actors on their private stage. So Quin taught the boy to speak, who afterwards became George III., and who was a very fair private player, but perhaps not equal with his brothers and sisters, and some of the young nobility who trod the stage for pastime, and gave occupation to painters and engravers to reproduce the mimic scene and the counterfeit presentments of those who figured therein.

It was in the reign of George III., and in the year 1777, that the year itself was inaugurated on the part of the fashionable amateurs by a performance of 'The Provoked Husband.' Lord Villiers was at the cost of getting it up, but that was nothing to a man who was the prince of macaronics, and who, as Walpole remarks, had 'fashioned away' all he possessed. The play, followed by a sort of *pose plastique,* called 'Pygmalion and the Statue,' was acted in a barn, expensively fitted up for the occasion, near Henley. Lord Villiers and Miss Hodges were Lord and Lady Townley. Walpole says, on hearsay, that 'it went off to admiration.' Mrs. Montagu, also on report, says: 'I suppose the merit of this entertainment was, that people were to go many miles in frost and snow, to see in a barn what would have been every way better at the theatre in Drury Lane or Covent Garden.' Walpole speaks of M. Texier's Pygmalion as ' inimitable.' The Frenchman was at that time much patronised in town for his ' readings.' Miss Hodges acted the Statue. Mrs. Montagu's sharp criticism takes this shape : ' Modern nymphs are so warm and yielding that less art than that of M. Texier might have animated the nymph. My niece will never stand to be made love to before a numerous audience.' The Lady Townley and Galatea of these gay doings sacrificed herself, we suppose, to these important duties. ' Miss Hodges' father,' writes Mrs. Montagu, ' is lately dead : her mother is dying. How many indecorums the girl has brought together in one *petite pièce* ! ' The play was not all the entertainment of the night, which was one of the most inclement of that pitiless winter. ' There was a ball,' says the lady letter-writer, ' prepared after the play, but the barn had so benumbed the vivacity of the company, and the beaux' feet were so cold and the noses of the belles were so blue, many retired to a warm bed at the inn at Henley, instead of partaking of the dance.' Walpole gives play to his fancy over these facts. ' Considering,' he says, ' what an Iceland night it was, I concluded the company and audience would all be brought to town in waggons, petrified, and stowed in a statuary's yard in Piccadilly.'

We have heard over and over again of such private theatres as Winterslow, near Salisbury, which was burnt down on the night after a performance in which Fox and similar spirits had acted with equal vivacity in tragedy and farce. Other incidents are to be found in Walpole and similar gossiping chroniclers of the time. None of those private theatres, however, can match with Wargrave, in Berkshire, where, in the last century, Lord Barrymore held sway during his brief and boisterous life. When Lord Barrymore succeeded to the lordship of himself, that 'heritage of woe,' he came before the world with a splendour so extravagant in its character that the world was aghast at his recklessness. Wild and audacious as was the character of this wayward boy's life, he was in some sort a gentleman in his vices. He was brave and generous and kindly hearted. Since his time we have had a line (now extinct, or effete in the infirmity and imbecility of a surviving member or two) of gentlemen who plunged into blackguardism as a relief from the burden of life. They would play loosely at cards, swindle a dear friend at horse-dealing, and half a dozen of them together would not be afraid to fall upon some helpless creature and beat him into pulp by way of a 'lark.' Lord Barrymore was simply a 'rake,' and he injured no man but himself. He came into the hunting field more like a king of France and Navarre than an English gentleman, and his negro trumpeters played fantasias in the woods, to the infinite surprise, no doubt, of the foxes. He kept perpetual open house, and Mrs. Delpini superintended it for him. What he most prided himself upon was his taste for the drama, and the way he carried it into effect made Wargrave brilliant and famous in its little day.

This noble youth began modestly enough. His first private theatre was in one of his own barns. The first piece played in it was 'Miss in her Teens,' in which he acted Flash; and no one of the illustrious performers, youth or maiden, was over seventeen years of age. Noble by birth, as all the amateur Thespians were, this performance was not given to an exclusively aristocratic audience, but to all the villagers and the peasantry in the vicinity of the village who cared to come. All came, and there was a pit of red cloaks and smock frocks, and ample provision of creature comforts for the whole barn. From this modest origin sprang the noble theatre which Cox of Covent Garden Theatre built for the earl at a cost of 60,000*l.* It was a marvellous edifice. For pantomimic performances it had traps and springs and other machinery that might satisfy the requirements of Mr. George Conquest himself, who practised gymnastics, for exercise, when he was a student at a German university, and who is now the first of gymnastic performers instead of being the profoundest of philosophers— though there is no reason why he may not be both.

The Wargrave theatre lacked nothing that could be wanted for its completeness. The auditorium was splendid. There was a saloon quite as superb, wherein the audience could sup like kings and the invited could afterwards dance. Between the acts of performance pages and lackeys, in scarlet and gold, proffered choice refreshments to the spectators, who were not likely to be hard upon players under a management of such unparalleled liberality. The acting company was made up of professional players—Munden, Delpini, and Moses Kean, among the men, with the best and prettiest actresses of the Richmond Theatre. Lord Barrymore and Captain Walthen were the chief amateurs. Low comedy and pantomime formed the 'walk' of my lord, who on one occasion danced a celebrated *pas Russe* with Delpini as it was then danced at the opera. Now and then the noble proprietor would stand disguised as a check-taker, and promote 'rows' with the farmers and their wives, disputing the validity of their letters of invitation. It was also his fond delight to mingle with them, in disguise again, as they wended homeward, listening to or provoking their criticism. He probably heard some unwelcome truths, for he could not have long escaped detection. Within doors the night's pleasures were not at an end with the play. Dancing, gambling, music, and folly to its utmost limits succeeded; and he, or *she*, was held in scorn who attempted to go to bed before 5 A.M. Indeed, such persons were not allowed to sleep if they did withdraw before the appointed hour. From five o'clock to noon was the Wargrave season for sleep. The company were consigned to the 'upper and lower barracks,' as the two divisions were called where the single and the married, or those who might as well have been, were billeted for the night.

Lord Barrymore did not confine himself to acting on a private stage. In August, 1790, he 'was so humble as to perform a buffoon dance and act scaramouch in a pantomime at Richmond for the benefit of Edwin *junior*, the comedian; and I,' writes Walpole, 'like an old fool, but calling myself a philosopher that loves to study human nature in all its disguises, went to see the performance!' Walpole used to call the earl 'the strolling player.' On the above occasion, however, there is one thing to be remembered: Lord Barrymore, invited to play the fool, condescended to that degradation in order to serve young Edwin, whose affection and filial duty towards a sick and helpless mother had won the noble amateur's regard.

Lord Barrymore married in 1792, in which

year the splendid theatre at Wargrave was pulled down. In March, 1793, he was, as captain of militia, escorting some French prisoners through Kent. On his way he halted at an inn to give them and his own men refreshment; which being done, he kissed the handsome landlady and departed in his phaeton, his groom mounting the horse Lord Barrymore had previously ridden. The man put a loaded gun into the carriage, and Lord Barrymore had not ridden far when it exploded and killed him on the spot. Thus ended, at the age of twenty-four years, the career of the young earl, who was the most indefatigable, if not the most able, amateur actor of his day.

Such examples fired less noble youths, who left their lawful callings, broke articles and indentures, and set up for themselves by representing somebody else. Three of our best bygone comedians belong to this class, and may claim some brief record at our hands.

Oxberry, who was distinguished for the way in which he acted personages who were less remarkable for their simplicity than for their silliness, was a pupil of Stubbs, the animal painter, and subsequently was in the house of Ribeau, the bookseller. The attractions of the private theatres in Queen Anne Street and Berwick Street were too much for him. Oxberry's first appearance was made at the former place, as Hassan, in the 'Castle Spectre.'

The well-known players, Mrs. W. West and John
Cooper, acted together as Alonzo and Leonora in
'The Revenge,' at a private theatre in Bath, to the
horror of their friends and the general scandalising
of the city of which they were natives.  The Bath
manager looked on the young pair with a business
eye, and the youthful amateurs were soon enrolled
among the professionals.  In their first stages, professionals scarcely reckon above amateurs.  They
play what they can, and such comic actors as Wilkinson and Harley are not the only pair of funny
fellows upon record who played the most lofty
tragedy in opposition to each other.  Little Knight,
as he used to be called, was, like Long Oxberry,
intended for art, but he too took to private acting,
and passed thence to the stage, where he was
supreme in peasants, and particularly rustics, of
sheer simplicity of character.  His Sim in 'Wild
Oats' was an exquisite bit of acting, and this is
said without any disparagement of Mr. D. James,
who recently acted the part at Mr. Belmore's benefit with a natural truthfulness which reminded old
play-goers of the 'real old thing.'  If Mr. Knight
did not succeed in pictorial art, he left a son who
did—the gentleman who so recently retired from
the secretaryship of the Royal Academy.  The
two names of Knight and Harley were, for a long
time, pleasant in the ears of the patrons of the
drama.  John Pritt Harley was intended for many

things, but amateur acting made a capital comedian
of him. His father was a reputable draper and
mercer—and jealous actors used to say that he sold
stays and that his son helped to make them. The
truth is that he was first devoted to surgery, but
Harley ' couldn't abide it.' Next he tried the law,
and sat on a stool with the edge of a desk pressing
into him till he could bear it no longer. There
was, at the time, a company of amateurs who performed in the old Lyceum, and there, and at other
private theatres, Harley worked away as joyously
as he ever played ; and worked harder still through
country theatres, learning how to starve as well as
act, and to fancy that a cup of tea and a penny
loaf made a good dinner—which no man could
make upon them. His opportunity came when, in
1815, Mr. Arnold, who had watched some part of
his progress, brought him out at the Lyceum—his
old amateur playing ground—as Marcelli, in ' The
Devil's Bridge.' Harley lived a highly-esteemed
actor and a most respectable bachelor. Some
little joking used to be pointed at him in print, on
account of an alleged attachment between him and
Miss Tree, the most graceful of dancers and of
columbines. But Miss Tree was a Mrs. Quin—
though she had scarcely seen her husband, since
she was compelled to marry him in her childhood.
The nicest pointed bit of wit was manufactured in
a hoaxing announcement of a benefit to be taken

by both parties. The pieces advertised were 'A Tale of *Mystery*,' and a 'Harley-Quinade.' The names of the parties could not have been more ingeniously put together in sport. Harley, though a mannerist, was an excellent actor to the last. When he was stricken with apoplexy, while playing Bottom, in the 'Midsummer Night's Dream,' at the Princess's Theatre, in Charles Kean's time, he was carried home, and the last words he uttered were words in his part: 'I feel an exposition to sleep coming over me.' And straightway the unconscious speaker slept—for aye !

We must not add to the grievances of Ireland by altogether overlooking Erin's private theatricals. From the day in 1544, when Bale's 'Pammachius' was acted by amateurs at the market cross of Kilkenny, to the last recent record of Irish amateur acting, in the 'Dublin Evening Mail,' this amusement has been a favourite one among the 'West Britons.' The practice did not die out at the Union. Kilkenny, Lurgan, Carton, and Dublin had their private stages. When the amateur actors played for charity's sake everybody took private boxes and nobody paid for them. In 1761, the 'Beggars' Opera' was played at the Duke of Leinster's (Carton). Dean Marly played Lockit, and wrote and spoke the prologue, in which the reverend gentleman thus alluded to himself :

But when this busy mimic scene is o'er
All shall resume the worth they had before ;
Lockit himself his knavery shall resign,
And lose the Gaoler in the dull Divine.

The above was not quite as dignified as Milton's
' Arcades,' played by the children of the Dowager
Countess of Derby, at her house, Harefield Place ;
or as 'Comus,' acted by the young Egertons before
the Earl of Bridgewater, at Ludlow Castle. Perhaps it was more amusing.

One of our own best amateur actresses was the
Princess Mary of Cambridge (now Duchess of Teck).
This excellent lady had once to commence the
piece (a musical piece, written for the occasion by
an amateur) on a private stage in one of the
noblest of our country mansions. An illustrious
audience was waiting for the curtain to go up ; but
the kindly-hearted princess was thinking of some
less illustrious folks, who were not among that
audience and whom she desired to see there, namely,
the servants of the household—as many as could
be spared. They had had much trouble, and she
hoped they would be allowed to share in the amusement. There was some difficulty ; but it was only
when she was informed that the servants were
really ' in front,' that the ' Queen of Hearts ' (her
part in the piece) answered that she was ready to
begin the play. She never acted better than on
this occasion

## *THE SMELL OF THE LAMPS.*

As we look at the two volumes of Mr. Planché's autobiography we experience a sensation of delight. They remind us of a story told of Maria Tree, long after she had become Mrs. Bradshaw, and was accustomed to luxuries unknown in her early and humble life. She was one night crossing the stage behind the curtain, on a short way to a private box, when she stopped for a moment, and, as she caught the well-known incense of the foot-lights, joyously exclaimed, 'The smell of the lamps! How I love it!' Therewith she spoke of the old times, when she worked hard—that is, 'played,' for the support of others as well as for her own support; and what a happy time it was, and how she wished it could all come over again! The noble peer who had the honour of escorting her, looked profoundly edified, smiled good-humouredly, and then completed his duty as escort. Here we open Mr. Planché's book, and catch from it a 'smell of the lamps.' Yes, there must have been—must be— something delicious in it to those who have achieved success. To old play-goers there is a

similar delight in books of stage reminiscences
which include memories of great actors whom
those play-goers have seen in their youth.  A few
of these still survive to talk of the old glories and
to prove by comparison of 'cast' that for the
costly metal of other days we have nothing now
but pinchbeck.  We have heard one of the old
gentlemen of the *ancien régime* talk, with unfeigned
emotion, of the way in which 'The Gamester' used
to be acted by Mrs. Siddons, John Kemble, Charles
Kemble, and George Frederick Cooke.  How ladies
sobbed and found it hard to suppress a shriek;
how gentlemen veiled their eyes to hide the impertinent tears, and tried to look as if nothing
were the matter; and, how people who had seen
the dreadful tragedy more than once, and dreaded
to witness it again, were so fascinated that they
would stand in the box-passages gazing through
the glass panels of the box doors, beholding the
action of the drama, but sparing themselves the
heartbreaking utterances of the chief personages.
Within a few weeks we have heard a veteran play-
goer give imitations of John Kemble in 'Coriolanus,' which he last played more than half a
century ago!  It had the perfect enunciation
which was the chief merit of the Kemble school;
it was dignified; it gave an idea of a grand actor,
and it was a pleasure conferred on the hearers
such as Charles Mathews the elder used to confer

on his audiences 'At Home,' when he presented them with Tate Wilkinson, and they were delighted to make acquaintance with the famous man who had so long before got, as the old Irishwoman said at Billy Fullam's funeral, his 'pit order at last.'

While we wait for a paper-cutter to open the closed pages of Mr. Planché's book, we will just remark that those were days when audiences were differently arranged to what they are now. In the little summer-house in the Haymarket, when stalls were not yet invented, the two-shilling gallery was the rendezvous of some of the richest tradesmen in Pall Mall and the neighbourhood around. At that period, London tradesmen lived and slept at their places of business. They did not pass their nights at a country house. London audiences were made up almost entirely of London people. In the present day, they are largely made up of visitors from the country. In proportion as travelling companies of actors of merit increase and continue to represent plays sometimes better than they are represented in London, country visitors will cease to go to 'the play,' as it is called, in the metropolis, and will find some other resort where they can shuffle off the mortal coil of tediousness which holds them bound during their absence from home.

In good old times the pit was the place, not

only for the critics, but for the most eminent men
of the day. Indeed, not only eminent men, but
ladies also, whose granddaughters, as they sweep
into the stalls, would think meanly of their grand-
mothers and grandfathers, and would shudder at
the thought of themselves, being in that vulgar
part of the house. It is an excellent vulgarity
that sits there. Nineteen out of twenty, perhaps
ninety out of a hundred, of persons in the pit are
the truest patrons of the drama; they pay for the
places; and, generally speaking, the places are
made as uncomfortable as if the occupiers were
intruders of whom the managers would be glad to
get rid.

The best proof of the quality of the old pittites
is to be found in the diary of the Right Hon. William Windham (1784–1810). One of the entries
in the first-named year records a breakfast with
Sir Joshua Reynolds, a visit to Miss Kemble, and
'went in the evening to the pit with Mrs. Lukin.'
The play was 'The Gamester.' A day or two
afterwards the great statesman went with Steevens
and Miss Kemble to see 'Measure for Measure.'
'After the play,' writes Windham, 'went with Miss
Kemble to Mrs. Siddons's dressing-room; met
Sheridan there.' What interest Windham took in
that actress is illustrated in another entry:
'Feb. 1, 1785. Drove to Mrs. Siddons in order to
communicate a hint on a passage in Lady Macbeth,

which she was to act the next night. Not finding her at home, went to her at the play-house.' Well might Mrs. Siddons write, on inviting Windham to tea : 'I am sure you would like it ; and you can't be to learn that I am truly sensible of the honour of your society.'

The pits in the London theatres have undergone as great a change, though **a** different one, as the pit at the opera, which now only nominally exists, if it exist at all. It is now an area of stalls ; the old price for admission is doubled, and the entertainment is not worth an eighth of what **is** charged for it compared with that of the olden time, when for an eight-and-sixpenny pit ticket you had Grisi, Mario, Lablache, and Tamburini, with **minor** vocalists, thorough artists, in the same **opera. What** a spectacle was the grand old house ! The old aristocracy had their boxes for the season, as they had their **town** and country houses. You got intimate with them by sight ; it was a pleasure to note how **the** beautiful young daughters of each family grew in gracefulness. You took respectful part in the marriages. At each opening season you marked whether the roses bloomed or paled upon the young cheeks, and you sympathised accordingly. You spoke of Lord Marlshire's look with **a** hearty neighbourly feeling, and you were glad that Lady Marlshire really seemed only the eldest sister of a group of beauties who were her daughters. As for the sons of those great families, they were in full dress, **sauntering** or gossiping in that Elysium ill-naturedly called 'Fops' Alley'; they were exchanging recognitions with friends and kinsmen in all parts of the house. If you heard a distant laugh—loud enough where the laughers were moved to it—you might be sure it was caused by Lord Alvanley, who was telling some absurdly jocose story to a group of noble Young Englanders **in** the pit passage under **the** boxes. We have seen the quiet entry of a quiet man into **a** private box make **quite a stir.** Every stranger felt **that the** quiet man **was a** man **of** mark; **he came to snatch a momentary joy,** and then **away** to affairs of **state again**; he was the prime **minister. Dozens of** opera-goers have recorded their *souvenirs* of **the** old glorious days when the opera, as they say, was an institution, opened only twice a week: whereas each house **is** merely an ordinary theatre, with audiences that are never, two nights running, chiefly made up of the same *habitués.* They have told what friendly interest used to be aroused when the Duchess of Kent and her daughter, the Princess Victoria, took their seats every opera night. We seem again to hear a ringing laugh, and **we know** it comes from the sparkling English **lady** with an Italian title, the Countess St. Antonio. **We** seem again to see that marvellously audacious-looking pair, Lady

Blessington and Count D'Orsay, gauging the house and appearing to differ as to conclusions. The red face of the Duchess of St. Albans and the almost as ruddy vessel from which her tea was poured have been described over and over again; and, in the records of other chroniclers we fancy that once more there come upon us the voices of two gentlemen who talked so above the singers that a remonstrant 'Hush!' went round the building. The offenders were the Duke of Gloucester and Sir Robert Wilson. The soldier would draw out of sight, and the prince would make a sort of apologetic remark in a voice a little higher than that which had given offence. These are reminiscences chronicled in the memoirs, diaries, and fugitive articles of old opera-goers.

Mr. Planché must have been among those ancient lovers of music and of song, and that he should record his experiences is a thing to be grateful for, especially as he writes of the battle and joys of life while he is still in harness and the wreathed bowl is in his hand. In 1818, he began with burlesque—'Amoroso, King of Little Britain,' written for amateurs, and taken by Harley, unknown to the author, to Drury Lane. In 1872, after fifty-four years of work, Mr. Planché executed the better portion of 'Babil and Bijou,' which, compared with 'Amoroso,' is as the *Great Eastern* steamer to a walnut-shell. We heartily welcome all chroniclers of an art that lives only in the artist, and never survives him in tradition. Our own collection begins with Downes, and Mr. Planché's emerald-green volumes will find room there. Scores of biographies are 'squeezing' room for him. Fred Reynolds's portrait seems to say, 'Let Planché come next to me.' As we look at those dramatic historians we are struck with their usefulness as well as their power of entertaining. For example, a paragraph in one of the most ancient of dramatic chronicles—the 'Roscius Anglicanus,' by old Downes, the prompter—is of infinite use to the reputation of Shakespeare. Dryden, who produced *his* version of 'The Tempest' to show how Shakespeare *ought* to have written it, maintained that after the Restoration our national poet was not much cared for by the people, and that for a long time two plays of Beaumont and Fletcher were acted for one of Shakespeare. In Downes's record the prompter registers the revival of 'Hamlet;' and, without any reference to Dryden, or knowledge, indeed, of his depreciation of Shakespeare, he states that the tragedy in question brought more money to the house and more reputation to the players than any piece by any other author during a great number of years.

To some nameless chronicler we owe a knowledge of the fact that Shakespeare's 'Hamlet' was played on board ship, in Shakespeare's time, by sailors. Why was this left unnoticed when the royal captain of the *Galatea* took the chair at the last Theatrical Fund dinner?  But for the chroniclers we should be ignorant that, just six hundred years ago, the Chester mysteries and passion-plays were at their highest point of attraction.  Indeed, they could never have been unattractive; for all those who undertook to witness the performance during about a month's season were promised to be relieved from hundreds of years of the fire of purgatory.  What a delicious feeling to the earnest play-goer, that the more regularly he went to the play on these occasions, the more pleasantly he would work out his salvation!  The different dramatic scenes were represented by the best actors in the Chester trading companies.  One would like to know on what principle the distribution of parts was made by the manager.  Why should the Tanners have been chosen to play the 'Fall of Lucifer'?  What virtue was there in the Blacksmiths, that they should be especially appointed to enact 'The Purification'? or, in the Butchers, that they should represent 'The Temptation'? or, in the Bakers, that they should be deemed the fittest persons to illustrate 'The Last Supper'?  One can understand the Cooks being selected for 'The Descent into Hell,' because they were accustomed to stand fire; but what of angelical or evangelical could be found exclusively in the Tailors, that they should be cast for 'The

'Ascension'?   Were the Skinners, whose mission it was to play 'The Resurrection,' not deemed worthy of going higher?   Or, were the Tailors lighter men, and more likely to rise with alacrity?

We are inclined to think that the idea of plays being naughty things and players more than naughty persons in the early days is a vulgar error.   Plays must have been highly esteemed by the authorities, or Manningtree in Essex (and probably many another place) would not have enjoyed its privilege of holding a fair by tenure of exhibiting a certain number of stage plays annually.

There was undoubtedly something Aristophanic in many of the early plays.   There was sharp satire, and sensitive ribs which shrank from the point of it.   When the Cambridge University preachers satirised the Cambridge town morals the burgesses took the matter quietly; but when the Cambridge University players (students) caricatured the town manners in 1601, exaggerating their defects on the University stage, there was much indignation.

The presence of Queen Elizabeth at plays in London, and the acting of them in the mansions which she honoured by a visit, are proofs of the dignity of the profession.   We have her, in the year last named, at one of the most popular of London theatres, with a bevy of fair listening maids of honour about her.  This was in her old age.  'I have just come,' writes Chamberlain to Charlton, 'from the Blackfriars, where I saw her at the play with all her *candida auditrices.'*  At Christmas time, Carlile writes to Chamberlain, 'There has been such a small court this Christmas, that the guard were not troubled to keep doors at the plays and pastimes.'

And if the name of Elizabeth should have a sweet savour to actors generally, not less delicious to dramatic memories should be the mayor of Abingdon, in that queen's time, who invited so many companies of players to give a taste of their quality in that town for fee and reward.  If any actor to whom the history of the stage be of interest should turn up at Abingdon, let him get the name of this play-loving mayor, and hang it over the fire-place of the best room of the Garrick, or rather of the club that *will* be—the social, cosey, comfortable, professional, not palatial nor swellish, but homelike house, that the Garrick was in its humbler and happier days.

Now the companies the Mayor had down to Abingdon included the Queen's players, the Earl of Leicester's players, the players of the Earl of Worcester, of Lord Sussex, of the Earl of Bath, of Lord Berkely, of Lord Shrewsbury, of Lord Derby, and of Lord Oxford.  Is there no one who can get at the names of these actors, and of the pieces they played—played for rewards varying from twenty pence to twenty shillings? Will that thoroughly English actor, one of the few accomplished comedians of the well-trained times now left to us, be the more successfully urged to the task, if we remind him that, in 1573, his professional namesake, Mr. Compton, took his players to Abingdon, and earned four shillings by the exercise of their talents?

The Elizabethan time was a very lively one. It had its theatrical cheats and its popular riots. We learn from State records that on the anniversary of the Queen's accession, November, 1602, 'One Verner, of Lincoln's Inn, gave out bills of a play on Bankside, to be acted by persons of account; price of entry, 2s. 6d. or 1s. 6d. Having got most of the money he fled, but was taken and brought before the Lord Chief Justice, who made a jest of it, and bound him over in 5l. to appear at the sessions. The people, seeing themselves deluded, revenged themselves on the hangings, chairs, walls, &c., and made a great spoil. There was much good company, and many noblemen.'

The Queen died in March, 1603. There were the usual 'blacks,' but the court and stage were brilliant again by Christmas. Early in January of the following year people were talking of the gay doings, the brilliant dresses, the noble dramas, the grand bear-baitings, the levity, dancing, and the golden play, which had solemnised the Christmas just ended.   Thirteen years later Shakespeare died, and in little more than half a century small spirits whispered that he was not such a great spirit himself after all.

In Mr. Planché's professional autobiography, which makes us as discursive as the biographer himself, there is a seeming inclination to overpraise some actors of the present time at the expense of those whom we must consider their superiors in bygone days.   As far as this may tend to show that there is no actor so good but that his equal may in time be discovered, we have no difference with the author of these ' Recollections.'   It is wonderful how speedily audiences recover the loss of their greatest favourites.   Betterton, who restored the stage soon after Monk had restored the monarchy, was called ' the glory and the grief' of that stage.   The glory while he acted and lived in the memories of those who had seen him act.   To the latter his loss was an abiding grief.   For years after Betterton's decease it was rank heresy to suppose that he might be equalled. Pope, in expressive, yet not the happiest of his verses, has alluded to this prejudice.   The prejudice, nevertheless, was unfounded.   Betterton remains indeed with the prestige of being an actor who has not been equalled in many parts, who has been excelled in none.   Old playgoers, who could compare him in his decline with young

Garrick in his vigour, were of different opinions as
to the respective merits of these two great masters
of their art.   We may fairly conclude that Garrick's
Hamlet was as 'great' as Betterton's; that the
latter's Sir John Brute was hardly equal to Garrick's Abel Drugger; and that the Beverley of the
later actor was as perfect an original creation as
the Jaffier of Betterton.

When Wilks made the 'Constant Couple, or a
Trip to the Jubilee,' a success by the spirit and
ease with which he played the part of Sir Harry
Wildair, Farquhar, the author of the comedy, said
'That he made the part will appear from hence:
whenever the stage has the misfortune to lose him
Sir Harry Wildair may go to the Jubilee.'   Nevertheless, Margaret Woffington achieved a new success for that play by the fire and joyousness of her
acting.   When Wilks died, poets sang in rapturous
grief of his politeness, grace, gentility, and ease;
and they protested that a supernatural voice had
been heard moaning through the air—

> Farewell, all manly Joy!
> And ah! true British Comedy, adieu!
> Wilks is no more.

Notwithstanding this, British comedy did not die;
Garrick's Ranger was good compensation for
Wilks's Sir Harry.

When Garrick heard of Mrs. Cibber's death, in
1766, he exclaimed, 'Mrs. Cibber dead!   Then

tragedy has died with her!'  At that very time a little girl of twelve years of age was strolling from country theatre to country theatre, and she was destined to be an actress of higher quality and renown than even Mrs. Cibber, namely, Sarah Siddons.  Mrs. Pritchard could play Lady Macbeth as grandly as Mrs. Siddons; and Mrs. Crawford (Spranger Barry's widow), who laughed at the 'paw and pause' of the Kemble school, was a Lady Randolph of such force and pathos that Sarah feared and hated her.  Not many years after Garrick had pronounced Tragedy and Cibber to have expired together, his own death was described as having eclipsed the harmless gaiety of nations, and Melpomene wept with Thalia for their common adopted son, and neither would be comforted.  But as Siddons was compensation for Mrs. Cibber, so the Kembles, to use an old simile, formed the very fair small change for Garrick.  When Kemble himself departed, his most ardent admirers or worshippers could not assert that his legitimate successor could not be found.  Edmund Kean had already supplanted him.  The romantic had thrust out the classic; the natural had taken place of the artificial; and Shakespeare, by flashes of the Kean lightning, proved more attractive than the stately eloquence of 'Cato,' or the measured cadences of 'Coriolanus.'

Edmund Kean, however, has never had a successor in certain parts. Mrs. F. Kemble has justly said of him : 'Kean is gone, and with him are gone Shylock, Richard, and Othello.' Mrs. Siddons, at her first coming, did not dethrone the old popular favourites. After she had withdrawn from the stage, Miss O'Neill cast her somewhat under the shadow of oblivion ; but when old Lady Lucy Meyrick saw Mrs. Siddons's Lady Macbeth in her early triumph, she acknowledged the fine conception of the character, but the old lady, full of ancient dramatic memories, declared that, compared with Mrs. Pritchard and Mrs. Cibber, Mrs. Siddons's grief was the grief of a cheesemonger's wife. Miss Hawkins is the authority for this anecdote, the weak point in which is that in Lady Macbeth the player is not called upon to exhibit any illustration of grief.

We have said that Kean never had a superior in certain parts. Elliston considered himself to be superior in one point ; and by referring to some particular shortcoming in other actors Elliston contrived to establish himself as *facile princeps* of dramatic geniuses—in his own opinion. This we gather from Moncrieff, whom Elliston urged to become his biographer. He would not interfere with Moncrieff's treatment of the subject. 'I will simply call your attention, my dear fellow,' said Elliston, 'to three points, which you *may* find worthy of notice, when you draw your parallels of

great actors.   Garrick could not sing ; I can.
Lewis could not act tragedy ; I can.   Mossop could
not play comedy ; I can.   Edmund Kean never
wrote a drama ; I have.'   In the last comparison
Elliston was altogether out.   In the cheap edition
of 'Their Majesties' Servants' I have inserted a
copy of a bill put up by Kean, in 1811, at York,
in the ball-room of the Minster Yard of which
city Edmund Kean and his young wife announced
a two nights' performance of scenes from plays,
imitations, and songs, the whole enacted by the
poor strolling couple.   In that bill Mr. Kean is
described as ' late of the Theatres Royal, Haymarket and Edinburgh, and author of " The Cottage
Foundling, or Robbers of Ancona," now preparing
for immediate representation at the theatre Lyceum.'
We never heard of this representation having taken
place.   Hundreds of French dramas once came
into the cheap book market from the Lyceum,
where they had been examined for the purpose of
seeing whether any of them could be made useful
in English dresses.   Some of them undoubtedly
were.   Kean's manuscript drama may still be lying
among the Arnold miscellanies ; if found, we can
only hope that the owner will make over 'The
Cottage Foundling *and* the Robbers of Ancona ' to
the Dramatic College.   The manuscript would be
treasured there as long as the College itself lasts.
How long that will be we cannot say ; probably as

long as the College serves its present profitable
purpose. We could wish that the *emeriti* players
had a more lively lookout. A view from its door-
way over the heath is as cheerful as that of an
empty house to the actor who looks through the
curtain at it on his benefit night!

Edmund Kean's loss has not been supplied as
Mrs. Siddons's was, to a certain extent, and to that
actress's great distaste, by Miss O'Neill; but Drury
Lane has flourished with and by its Christmas
pantomimes. Audiences cannot be what they
were in Mr. Planché's younger days. They
examine no coin that is offered to them. They
take what glitters as real currency, and are
content. When we were told the other day of a
player at the Gaiety representing Job Thornberry
in a moustache, we asked if the pit did not shave
him clean out of the comedy? Job Thornberry in
a moustache! 'Well,' was the rejoinder, 'he only
follows suit. He imitates the example of Mr.
Sothern, who played Garrick in a moustache.'
We were silent, and thought of the days when
actors dressed their characters from portraits, as
William Farren did his Frederick and his Charles
XII.

If Mr. Planché's book had not been as sug-
gestive as it is purely historical we should not have
been so long coming to it. But he records a fact
or makes a reflection, and straightway a reader,

who has long memories of books or men, goes far back into older records in search of contrasts or of parallels. We come to him now definitely, and do not again mean to let him go, as far as his dramatic experiences are concerned. Mr. Planché makes even his birth *theatrical*; he says, 'I believe I made my first appearance in Old Burlington Street on the 27th of February, 1796, about the time the farce begins' (used to begin?) ' at the Haymarket, that is, shortly after one o'clock in the morning.' The Haymarket season, however, ran at that time only from June to September. In spite of ourselves, Mr. Planché's record of his birth leads us to a subject that is, however, in connection with the record. We find that Mr. Planché was not only of the Kemble and Kean periods, since which time the stage has been ' nothing' especial, but that he was born under both. On the night of his birth John Kemble played Manly in 'The Plain Dealer,' with a cast further including Jack Bannister, the two Palmers, Dodd, Suett, and Mrs. Jordan! Think of the dolls and puppets and groups of sticks whom people are now asked to recognise as artists, and who gain more in a night than the greatest of the above-named players earned in a week. A few nights later Edmund Kean, if he himself is to be credited rather than theatrical biographers, made his first appearance on any stage as the ' Robber's Boy' on the first night the

' Iron Chest ' was acted—a play in which the boy was destined to surpass, in Sir Edward Mortimer, the original representative, John Kemble. At the other house little Knight, the father of the present secretary of the Royal Academy, made his *début* in London ; and the father of Mr. Macready was playing *utility* with a finish that, if he were alive to do it now, would entitle him to a name on ' posters ' three feet high, and to the sarcasm of managers, who readily pay comedians who ' draw ' and laugh at *them* and at the public who are drawn by them. But here is Mr. Planché waiting.

Well ! he seems to have been backward in speaking ; though he says, as a proof to the contrary, that he spoke Rolla's speech to his soldiers shortly after he had found his own. ' Pizarro,' we will observe, was not produced till 1799, and was not printed *then.* But, on the other hand, Mr. Planché, like Pope, seems to have lisped in numbers, for at ten he wrote odes, sonnets, and particularly an address to the Spanish patriots, which he describes as ' really terrible to listen to.' When he passed into his teens, the serious question of life turned up. He could not be made to be a watchmaker, the calling of his good father, a French refugee. Barrister, artist. geometrician, cricketer, were vocations which were considered and set aside. His tutor in geometry died before the pupil could discover the quadrature of the

circle ; and the other callings not seeming to give
him a chance, Mr. Planché bethought himself that,
as he was fond of writing, he was especially qualified to become a bookseller.   It was while he was
learning this *métier* that his dramatic propensities
were further developed.   They had begun early ;
he had been ' bribed to take some nasty stuff when
an urchin, on one occasion, by the present of a
complete harlequin's suit, mask, wand, and all, and
on another by that of a miniature theatre and
strong company of pasteboard actors,' in whose
control he enjoyed what Charles Dickens longed to
possess—a theatre given up to him, with absolute
despotic sway, to do what he liked with, house,
actors and pieces, monarch of all he surveyed.
Mr. Kent has published this ' longing ' in his
' Charles Dickens as a Reader,' and added one
shadow on Dickens's character to the many which
Mr. Forster has made public, and which thoughtful
biographers ought to have suppressed.   We allude
particularly to where Dickens describes his mother
as advertising to receive young ladies as pupils in
a boarding school, without having the means to
make preparations for their reception ; also his
showing-up of his own father as Micawber ; and
above all, his recording that he never had forgiven
and never would forgive his mother for wishing
him to go back to his humble work at the
blacking-maker's instead of to school.   The light

which thoughtless worshippers place before their
favourite saint often blackens him at least as much
as it does him honour.

While under articles with the bookseller Mr.
Planché amused himself as amateur actor at the
then well-known private theatres in Berwick
Street, Catherine Street, Wilton Street, and
Pancras Street. The autobiographer says he there
' murdered many principal personages of the acting
drama in company with several accomplices who
have since risen to deserved distinction upon the
public boards.' He adds, the probability, had he
continued his line of art, of his becoming by this
time ' a very bad actor, had not " the sisters three
and such odd branches of learning " occasioned me
by the merest accident to become an indifferent
dramatist.' He says jocosely that finding nothing
in Shakespeare or Sheridan worthy of him, he
wrote for amateurs the burlesque entitled
' Amoroso, King of Little Britain,' which one of
the company showed to Harley, who at once put
it on the stage of Drury Lane in April 1818.
There, night after night, Queen Coquetinda
stabbed Mollidusta, King Amoroso stabbed the
Queen, Roastando stabbed Amoroso, who however
stabbed *his* stabber, the too amorous cook—all to
excellent music and capitally acted, whether in the
love-making, the killing, or the recovery. Drury
Lane Theatre is described by Mr. Planché as being

at the time 'in a state of absolute starvation.'
Yet it was a season in which Kean led in tragedy
and Elliston in comedy, and David Fisher played
Richard and Hamlet as rival to the former, and
little Clara Fisher acted part of Richard the Third
in 'Lilliput.' Drury Lane had not had so good a
company for years ; and besides revived pieces of
sterling merit it brought out 'Rob Roy the
Gregarach,' and the 'Falls of Clyde ;' and Kean
played Othello and Richard, Hamlet and Reuben
Glenroy, Octavian and Sir Giles, Shylock and
Luke, Sir Edward Mortimer and King John,
Oroonoko, Richard Plantagenet ('Richard Duke
of York'), and Selim ('Bride of Abydos') ;
Barabbas ('Jew of Malta'), Young Norval,
Bertram, and, for his benefit, Alexander the Great,
Sylvester Daggerwood, and Paul in 'Paul and
Virginia.' Nevertheless the success of 'Amoroso'
was the *popular* feature of that Drury Lane season.
It made Mr. Planché become a dramatist in earnest.
'At this present date,' he says, 'I have put upon
the stage, of one description and another, seventy-
six pieces.'

## *A LINE OF FRENCH ACTRESSES.*

THE English stage has not been wanting in an illustrious line of right royal queens of tragedy. Mrs. Barry is the noble founder, and perhaps the noblest queen of that brilliant line. Then came Mrs. Cibber, Mrs. Pritchard, Mrs. Spranger Barry (Mrs. Crawford), Mrs. Siddons (who hated Mrs. Crawford for not abdicating), and Miss O'Neill, whom Mrs. Siddons equally disliked for coming after her.

With all these the lovers of dramatic literature are well acquainted. Of the contemporary line of French tragedy queens very little is known in this country ; nevertheless the dynasty is one of great brilliancy, and the details are not without much dramatic interest.

In the year 1644, in the city of Rouen, there lived a family named Desmares, which family was increased in that year by the birth of a little girl who was christened Marie. Corneille, born in the same city, was then eight-and-thirty years of age. Rouen is now proud of both of them—poet and actress. The actress is only known to fame by her married name. The clever Marie Desmares became the wife of the player, Champmeslé. Monsieur was to Madame very much what poor Mr. Siddons was to his illustrious consort. Madame, or Mademoiselle, or *La* Champmeslé, as she was called indifferently, associated with Corneille by their common birth-place, was more intimately connected with Racine, who was her senior by five years. La Champmeslé was in her twenty-fifth year when she made her *début* in Paris as Hermione, in Racine's masterpiece, 'Andromaque.' For a long time Paris could talk of nothing but the new tragedy and the new actress. The part from which the piece takes its name was acted by Mdlle. Duparc, whom Racine had carried off from Molière's company. The author was very much interested in this lady, the wife of a M. Duparc. Madame was, when a widow, the mother of a very posthumous child indeed. The mother died. She was followed to the grave by a troop of the weeping adorers of her former charms, 'and,' says Racine, alluding to himself, 'the most interested of them was half dead as he wept.'

The poet was aroused from his grief by a summons from the king, who, in presence of the sensitive Racine's bitterest enemy, Louvois, accused him of having robbed and poisoned his late mistress. The accusation was founded on information given by the infamous woman, Voisin, who was a poisoner by passion and profession, and was executed for her devilish practices. The information was found to be utterly false, and Racine, absolved, soon found consolation and compensation.

He became the master of La Champmeslé, and taught her how to play the heroines of the dramas which he wrote expressly for her. She, in her turn, became the mistress of her tutor. Of his teaching indeed she stood in little need, except to learn from him his ideas and object, as author of the play. She was not only sublime, but La Champmeslé was the first sublime actress that had hitherto appeared on the French stage. Madame de Sévigné wrote to her daughter :—

La Champmeslé is something so extraordinary that you have never seen anything like it in all your life. One goes to hear the actress, and not the play. I went to see ‘ Ariadne ’ for her sake alone. The piece is inspired : the players execrable. But as soon as La Champmeslé comes upon the stage a murmur of gladness runs throughout the house, and the tears of the audience flow at her despair.

The magic of the actress lured Madame de Sévigné's son, the young Marquis, from the side of Ninon de l'Enclos. ‘ He is nothing but a pumpkin fricasseed in snow,’ said the perennial beauty. After the young nobleman thought proper to inform his mother of the interest he took in La Champmeslé, Madame de Sévigné was so proud that she wrote and spoke of her son's mistress as her daughter-in-law ! To her own daughter she wrote as follows of the representation of Racine's ‘ Bajazet,’ in which La Champmeslé acted Roxane :

The piece appeared to me fine. My daughter-in-law



M

seemed to me the most miraculously good actress I had ever seen ; a hundred thousand times better than Des Œillets ; and I, who am allowed to be a very fair player, am not worthy of lighting the candles for her to act by. Seen near, she is plain, and I am not astonished that my son was 'choked' at his first interview with her; but when she breaks into verse she is adorable.  I wish you could have come with us after dinner; you would not have been bored.  You would probably have shed one little tear, since I let fall a score.  You would have admired your sister-in-law.

Two months later the mother sent to her daughter a copy of the piece, and wrote : 'If I could send you La Champmeslé with it you would admire it, but without her it loses half its value.'

Racine, as Madame de Sévigné said, wrote pieces for his mistress, and not for posterity.  'If ever,' she remarked, ' he should become less young, or cease to be in love, it will be no longer the same thing.'  The interpreter of the poet produced her wonderful effects dressed in exaggerated court costume, and delivering her *tirades* in a cadenced, sing-song, rise-and-fall style, marking the rhymes rather than keeping to the punctuation.  It was the glory of the well-educated *arlequin* and *columbine*, ' dans leur Hostel de Bourgogne,' to act whole scenes of mock tragedy in the manner of La Champmeslé and her companions.  It was such high-toned burlesque as the gifted Robson's Medea was to the Medea of Ristori.

Lovers consumed fortunes to win the smiles they sought from the plain but attractive actress. Dukes, courtiers, simple gentlemen, flung themselves and all they had at her feet. La Fontaine wrote verses in worship of her, when he was not helping her complaisant husband to write comedies. Boileau, in the most stinging of epigrams, has made the conjugal immorality immortal, and de Sévigné has made the nobly-endowed actress live for ever in her letters.

After Racine shut his eyes, as complaisantly as the husband, to the splendid infidelities of La Champmeslé—when temptation was powerless, and religion took the place of passionate love—he moralised on the sins of his former mistress. 'The poor wretch,' he wrote contemptuously to his son, ' in her last moments, refused to renounce the stage.' Without such renunciation the Church barred her way to heaven! Racine, however, was misinformed. La Champmeslé died (1698) like so many of her gayest fellows, ' *dans les plus grands sentiments de piété.*' Her widowed husband, when the rascal quality died out of him, kept to drink, and he turned now and then to devotion. One morning, in the year 1708, he went to the church of the Cordeliers, and ordered two masses for the repose of the souls of his mother and of his wife ; and he put thirty sous into the hand of the *sacristain* to pay for them. The man offered him ten sous as

change.   But M. Champmeslé put the money back :
' Keep it,' he said, ' for a third mass for myself.   I
will come and hear it.'   Meanwhile he went and
sat at the door of a tavern (*L'Alliance*) waiting for
church time.   He chatted gaily with his comrades,
promised to join them at dinner, and  as he rose to
his feet he put his hand to his head, uttered a faint
shriek, and fell dead to the ground.

As Racine formed La Champmeslé, so did the
latter form her niece as her successor on the stage
—Mdlle. Duclos, who reigned supreme ; but she
was a less potential queen of the drama than her
mistress.   Her vehemence of movement once
caused her to make an ignoble fall as she was playing Camille in ' Les Horaces.'   Her equally vehe-
ment spirit once carried her out of her part altogether.   At the first representation of La Motte's
' Inés de Castro ' the sudden appearance of the
children caused the pit to laugh and to utter some
feeble jokes.   Mdlle. Duclos, who was acting Inés,
was indignant.   ' Brainless pit ! ' she exclaimed,
' you laugh at the finest incident in the piece ! '
French audiences are not tolerant of impertinence
on the stage ; but they took this in good part,
and listened with interest to the remainder of the
play.

Mdlle. Duclos, like her aunt, chanted or reci-
tatived her parts.   The French had got accustomed
to the sing-song cadences of their rhymed plays,

when suddenly a new charm fell upon their delighted ears. The new charmer was Adrienne
Lecouvreur—a hat-maker's daughter, an amateur
actress, then a strolling player. In 1717 she burst
upon Paris, and in one month she enchanted the
city by her acting in Monimia, Electra, and
Bérénice, and had been named one of the king's
company for the first parts in tragedy and comedy.
Adrienne's magic lay in her natural simplicity.
She spoke as the character she represented might
be expected to speak. ·This natural style had been
suggested by Molière, and had been attempted by
Baron, but unsuccessfully. It was given to the
silver-tongued Adrienne to subdue her audience by
this exquisite simplicity of nature. The play-going
world was enthusiastic. Whence did the new
charmer come? She came from long training in
the provinces, and was the glory of many a provincial city before, in 1717, she put her foot on the
stage of the capital, and at the age of twenty-seven
began her brilliant but brief artistic career of thirteen years. Tracing her early life back, people
found her a baby, true child of Paris. In her little-
girlhood she saw 'Polyeucte' at the playhouse
close by her father's house. She immediately got
up the tragedy, with other little actors and actresses.
Madame la Présidente La Jay, hearing of the
ability of the troupe and of the excellence of
Adrienne as Pauline at the rehearsals in a grocer's

warehouse, lent the court-yard of her hotel in the Rue Garancière, where a stage was erected, and the tragedy acted, in presence of an audience which included members of the noblest families in France. All Paris was talking of the marvellous skill of the young company, but especially of Adrienne, when the association called the 'Comédie Française,' which had the exclusive right of acting the legitimate drama, arose in its spite, screamed 'Privilege!' and got the company suppressed.

The little Adrienne, however, devoted herself to the stage; and when she came to Paris, after long and earnest experience in the provinces, her new subjects hailed their new queen—queen of tragedy, that is to say; for when she took comedy by the hand the muse bore with, rather than smiled upon her; and, wanting sympathy, Adrienne felt none. Outside the stage her heart and soul were surrendered to the great soldier and utterly worthless fellow, Maurice de Saxe. He was the only man to whom she ever gave her heart; and he had given his to so many there was little left for her worth the having. What little there was was coveted by the Princesse de Bouillon. Adrienne died while this aristocratic rival was flinging herself at the feet of the handsome Maréchal; and the wrathful popular voice, lamenting the loss of the dramatic queen, accused the princess of having poisoned the actress.

Adrienne Lecouvreur (whose story has been twice told in French dramas, and once marvellously illustrated by the genius of Rachel), before she made her exit from the world, thought of the poor of her district, and she left them several thousands of francs. The curé of St.-Sulpice was told of the death and of the legacy. The good man took the money and refused to allow the body to be buried in consecrated ground. Princes of the church went to her *petits soupers*, but they would neither say 'rest her soul' nor sanction decent rest to her body; and yet charity had beautified the one, as talent and dignity had marked the other. The corpse of this exquisite actress (she was only forty when she died) was carried in a *fiacre*, accompanied by a faithful few, to a timber yard in the Faubourg St.-Germain; a hired porter dug the shallow grave of the tragedy queen; and I remember, in my youthful days, a stone post at the corner of the Rue de Bourgogne and the Rue de Grenelle which was said to stand over the spot where Monimia had been so ingloriously buried. It was then a solitary place, significantly named La Grenouillière.

And when this drama had closed, a valet of Baron, the great tragedian, looked at an old woman who attended in a box lobby of the Comédie Française, and they mutually thought of their daughter as the successor to poor Adrienne Lecouvreur. Their name was Gaussem;

but when, a year after Adrienne's death, they succeeded in getting the young girl—eighteen, a flower of youth, beauty, and of simplicity, most exquisite, even if affected—they changed their name to Gaussin.   As long as she was young, Voltaire intoxicated her with the incense of his flattery.   He admired her Junie, Andromaque, Iphigénie, Bérénice; but he worshipped her for her perfect acting in parts he had written— Zaïre (in which there is a 'bit of business' with a veil, which Voltaire stole from the 'handkerchief' in 'Othello,' the author of which he pretended to despise)—Zaïre, Alzire; and in other characters Voltaire swore that she was a miracle of acting.   But La Gaussin never equalled Adrienne. She surpassed Duclos in 'Inés de Castro:' she was herself to be surpassed by younger rivals. At about forty Voltaire spoke of his once youthful idol as *that old girl!*

La Gaussin had that excellent thing in woman —a sympathetic voice.   Her pathos melted all hearts to the melodious sorrow of her own.   In Bérénice, her pathetic charm had such an effect on one of the sentinels, who, in those days, were posted at the wings, that he unconsciously let his musket fall from his arm.   Her eyes were as eloquent as her voice was persuasive.   In other respects, Clairon (an actress) has said of her that La Gaussin had instinct rather than intelligence, with beauty, dignity, gracefulness, and an invariably winning manner which nothing could resist. Her great fault, according to the same authority, was sameness. Clairon added that she played Zaïre in the same manner as she did Rodogune. It is as if an English actress were to make no difference between Desdemona and Lady Macbeth.

When La Gaussin had reached the age of forty-seven the French pit did what the French nation invariably does—smote down the idol which it had once worshipped. The uncrowned queen married an Italian ballet dancer, one Tevolaigo, who rendered her miserable, but died two years before her, in 1767. It is, however, said that Mdlle. La Gaussin was led to withdraw from the stage out of sincerely religious scruples. A score of French actresses have done the same thing, and long before they had reached the *quarantaine.*

There is a good illustration of how unwilling the French audiences were to lose a word of La Gaussin's utterances in Cibber's 'Apology.' 'At the tragedy of "Zaïre,"' he says, 'while the celebrated Mdlle. Gossin (*sic*) was delivering a soliloquy, a gentleman was seized with a sudden fit of coughing, which gave the actress some surprise and interruption, and, his fit increasing, she was forced to stand silent so long that it drew the eyes of the uneasy audience upon him;

when a French gentleman, leaning forward to him, asked him if this actress had given him any particular offence, that he took so public an occasion to resent it? The English gentleman, in the utmost surprise, assured him that, so far from it, he was a particular admirer of her performance; that his malady was his real misfortune, and that if he apprehended any return of it he would rather quit his seat than disoblige either the actor or the audience.' Colley calls this the ' publick decency' of the French theatre.

The Mdlle. Clairon, named above, took up the inheritance which her predecessor had resigned. Claire Joseph Hippolyte Legris de Latude were her names; but, out of the first, she made the name by which she became illustrious. Her life was a long one—1723-1803. She acted from childhood to middle age; first as sprightly maiden, then in opera, till Rouen discovered in her a grand *tragédienne*, and sent her up to Paris, which city ratified the warrant given by the Rouennais. She made her first appearance as Phèdre, and the Parisians at once worshipped the new and exquisite idol.

The power that Mdlle. Clairon held over her admirers, the sympathy that existed between them, is matter of notoriety. She was once acting Ariane in Thomas Corneille's tragedy, at Marseilles, to an impassioned southern audience.

In the last scene of the third act, where she is eager to discover who her rival can be in the heart of Theseus, the audience took almost as eager a part; and when she had uttered the lines in which she mentions the names of various beauties, but does not name, because she does not suspect, her own sister, a young fellow who was near her murmured, with the tears in his eyes, 'It is Phædra! it is Phædra!'—the name of the sister in question. Clairon was one of those artists who conceal their art by being terribly in earnest. In her days the pit stood, there were no seats; *parterre* meant exactly what it says, 'on the ground.' The audience there gathered as near the stage as they could. Clairon, in some of her most tragic parts, put such intensity into her acting that as she descended the stage, clothed in terror or insane with rage, as if she saw no pit before her and would sweep through it, the audience there actually recoiled, and only as the great actress drew back did they slowly return to their old positions.

The autobiographical memoirs of Mdlle. Clairon give her rank as author as well as actress. Her style was declamatory, rather heavy, and marked by dramatic catchings of the breath which were among the faults that weaker players imitated. It was the conventional style, not to be rashly broken through in Paris; she accordingly first

tried to do so at Bordeaux in 1752.    ‘ I acted,’ she
tells us, ‘ the part of Agrippina, and from first to last
I played according to my own ideas.    This simple,
natural, unconventional style excited much surprise in the beginning ; but, in the very middle
of my first scene, I distinctly heard the words
from a person in the pit, “ That is really fine ! ” ’
It was an attempt to change the sing-song style,
just as Mdlle. Clairon attempted to change the
monotonous absurdity of the costume worn by
actresses ; but she was preceded by earlier re-
formers, Adrienne Lecouvreur, for instance.    Her
inclination for natural acting was doubtless confirmed on simply hearing Garrick recite passages
from English plays in a crowded French drawing-
room.    She did not understand a word of English,
but she understood Garrick’s expression, and, in
her enthusiasm, Mdlle. Clairon kissed Roscius, and
then gracefully asked pardon of Roscius’s wife for
the liberty she had taken.

It is said that Clairon was one of those
actresses who kept themselves throughout the
day in the humour of the character they were to
act at night.    It is obvious that this might be
embarrassing to her servants and unpleasant to
her friends, family, and visitors.    A Lady Macbeth
vein all day long in a house would be too much of
a good thing ; but Mdlle. Clairon defended the
practice, as others did : ‘ How,’ she would say,

'could I be exalted, refined, imperial at night, if through the day I had been subdued to grovelling matters, every-day commonness, and polite servility?' There was something in it; and in truth the superb Clairon, in ordinary life, was just as if she had to act every night the most sublimely imperious characters. With authors she was especially arbitrary, and to fling a manuscript part in the face of the writer, or to box his ears with it, was thought nothing of. Even worse than that was ' only pretty Fanny's way.'

The cause of Mdlle. Clairon's retirement from the stage was a singular one. An actor named Dubois had been expelled from membership with the company of the Théâtre Français, on the ground that his conduct had brought dishonour on the profession. An order from the King commanded the restoration of Dubois, till the question could be decided. For April 15, 1765, the 'Siege of Calais' was accordingly announced, with Dubois in his original character. On that evening, Lekain, Molé, and Brizard, advertised to play, did not come down to the theatre at all. Mdlle. Clairon arrived, but immediately went home. There was an awful tumult in the house, and a general demand that the deserters should be clapped into prison. The theatre was closed : Lekain, Molé, and Brizard suffered twenty-four days' imprisonment, and Mdlle.

Clairon was shut up in Fort l'Évêque. At the re-opening of the theatre Bellecourt offered a very humble apology in the names of all the company ; but Mdlle. Clairon refused to be included, and she withdrew altogether from the profession.

On a subsequent evening, when she was receiving friends at her own house, the question of the propriety of her withdrawal was rather vivaciously discussed, as it was by the public generally. Some officers were particularly urgent that she should return, and play in the especially popular piece the 'Siege of Calais.' 'I fancy, gentlemen,' she replied, 'that if an attempt was made to compel you to serve with a fellow-officer who had disgraced the profession by an act of the utmost baseness, you would rather withdraw than do so ? ' 'No doubt we should,' replied one of the officers, ' but we should not withdraw on a day of *siege.*' Clairon laughed, but she did not yield. She retired in 1765, at the age of forty-two.

Clairon, being great, had many enemies. They shot lies at her as venomous as poisoned arrows. They identified her as the original of the shameless heroine in the 'Histoire de Frétillon.' With her, however, love was not sporadic. It was a settled sentiment, and she loved but one at a time ; among others, Marmontel (see his Memoirs), the Margrave of Anspach, and the comedian Larive. After all, Clairon had a divided sway. The rival queen was Marie Françoise Dumesnil. The latter was much longer before the public. The life of Mademoiselle Dumesnil was also longer, namely, from 1711 to 1803. Her professional career in Paris reached from 1737, when she appeared as Clytemnestra, to 1776, when she retired. For eleven years after Clairon's withdrawal Dumesnil reigned alone. She was of gentle blood, but poor; she was plain, but her face had the beauty of intelligence and expression. When Garrick was asked what he thought of the two great *tragédiennes*, Clairon and Dumesnil, he replied, 'Mdlle. Clairon is the most perfect actress I have seen in France.' 'And Mdlle. Dumesnil?' 'Oh!' rejoined Garrick, 'when I see Mdlle. Dumesnil I see no actress at all. I behold only Semiramis and Athalie!'—in which characters, however, she for many years wore the *paniers* that were in vogue. She is remembered as the first tragic actress who actually ran on the stage. It was in 'Mérope,' when she rushed to save Ægisthe, exclaiming, 'Hold! he is my son!' She reserved herself for the 'points,' whether of pathos or passion. The effect she produced was the result of nature; there was no art, no study. She exercised great power over her audiences. One night having delivered her famous line in Clytemnestra,

Je maudirais les dieux, s'ils me rendaient le jour,

an old captain standing near her clapped her on the back, with the rather rough compliment of 'Va-t-en chienne, à tous les diables!' Rough as it was, Dumesnil was delighted with it. On another occasion, Joseph Chénier, the dramatist, expressed a desire, at her own house, to hear her recite. It is said that she struck a fearful awe into him, as she replied, 'Asséyez-vous, Néron, et prenez votre place!'—for, as she spoke, she seemed to adopt the popular accusation that Joseph had been accessory to the guillotining of his brother, the young poet, André Chénier. Her enemies asserted that Dumesnil was never 'up to the mark' unless she had taken wine, and a great deal of it. Marmontel insists that she caused his 'Héraclides' to fail through her having indulged in excess of wine; but Fleury states that she kept up her strength during a tragedy by taking chicken broth with a little wine poured into it.

Mademoiselle Dumesnil retired, as we have said, in 1776. The stage was next not unworthily occupied by Mdlle. Raucourt. But meanwhile there sprang up two young creatures destined to renew the rivalry which had existed between Clairon and Dumesnil. While these were growing up the French Revolution, which crushed all it touched, touched the Comédie Française, which fell to pieces. It pulled itself together, after a manner, but it was neither flourishing nor easy under the republic.

The French stage paid its tribute to prison and to scaffold.

When the storm of the Revolution had swept by, that stage became once more full of talent and beauty. Talma reappeared, and soon after three actresses set the town mad. There was Mdlle. Georges, a dazzling beauty of sixteen, a mere child, who had come up from Normandy, and who knew nothing more of the stage than that richly dressed actors there represented the sorrows, passion, and heroism of ancient times. Of those ancient times she knew no more than what she had learned in Corneille and Racine. But she had no sooner trod the stage, as Agrippina, than she was at once accepted as a great mistress of her art. Her beauty, her voice, her smile, her genius and her talent, caused her to be hailed queen ; but not quite unanimously. There was already a recognised queen of tragedy on the same stage, Mdlle. Duchesnois. This older queen (originally a dress-maker, next, like Mrs. Siddons, a lady's-maid), was as noble an actress as Mdlle. Georges, but her noble style was not supported by personal beauty. She was, perhaps, the ugliest woman that had ever held an audience in thrall by force of her genius and ability alone. While song-writers celebrated the charms of Mdlle. Georges, portrait-painters, too cruelly faithful, placed the sublime ugliness of Mdlle. Duchesnois in the shop windows. There she was to be seen in character, with one of the lines she had to utter in it, as the epigraph :

Le roi parut touché de mes faibles attraits.

Even Talleyrand stooped to point a joke at her expense. A certain lady had no teeth. Mdlle. Duchesnois *had*, but they were not pleasant to see. 'If,' said Talleyrand, alluding to the certain lady, 'If Madame —— had teeth, she would be as ugly as Mdlle. Duchesnois.'

Between these two queens of tragedy the company of the Théâtre Français were as divided in their allegiance as the public themselves. The Emperor Napoleon and Queen Hortense were admirers of Mdlle. Georges; he covered her with diamonds, and he is said to have lent her those of his wife Josephine, who was the friend of Mdlle. Duchesnois. Bourbonites and Republicans also adopted Mdlle. Duchesnois, who was adopted by Mdlle. Dumesnil. Talma paid allegiance to the same lady, while Lafon swore only by Mdlle. Georges, in whose behalf Mdlle. Raucourt once nearly strangled Duchesnois. In society, every member of that awful institution was compelled to choose a side and a night. One queen played on a Monday, the other on a Wednesday; Mdlle. Georges on a Friday, and Duchesnois again on Sunday; and on the intervening nights the brilliant muse of comedy, Mdlle. Mars (as the daughter of

Monvel, the actor, always called herself), came and made Paris ecstatic with her Elmire, her Célimène, and other characters. Of these three supreme actresses, Mdlle. Mars alone never grew old on the stage, in voice, figure, movement, action, feature, or expression. I recollect her well at sixty, creating the part of Mdlle. de Belleisle, a young girl of sixteen ; and Mdlle. Mars that night was sixteen, and no more. It was only by putting the *binocle* to the eyes that you might fancy you saw something older ; but the voice ! It was the pure, sweet, gentle, penetrating, delicious voice of her youth— ever youthful. Jules Janin describes the nights on which the brilliant and graceful Mdlle. Mars acted as intervals of inexpressible charm, moments of luxurious rest. Factions were silenced. The two queens of tragedy were forgotten for a night, and all the homage was for the queen of comedy.

The beauty, youth, and talent of Mdlle. Georges would probably have secured her seat on an undisputed throne, only for the caprices that accompany those three inestimable possessions. The youthful muse suddenly disappeared. She rose again in Russia, whither she had been tempted by the imperial liberality of Alexander the Czar. She was queening it there in more queenly fashion than ever ; her name glittered on the walls of Moscow, when the Grand Army of France scattered all such glories and wrecked its own.   A quarter of a million of men perished in that bloody drama, but the tragedy queen contrived to get safe and sound over the frontier.

Thenceforth she gleamed like a meteor from nation to nation.  Mdlle. Duchesnois and Mdlle. Mars held the sceptres of tragedy and comedy between them.  They reigned with glory, and when their evening of life came on they departed with dignity—Duchesnois in 1835.  The more impetuous Mdlle. Georges flashed now here now there, and blinded spectators by her beauty, as she dazzled them by her talent.  The joy of acting, the ecstasy of being applauded, soon became all she cared for.   One time she was entrancing audiences in the most magnificent theatres ; at another, she was playing with strollers on the most primitive of stages ; but always with the same care. Now, the Parisians hailed the return of their queen ; in a month she was acting Iphigenia to the Tartars of the Crimea !

When the other once youthful queens of tragedy and comedy were approaching the sunset glories of their reigns, Mdlle. Georges, in her mature and majestic beauty too, seized a new sceptre, mounted a new throne, and reigned supreme in a new kingdom.  She became the queen of drama—not melodrama—of that prose tragedy, which is full of action, emotion, passion, and strong contrasts. Racine and Corneille were no longer the fountains at which she quaffed long draughts of inspiration. New writers hailed her as their muse and interpreter. She was the original Christine at Fontainebleau, in Dumas's piece so named; and Victor Hugo wrote for her his terrible 'Mary Tudor' and his 'Lucretia Borgia.' It was a delicious terror, a fearful delight, a painful pleasure, to see this wonderful woman transform herself into those other women, and seem the awful reality which she was only — but earnestly, valiantly, artistically—acting. She could be everything by turns: proud and cruel as Lady Macbeth; tender and gentle as Desdemona. Mdlle. Georges, however, found a rival queen in-drama, as she had done in tragedy—Madame Allan Dorval, who made weeping a luxury worth the paying for. Competitors, perhaps, rather than rivals. There was concurrency, rather than opposition. One of the prettiest incidents in stage annals occurred on the occasion of these artists being twice 'called,' after a representation of 'Mary Tudor,' in which Mdlle. Georges was the Queen and Madame Dorval Lady Jane Grey. After the two actresses had gracefully acknowledged the ovation of which they were the objects, Madame Dorval, with exquisite refinement and noble feeling, kissed the hand of Mdlle. Georges, as if she recognised in her the still supremely reigning queen. It was a pleasure to see this; it is a pleasure to remember it; and it is equally a pleasure to make record of it here.

When all this brilliant talent began to be on the wane, and play-goers began to fear that all the thrones would be vacant, a curious scene used to occur nightly in summer time in the Champs Élysées. Before the seated public, beneath the trees, an oldish woman used to appear, with a slip of carpet on her arm, a fiddle beneath it, and a tin cup hanging on her finger. She was closely followed by a slim, pale, dark, but fiery-eyed girl, whose thoughts seemed to be with some world far away. When the woman had spread the carpet, had placed the cup at one corner, and had scraped a few hideous notes on the fiddle, the pale dark-eyed girl advanced on the carpet and recited passages from Racine and Corneille. With her beautiful head raised, with slight, rare, but most graceful action, with voice and emphasis in exact accord with her words, that pale-faced, inspired girl, enraptured her out-of-door audience. After a time she was seen no more, and it was concluded that her own inward fire had utterly consumed her, and she was forgotten. By-and-by there descended on the deserted temple of tragedy a new queen—nay, a goddess, bearing the name of Rachel. As the subdued and charmed public gazed and listened and sent up their incense of praise and their shout of adulation, memories of the pale-faced girl who

used to recite beneath the stars in the Champs
Élysées came upon them. Some, however, could
see no resemblance. Others denied the possibility
of identity between the abject servant of the muse
in the open air, and the glorious, though pale-faced,
fiery-eyed queen of tragedy, occupying a throne
which none could dispute with her. When half
her brief, splendid, extravagant, and not blameless
reign was over, Mdlle. Rachel gave a 'house-
warming' on the occasion of opening her new and
gorgeously-furnished mansion in the Rue Troncin.
During the evening the hostess disappeared, and
the *maître d'hôtel* requested the crowded company
in the great saloon so to arrange themselves as to
leave space enough for Mdlle. Rachel to appear at
the upper end of the room, as she was about to
favour the company with the recital of some passages from Racine and Corneille. Thereupon entered an old woman with strip of carpet, fiddle,
and tin pot, followed by the queen of tragedy, in
the shabbiest of frocks, pale, thoughtful, inspired,
and with a sad smile that was not altogether out of
tune with her pale meditations; and then, the
carpet being spread, the fiddle scraped, and the
cup deposited, Rachel trod the carpet as if it were
the stage, and recited two or three passages from
the masterpieces of the French masters in dramatic
poetry, and moved her audience according to her
will, in sympathy and delight. When the hurri-

cane of applause had passed, and while a murmuring of enjoyment seemed as its softer echo, Rachel stooped, picked up the old tin cup, and, going round with it to collect gratuities from the company, said, ' Anciennement, c'était pour maman ; à présent, c'est pour les pauvres.'

The Rachel career was of unsurpassable splendour. Before it declined in darkness and set in premature painful death, the now old queen of tragedy, Mdlle. Georges, met the sole heiress of the great inheritance, Mdlle. Rachel, on the field of the glory of both. Rachel was then at the best of her powers, at the highest tide of her triumphs. They appeared in the same piece, Racine's ' Iphigénie.' Mdlle. Georges was Clytemnestre ; Rachel played Ériphile. They stood in presence, like the old and the young wrestlers, gazing on each other. They each struggled for the crown from the spectators, till, whether out of compliment, which is doubtful, or that she was really subdued by the weight, power, and majestic grandeur of Mdlle. Georges, Ériphile forgot to act, and seemed to be lost in admiration at the acting of the then very stout, but still beautiful, mother of the French stage.

The younger rival, however, was the first to leave the arena. She acted in both hemispheres, led what is called a stormy life, was as eccentric as she was full of good impulses, and to the last she

knew no more of the personages she acted than
what she learned of them from the pieces in which
they were represented.  Rachel died utterly ex
hausted.  The wear and tear of her professional life
was aggravated by the want of repose, the restless-
ness, and the riot of the tragedy queen at home.
She was royally buried.  In the *foyer* of the Théâtre
Français Rachel and Mars, in marble, represent
the Melpomene and Thalia of France.  They are
both dead and forgotten by the French public.

For years after Mdlle. Duchesnois had vanished
from the scene, Mdlle. Georges may be said to
have languished out her life.  One day of snow
and fog, in January 1867, a funeral procession
set out from Passy, traversed the living city of
Paris, and entered through the mist the city
of the dead, Père la Chaise.  Alexandre Dumas
was chief mourner.  'In that coffin,' said Jules
Janin, 'lay more sorrows, passions, poetry, and
hopes than in a thousand proud tombs in the
cemetery of Père la Chaise.'  She who had
represented and felt and expressed all these sentiments, emotions, and ideas, was the last survivor
of the line of dramatic queens in France.

That line had its Lady Jane Grey, its queen
for an hour; one who was loved and admired
during that time, and whose hard fate was de-
plored for full as long a period.  About the
year 1819–20 there appeared at the Odéon a

Mdlle. Charton. She made her *début* in a new piece, 'Lancastre,' in which she acted Queen Elizabeth. Her youth and beauty, combined with extraordinary talent, took the public mind prisoner. Here was a young goddess who would shower delight when the maturer divinities had gone back to Olympus. The lithographed portrait of Mdlle. Charton was in all the shops and was eagerly bought. Suddenly she ceased to act. A jealous lover had flung into that beautiful and happy face a cup of vitriol, and destroyed beauty, happiness, and partially the eyesight, for ever. The young actress refused to prosecute the ruffian, and sat at home suffering and helpless, till she became 'absorbed in the population'—that is to say, starved, or very nearly so. She had one poor female friend who helped just to keep her alive. In this way the once proud young beauty literally went down life into old age and increase of anguish. She dragged through the horrible time of the horrible Commune, and then she died. Her body was carried to the common pauper grave at Montmartre, and one poor actor who had occasionally given her what help he could, a M. Dupuis, followed her to that bourn.

Queens as they were, their advent to such royalty was impeded by every obstacle that could be thrown in their way. The 'Society' of French actors has been long noted for its cruel illiberality and its mean jealousy, especially the 'Society' that has been established since the Revolution— or, to speak correctly, during the Revolution which began in 1789, and which is now in the eighty-fourth year of its progress. The poor and modest Duchesnois had immense difficulty in being allowed to appear at all. The other actors would not even speak to her. When she was 'called' by an enthusiastic audience no actor had the gallantry to offer a hand to lead her forward. A poor player, named Florence, at length did so, but on later occasions he was compelled to leave her to 'go on' alone. When Mdlle. Rachel, ill-clad and haggard, besought a well-known *sociétaire* to aid her in obtaining permission to make her *début* on the stage of the Théâtre Français, he told her to get a basket and go and sell flowers. On the night of her triumph, when she *did* appear, and heaps of bouquets were flung at her feet, on her coming forward after the fall of the curtain, she flung them all into a basket, slung it from her shoulders, went to the actor who had advised her to go and vend flowers, and kneeling to him, asked him, half in smiles and half in tears, if he would not buy a nosegay! It is said that Mdlle. Mars was jealous of the promise of her sister, Georgina. Young *débutantes* are apt to think that the aged queens should abandon the parts of young princesses, and when the young *débutantes* have become old they are amazed at the impertinence of new comers who expect them to surrender the juvenile characters. The latest successful *débutante*, Mdlle. Rousseil and M. Mounae Sully, are where they now are in spite of their fellows who were there before them.

## SOME ECCENTRICITIES OF THE FRENCH STAGE.

THE future historian of the French Stage will not want for matter to add to a history which has already had many illustrators and writers. Just a year ago, I saw a magnificent funeral pass from the church of Notre Dame de Lorette. ' *C'est Lafont, le grand Comédien!* ' was the comment of the spectators. ' Poor Glatigny! ' said another, ' was not thus buried—like a prince! ' Wondering who Glatigny might be, I, in the course of that day, took up a French paper in the reading-room of the Grand Hôtel, in which the name caught my eye, and I found that Glatigny had been one of the eccentric actors of the French stage. He was clever, but reckless; he had a bad memory, but when it was in fault, he could *improvise*—with impudence, but effect.

Glatigny once manifested his improvising powers in a very extraordinary manner. The story, on the authority of the Paris papers, runs thus:

Passing in front of the Mont-Parnasse Theatre, he saw the name of his friend Chevilly in the play-bill. Glatigny entered by the stage-door, and asked to see him. He was told that Chevilly was on the stage, and could not be spoken to; he was acting in Ponsard's 'Charlotte Corday.' Glatigny, thereupon, and to the indignant astonishment of the manager, coolly walked forward to the side of Chevilly, as the latter was repeating the famous lines—

> Non, je ne crois pas, moi,
> Que tout soit terminé quand on n'a plus de roi ;
> C'est le commencement.

As Chevilly concluded these words, he stared in inexpressible surprise at Glatigny, and exclaiming : 'What, you here!' shook him cordially by the hand, as if both were in a private room, and not in the presence of a very much perplexed audience. The audience did not get out of their perplexity by finding that Ponsard's play was altogether forgotten, and that the two players began talking of their private affairs, walking up and down the stage the while, as if they had been on the boulevards or in the gardens of the Tuileries. At length, said Glatigny, 'I am afraid, that I perhaps intrude?' 'Not at all !' said Chevilly. 'I am sure I do,' rejoined Glatigny, ' so farewell. When you have finished, you will find me at the café, next door.' The eccentric player had reached the wing, when he returned, saying : 'By-the-by, before we part, shall we sing together a little *couplet de facture?*'

'With all my heart,' was the reply; and both of them, standing before the foot-lights, sang a verse from some old vaudeville, on the pleasure of old friends meeting unexpectedly, and which used to bring the curtain down with applause.

At this duet, the public entered into the joke— they could not hiss, for laughing,—and the most joyous uproar reigned amongst them, till Glatigny retired as if nothing had happened, and Chevilly attempted seriously to resume his part in 'Charlotte Corday.'

There was a serious as well as a comic tinge in Glatigny's experiences. On one morning in February, 1869, some country folk, returning from the market at Tarbes, saw a man stretched fast asleep on the steps of the theatre. It was early dawn, and snow was gently falling. The peasants shook the sleeper, told him, when half awake, of the danger he was in by thus exposing himself, and asked him what he was doing there? 'Well,' said Glatigny, 'I am waiting for the manager;' he turned round to go to sleep again, and the country folk left him to his fate. Later in the day, he shook himself, by way of toilet and breakfast, and made his call upon the manager. 'My name,' he said, 'is Albert Glatigny. I am a comedian and a poet. At the present moment, I have no money, but am terribly hungry. Have you any vacancy in your company, leading tragedian or lamp-cleaner?' The manager asked him if he was perfect in the part of Pylades. 'Thoroughly so!' was the answer. 'All the better,' said the manager; 'we play "Andromaque," to-night; my Pylades is ill. You will replace him. Good morning!'

When the evening came, Glatigny put on the Greek costume, and entered on the stage, without knowing a single line of his part. That was nothing. When his turn came, he improvised a little reply to Pyrrhus. Glatigny now and then had a line too short by a syllable or two, but he made up for it by putting a syllable or two over measure in the line that followed. He knew the bearing of the story, and he improvised as naturally as if he were taking part in a conversation. The audience was not aware of anything unusual. The manager who, at first, was ready to tear his hair from his head, wisely let Glatigny take his own course, and when the play was ended he offered the eccentric fellow an engagement, at the stupendous salary of sixty francs a month!

Never was there a man who led a more unstable and wandering life. One day, he would seem fixed in Paris; the week after he was established in Corsica; and after disappearing from the world that knew him, he would turn up again at the Café de Suède, with wonderful stories of his errant experiences. With all his mad ways there was no lack of method in Glatigny's mind when he chose to dis-

cipline it.  French critics speak with much favour
of the grace and sweetness of his verses, and quote
charming lines from his comedy, 'Le Bois,' which
was successfully acted at the Odéon.  Glatigny had
a hard life withal.  It was for bread that he became
a strolling player,—that he gave some performances
at the Alcazar, as an improvisatore—and, finally,
that he woke up one fine morning, with republican
opinions.

Probably not a few play-goers among us who
were in Paris in 1849 will forget the first representation of 'Adrienne Lecouvreur,' in the April of
that year.  Among the persons of the drama was
the Abbé de Chazeuil, which was represented by
M. Leroux, and well represented; a perfect *abbé de
boudoir*, loving his neighbour's wife, and projecting
a revolution by denouncing the fashion of wearing
patches!  M. Leroux, like Michonnet in the play,
was eager to become a *sociétaire* of the Théâtre
Français, but (like poor Firmin, whose memory was
not so blameless as his style and genius—and who
committed suicide, like Nourrit, by flinging himself
out of the window of an upper storey) Leroux was
not a 'quick study,' and, year by year, he fell into
the background, and had fewer parts assigned to
him.  The actor complained.  The answer was
that his memory was not to be trusted.  He rejoined
that it had never been trustworthy, and yet he had
got on, in a certain sense, without it.  The rejoinder

was not accepted as satisfactory. The oblivious player (with all his talent) fell into oblivion. He not only was not cast for new parts, but many of his old ones that he had really got by heart were consigned to other members of the company. Leroux was, before all things, a Parisian, and yet, in disgust, he abandoned Paris. He wandered through the provinces, found his way to Algiers, and there, after going deeper and deeper still, did not forget one thing for which he had been cast in the drama of life—namely, his final exit.

Political feeling has often led to eccentric results on, and in front of, the French stage. With all the Imperial patronage of the drama, the public never lost an opportunity of laughing at the vices of the Imperial *régime*. When Ponsard's 'Lucréce' was revived at the Odéon, the public were simply bored by Lucretia's platitudes at home and the prosings of her husband in the camp. But when Brutus abused the Senate, and scathing sarcasm was flashed against the extravagance of the women of the court, and their costume, the pit especially, the house generally, burst forth into a shout of recognition and derision. It is to be observed that the acute Emperor himself often led the applause on passages which bore political allusions, and which denounced tyranny in supreme lords or in their subordinates. When the Emperor did not take the initiative, the people did. At the first representation of Augier's

'La Contagion,' there was a satirical passage against England. The audience accepted it with laughter; but when the actor **added** : 'After all, the English are our best friends, and are a free people!' the phrase was **received** with a thundering *Bravo!* from the famous Pipe-en-bois, who sat, wild and dishevelled, **in** the middle **of** the pit, and **whose** exclamation aroused tumultuous echoes. **At** another passage, 'There comes a time when baffled truths are affirmed by thunder-claps!' the audience tried to encore **the phrase.** M. Got was too well-trained an actor to be guilty of obeying, but the house **shouted,** '*Vivent les coups de tonnerre!*' 'Thunder-claps **for ever!**' and **the** passive Cæsar looked **cold and unmoved** across that turbulent pit.

The French public is cruel to its idols whose powers have **passed** away. The French stage is ungrateful **to** its old patrons who can no longer confer patronage. When the glorious three days of 1830 had overthrown the Bourbon Charles X., King of France and Navarre, and put in his place Louis Philippe, King of the French, and the 'best **of** republics,' the actors at the Odéon inaugurated their first representation under the 'Revolution' by acting Pichat's tragedy of 'William Tell' and Molière's 'Tartuffe.' **All** the actors were ignoble enough to associate themselves with the downfall of a dynasty many kings of which had been liberal benefactors of the drama. In 'William Tell' Ligier stooped to the anachronism of wearing a tri-coloured rosette on the buffskin tunic of Tell.  In ' Tartuffe ' all the actors and actresses but one wore the same sign of idiocy.  Tartuffe himself wore the old white ribbon of the Bourbons, but only that the symbol which once was associated with much glory might be insulted in its adversity.  Dorine, the servant, tore the white rosette from Tartuffe's black coat amid a hurricane of applause from the hot-headed heroes of the barricades, who had by fire, sword, artillery, and much slaughter, set on the throne the ' modern Ulysses.'  Eighteen years later, that Ulysses shared the fate of all French objects of idolatry, and was rudely tumbled down from his high estate.  At the Porte St. Martin, Frederic Lemaître played a chiffonier in one of the dramas in which he was so popular.  In his gutter-raking at night, after having tossed various objects over his shoulder into his basket, he drove his crook into some object which he held up for the whole house to behold.  It was a battered kingly crown, and when, with a scornful chuckle, he flung it among the rags and bones in the basket on his back, the vast mob of spectators did not hiss him from the stage ; they greeted the unworthy act by repeated salvoes of applause !

Turning from eccentric actors to eccentric pieces, there may be reckoned among the latter a piece called ' Venez,' which was first produced, a

few years ago, at Liége. A chief incident in the
piece is where a pretty actress, seeking an engagement, is required by the young manager, as a test
of her competency, to give to the above word as
many varied intonations as might be possible. One
of these proves to be so exquisitely seductive that
the manager offers a permanent engagement for life,
which is duly accepted. From Liége to Compiègne
is a long step, but it brings us to another eccentricity. Nine years ago, at one of the Imperial
revels there, certain of the courtiers and visitors
acted in an apropos piece, named 'Les Comment-
aires de César.' The Prince Imperial represented
the Future, without having the slightest idea of it.
Prosper Mérimée, Academician, poet, and historian,
acted the Past, of which he had often written so
picturesquely. In the more farcical part which
followed the prologue, the most prominent personage was the Princesse de Metternich (wife of the
Austrian ambassador), who played the part of a
French cabman out on strike. She tipped forth the
Paris slang, and sang a character song, with an
audacity which could not be surpassed by the
boldest of singing actresses at any of the popular
minor theatres. The august audience were convulsed at this manifestation of high dramatic art—
in its way! These fêtes led to much extravagance
in dress, and to much contention thereon between
actresses and managers.

The directors of the Palais Royal Theatre have frequently been at law with their first ladies. Mdlle. Louisa Ferraris, in 1864, signed an engagement to play there for three years at a salary beginning at 2,400 francs, and advancing to 3,000 and 3,600 francs, with a forfeit clause of 12,000 francs. The salary would hardly have sufficed to pay the lady's shoemaker. In the course of the engagement the 'Foire aux Grotesques' was put in rehearsal. In the course of this piece Mdlle. Ferraris had to say to another actress, 'I was quite right in not inviting you to my ball, for you could not have come in a new dress, as you owe your dressmaker 24,000 francs!' As this actress was really deeply indebted to that important personage, she begged that this speech, which seemed a deliberate insult to her, might be altered. Mdlle. Ferraris, in spite of the authors, who readily changed the objectionable phrase, continued, however, to repeat the original words. As she was peremptorily ordered to omit them she flung up her part, whereupon the directors applied to the law to cancel her engagement for breach of contract, and to award them 12,000 francs damages. Mademoiselle repented and offered to resume the part. On this being declined she entered a cross action to gain the 12,000 francs for breach of contract on the directors' side. The Tribunal de Commerce, after consideration, cancelled the engagement, but condemned Mdlle. Ferraris to pay 2,000 francs damages and the costs of suit. It is to the stage, and not to the empress, that inordinate luxury in dress is to be attributed. Sardou, in 'La Famille Bénoiton,' has been stigmatised as the forerunner of such an exaggerated luxury that no private purse was sufficient to pay for the toilette of a woman whose maxim was, *La mode à tout prix.*

Two or three years ago there was an actress at the Palais Royal Theatre known as Antonia de Savy. Her real name was Antoinette Jathiot. Her salary was 1,200 francs for the first year, 1,800 francs for the second: not three-and-sixpence a night in English money. But out of the three-and-sixpences Mdlle. Antonia was bound to provide herself with 'linen, shoes, stockings, head-dresses, and all theatrical costumes requisite for her parts, except foreign costumes totally different from anything habitually worn in France.' For any infringement of these terms Mademoiselle was to pay a fine of 10,000 francs—about her salary for half-a-dozen years. Circumstances led Antonia to be wayward, and the management entered on a suit for the cancelling of the engagement on the ground of her refusing to play a particular part, and her unpunctuality. Her counsel, M. G. Chaix d'Est Ange, pleaded that the lady was a minor, that her father had not given his consent to such an engagement, and that it was an imposition on her youth and

inexperience.  The other side replied that Mdlle.
Jathiot had ceased to be a minor since the engagement was signed ; that as to her inexperience, she
was a very experienced young lady in the ways of
Parisian life ; that the engagement was concluded 
with her because she dressed in the most magni-
ficent style, and that it would be profitable to the
theatre as well as to herself to exhibit those magnificent dresses on the stage ; and that as to her
respected sire, he was a humble clerk, living in a
garret in the Rue Saint-Lazare, and had no control
whatever over a daughter who lived in the style of
a princess, spent fabulous sums in maintaining it,
and had the most perfect ' turn-out ' in the way of
carriage, horses, and servants in the French capital.
The plaintiffs asked to be relieved from this modest
young lady, and to be awarded damages for her
insubordination and unpunctuality.  The Tribunal
de Commerce ordered the engagement to be cancelled, and the defendant to pay 1500 francs
damages and the costs of suit.  But the Imperial
Court of Appeal took another view of the case.
They refused in any way to sanction such an im-
moral notion as that the terms of the contract were
not disadvantageous for the minor because it was
known that she got her living in a way that could
not be avowed.  They quashed the judgment of
the Tribunal de Commerce, and ordered the managers of the Palais Royal to pay all the costs.

The most singular of all law cases between French actresses and managers was one the names of the parties to which have slipped out of my memory. It arose out of the refusal of a young actress, who had not lost her womanly modesty, to 'go on' in the dress provided for her, which would hardly have afforded her more covering than a postage-stamp. In the lawsuit which followed this act of insubordination, the modest young lady was defeated, and was rebuked by the magistrate for infringing the laws of the stage, of which the manager was the irresponsible legislator! The actress preferred the cancelling of her engagement to the degradation of such nightly exposure as was demanded by the manager and was sanctioned by the magistrate.

I have said above that the eccentric extravagance of dress—the other extreme from next to none at all—was not a consequence of an example set by the empress. But there is something to be said on both sides. Only two years ago Mdlles. Fargueil, Bernhardt, and Desclées made public protest against the *pièces aux robes*, in which they were required to dress like empresses (of fashion) at their own expense. They traced the ruinous custom to the period when the Imperial Court was at Compiègne, and when the actresses engaged or 'invited' to play to the august company there were required by the inexorable rule of the Court to obey the sumptuary laws which regulated costume.   Every lady was invited for three days; each day she was to wear three different dresses, and no dress was to be worn a second time.  Count Bacciochi, the grand chamberlain, kept a sharp eye on the ladies of the drama.  Histrionic queens and countesses were bound to be attired as genuinely as the historical dignitaries themselves.  The story might be romance, the outward and visible signs were to be all reality.  The awful Grand Chamberlain once banished an actress from the Court stage at Compiègne for the crime of wearing mock pearls when she was playing the part of a duchess!

This evil fashion, insisted on by dreadful Grand Chamberlains, was adopted by Paris managers, who hoped to attract by dresses—the very skirt of any one of which would swallow more than a *vicaire's* yearly income—and by a river of diamonds on a fair neck, whatever might be in the head above it. A young actress who hoped to live by such salary as her brains alone could bring her, and who would presume to wear sham jewellery or machine-made lace, was looked upon as a poor creature who would never have a reputation—that is, such a reputation as her gorgeously attired sisters, who did not particularly care to have *any* but that for which the most of them dressed themselves. When the empire fell the above-named actresses thought that a certain republican simplicity might properly take the place of an imperial magnificence. Or they maintained that if stage-ladies were required to find stage-dresses that cost twenty times their salary, the cost of providing such dresses should fall on the stage-proprietors, and not on the stage-ladies. It is said that the bills Mdlle. Fargueil had to pay for her dresses in 'La Famille Bénoiton' and 'Patrie' represented a sum total which, carefully invested, would have brought her in a comfortable annuity! This may be a little exaggerated, but the value of the dresses may be judged of from one fact, namely, that the Ghent lace which Mdlle. Fargueil wore on her famous blue dress in 'La Famille Bénoiton' was worth very nearly 500*l.*

How the attempt to introduce 'moderation' into the stage laws of costume has succeeded, the most of us have seen. It has not succeeded at all. Certain actresses are proud to occupy that bad pre-eminence from which they are able to set the fashion. '*Mon chancelier vous dira le reste!*'

One of the eccentricities of the modern French stage is the way in which it deals with the most delicate, or, rather, the most indelicate subjects and people. The indelicate people and subject may indeed be coarsely represented and outspoken, but they must observe certain recognised, though undefined rules. There must be an innocent young lady among the wicked people, and the lady (the *ingénue*) and her ingenuousness must be respected. One fly may taint a score of carcases and make a whole pot of ointment stink, but one *ingénue* keeps a French piece of nastiness comparatively pure, and the public taste for the impure is satisfied with this little bit of sentimentality. The subjects which many French authors have brought on the stage do not, it is to be hoped, hold a true mirror up to French nature. If so, concubinage, adultery, and murder reign supreme. The changes have been rung so often on this triple theme that an anonymous writer has proposed that the theme should be represented, once for all, in something of the following form, and that dramatic authors should then turn to fresh woods and pastures new : ' Scene.— A Drawing-room ; a married lady is seated, her lover at her feet ; the folding-door at back opens, and discovers husband with a double-barrelled revolver. He fires and kills married lady and her lover. Husband then advances and contemplates his victims. After a pause, he exclaims : " A thousand pardons ! I have come to a room on the wrong flat ! " Curtain slowly descends.' This represents quite as faithfully the iniquities which, according to the modern French drama, prevail universally in society, as the dramas of Florian achieve the mission which was assigned to him of illustrating *les petites vertus de tous les jours*—the little virtues of everyday life.

The name of Mademoiselle Aimée Desclées
reminds me of our Lord Chamberlain. Extremes
meet, in the mind as well as elsewhere! That
actress, who, after many years of hard struggle,
floated triumphantly as La Dame aux Camélias, and
after a few years' progress over sunny seas slowly
sank in sight of port, was discovered and brought
out by M. Dumas *fils*. A year or two ago she
came to London with his plays, the above 'Dame,'
the 'Princesse Georges,' the 'Visite de Noces,'
and some others. But they stank in the nostrils of
our Lord Chamberlain, and he would no more
allow them to be produced than the Lord Mayor
would allow corrupt meat to be exposed for sale in
a City market. Great was the outcry that arose
thereupon, from the French inhabitants, and some
of the ignorant natives of London. The Chamberlain's prudery and English delicacy generally were
made laughing-stocks. But, gently! Is it known
that the French themselves have raised fiercer outcry against plays which our Lord Chamberlain has
refused to license than ever Jeremy Collier raised
against that disgusting school of English comedy
which Dryden founded, and the filth of which was
not compensated for by the wit, such as it is, of
Congreve, or the humour, if it may be so called, of
Wycherly? The *Gaulois* and the *Figaro*, papers
which cannot be charged with over straitlacedness,
have blushed at the adulterous comedy of France

as deeply as the two harlequins at Southwark Fair
blushed at the blasphemy of Lord Sandwich.   A
French critic, M. Fournier, referring to the 'Visite
de Noces' of the younger Dumas, remarks that
'the theatre ought not to be a surgical operating
theatre, or a dissecting-room.  There are opera-
tions,' he adds, 'which should not be performed
on the stage, unless, indeed, a placard be posted at
the doors, "Women not admitted!"'   With respect to this suggestion, M. Hostein, another critic,
says: 'People ask if the "Visite de Noces" be
proper for ladies to see.  Men generally reply with
an air of modesty, that no woman who respects
herself would go to see it.  Capital puff!' exclaims
M. Hostein, 'they flock to it in crowds!' Not *all*,
however.  Not even all men.  Men with a regard
for 'becomingness' are warned by indignant French
critics.  The dramatic critic of the 'France'
thus vigorously speaks to the point: 'We say it
with regret, with sadness, in no other country, no
other civilised city, in no other theatre of Europe,
would the new piece of M. Dumas *fils* be possible,
and we doubt whether there could be found elsewhere than in Paris a public who would applaud
it even by mistake.  The "Visite de Noces" has
obtained a striking and decided success; so much
the worse for the author and for us.  If our tastes,
if our sentiments, if our conscience be so perjured
and perverted that we accept without repugnance

and encourage with our cheers such pictures, we are truly *en décadence.'* Such is the judgment of the leading critics. One of them, indeed, tersely said, 'the piece will have a success of indignation and money.' The public provided both, and the author accepted the latter. The women who were of his audience and were *not* indignant were of the same nature as those who listen to cases in our divorce courts. But the Lord Chamberlain is fully justified in refusing a licence to play French pieces which French critics have denounced as degrading to the moral and the national character. The only fault to be found is in the manner of the doing it; which in the Chamberlain's servants takes a rude and boorish expression. Meanwhile, let us remark that the attention of the Lord Chamberlain might well be directed to other matters under his control. If a fire, some night, break out in a crowded theatre (where, every night, there is imminent peril) he will be asked if he had officially done all in his power to prevent such a calamity. And if he were to put restraint on the performances of certain licenced places of amusement, husseydom might deplore it, but there would be one danger the less for young men for whose especial degradation these entertainments seem at present to be permitted. While this matter is being thought of, a study of that old-fashioned book 'The Elegant Letter-Writer,' would perhaps improve the style of the Chamberlain's *subs*, and would not be lost on certain young gentlemen of Oxford.

If not among the eccentricities—at least among the marvels of modern French-actress life—may be considered the highly dramatic entertainments given by some of the ladies in their own homes.

Like the historical tallow-chandler, who, after retiring from business, went down to the old manufactory on melting days, the actor, generally speaking, never gets altogether out of his profession. Some who retire give 'readings,' or return periodically to the stage, after no end of 'final farewells' for positively the last time, and nothing is more common than to see concert singers (on holiday) at concerts. French actresses have been especially addicted to keeping to their vocation, even in their amusements. If they are not at the theatre they have private theatricals at home; and, if not private theatricals, at least what comes next to them, or most nearly resembles them.

In the grand old days of the uninterrupted line of French actresses there was a Mdlle. Duthé, who was first in the second line of accomplished players. She was of the time of, and often a substitute for, Mdlle. Clairon. The latter was never off the stage. She was always acting. When she was released from Fort l'Évêque, where she had been imprisoned for refusing to act with Dubois, whom she considered as a disgrace to the profession, Clairon said to a bevy of actresses in her heroic way, 'The King may take my life, or my property, but not my honour!' 'No, dear,' responded the audacious Sophie Arnould, 'certainly not. Where there is nothing, the King loses his rights!' Mdlle. Duthé belonged to these always-acting actresses. She is the first on record who gave a *bal costumé*—a ball to which every guest was to come in a theatrical or fancy dress. This was bringing amateur acting into the ball-room. The invitation included the entire company of the Théâtre Français, every one of whom came in a tragedy suit. The non-professionals, authors, artists, *abbés, noblesse,* and *gentilshommes* also donned character dresses; and ball and supper constituted a wonderful success. An entertainment similar to the above was given when Louis Philippe was king, by Mdlle. Georges, the great *tragédienne.* All who were illustrious in literature, fine arts, diplomacy, and so forth, elbowed one another in the actress's suite of splendid rooms. Théophile Gautier, we are told, figured as an incroyable, Jules Janin as a Natchez Indian, and Victor Hugo, who now takes the 'Radical' parts, was present *en Palicare.* But the most striking of what may be called these amateur theatrical balls was given last April by M. and Mdme. Judic, or rather by the latter, in the name of both. According to the 'Paris Journal,' such things are easily done—if you are able to do them. If you have

an exquisitely arranged house, though small, you
may get three hundred dancers into it with facility.
You have only, if your house is in France, to send
for Belloir, who will clap a glass cover to your
court-yard, lay carpets here, hang tapestry there,
place mirrors right and left from floor to ceiling,
and scatter flowers and chandeliers everywhere,
and the thing is done—particularly if you have
an account at your bankers'. Something like this
was done on the night of Saturday, April 19, 1873,
when ' La Rosière d'ici ' invited her guests to come
in theatrical array to her ball, which was to begin
at midnight. According to the descriptions of
this spring festival, which were circulated by oral
or printed report, not every one was invited who
would fain have been there. The select company
numbered the choicest of the celebrities of the
stage, art, and literature (with few exceptions), and
*therefore* the ' go ' and the gaiety of the *fête* never
paused for a single instant.

As for the costumes, says Jehan Valter, they who did
not see the picturesque, strange, and fantastic composition,
have never seen anything. Never was coachman so perfect a coachman as Grénier. Never was waggoner more
waggoner than Grévin. Moreover, there were peasants
from every quarter of the world, of every colour, and of
every age. There were stout market porters, incroyables,
jockeys, brigands, waltzing, schottisching, and mazourka-
ing; for the dance went fast and furious on that memorable evening (or rather, Sunday morning). And no

wonder, for among the ladies were Madame Judic, in the costume of a village bride; with Mesdames Moissier, Gabrielle Gautier, Massart, and Gérandon, as the brides-maids. Alice Regnault was a châtelaine of the mediæval period, Hielbron and Damain (the latter, the younger of the sister actresses of that name, who played so charmingly little conversational pieces in English drawing-rooms during the Franco-German war), were country lasses; and, among others, were Blanche D'Antigny, Debreux, Léontine Spelier, Esther David, Gournay, &c., &c.—in short, all the young and pretty actresses of the capital were present. At four o'clock in the morning a splendid supper brought all the guests together, after which dancing was resumed till seven. The festival terminated by the serving of a *soupe à l'oignon à la paysanne*; this stirrup-cup of rustic onion soup was presented in little bowls, with a wooden spoon in each! The sun had been up a very long time before the last of the dancers, loth to depart, had entered their carriages on their way home.

Such is the newest form in which theatrical celebrities get up and enjoy costume-balls after their fashion.

One eccentric matter little understood in this country is co-operation, or collaboration, in the production of French pieces. There is an old story of an ambitious gentleman offering M. Scribe many thousand francs to be permitted to have his name associated with that of M. Scribe as joint authors of a piece by the former, of which the ambitious gen-tleman was to be allowed to write a line, to save his honour. Scribe wrote in reply that it was against Scripture to yoke together a horse and an ass. 'I should like to know,' asked the gentleman, 'what right you have to call me a horse?' This showed that the gentleman had wit enough to become a partner in a dramatic manufactory. Indeed, much less than wit—a mere idea, is sufficient to qualify a junior partner. The historian of 'La Collaboration au Théâtre,' M. Goizot, states that a young provincial once called on Scribe with a letter of introduction and a little comedy, in manuscript. Scribe talked with him, promised to read the piece, and civilly dismissed him. The provincial youth returned *au pays*, hoped, waited, and despaired; finally, at the end of a year, he went up to Paris, and again called on M. Scribe. With difficulty the dramatist recognised him ; with more difficulty could he recollect the manuscript to which his visitor referred, but after consulting a note-book, he took out a manuscript vaudeville of his own and proposed to read it to the visitor. It was that of his popular piece 'La Chanoinesse.' The visitor submitted, but he became delighted as he listened. The reading over, he ventured to refer to his own manuscript. 'I have just read it to you,' said Scribe, 'with my additions. Your copy had an idea in it ; ideas are to me everything. I have made use of yours, and you and I are authors of "La Chanoinesse."'

Collaboration rarely enables us to see the share

of each author in the work. The bouquet we fling to the successful pair is smelt by both. The lately deceased Mr. P. Lébrun made the reception speech when M. Émile Angier was admitted to one of the forty seats of the French Academy. There was a spice of sarcasm in the following words addressed to one of the two authors of ' Le Gendre de M. Poirier :' ' What is your portion therein? and are we not welcoming, not only yourself, to the Academy, but also your *collaborateur* and friend ?' The fact is that in the highest class of co-operative work the work itself is founded on a single thought. The thought is discussed through all its consequences, till the moment for giving it dramatic action arrives, and then the pens pursue their allotted work. There is, however, another method. MM. Legouvé and Prosper Dinaux wrote their drama of ' Louise de Lignerolles ' in this way. The two authors sat face to face at the same table, and wrote the first act. The two results were read, compared, and finally, out of what was considered the best work in the two, a new act was selected with some new writing in addition. Thus three acts were really constructed to build up one. This ponderous method is not followed by many writers. Indeed, how some co-operative dramatists work is beyond conjecture. A vaudeville in one act sometimes has four authors; indeed, several of these single-act pieces have been advertised as the work of a dozen;

in one case, according to M. Goizot, of *sixteen*
authors, who probably chatted, laughed, drank,
and smoked the piece into existence at a café ; and
the piece becoming a reality, the whole company
of revellers were named as the many fathers of
that minute bantling.

Undoubtedly the most marvellous example of
dramatic eccentricity that was ever put upon record is the one which tells us of a regular performance by professional actors in a public theatre,
before an ordinary audience, who had extraordinary
interest in the drama.  The locality was in Paris,
in the old theatre of the Porte Saint-Martin.  The
piece was the famous melodrama, ' La Pie Voleuse,'
on which Rossini founded ' La Gazza Ladra,' and
which, under the name of ' The Maid and the
Magpie,' afforded such a triumph to Miss Kelly as
that lady may remember with pride ; for we believe
that most accomplished and most natural of all
actresses still survives—or was surviving very lately
—with two colleagues at least of the olden time,
Mrs. W. West and Miss Love.  When ' La Pie
Voleuse ' was being acted at the above-named
French theatre, the allied armies had invaded
France ; a portion of the invading force had entered
Paris.  The circumstance now to be related is best
told on French authority.  An English writer might
almost be suspected of calumniating the French
people by narrating such an incident, unsupported

by reference to the source from which he derived it. We take it from one of the many dramatic *feuilletons* of M. Paul Foucher, an author of several French plays, a critic of French players and play-writers, and a relative, by marriage, of M. Victor Hugo. This is what M. Paul Foucher tells us: ' On the evening of the second entry of the foreign armies into Paris, the popular melodrama " La Pie Voleuse," was being acted at the Porte Saint-Martin. There was one thousand eight hundred francs in the house, which at that time was considered a handsome receipt. During the performance the doors were closed, because the rumbling noise of the cannon, rolling over the stones, interrupted the interest of the dialogue, and it rendered impossible the sympathetic attention of the audience.' Frenchmen there were who were ashamed of this heartless indifference for the national tragedy. Villemot was disgusted at this elasticity of the Parisian spirit, and he added to his rebuke these remarkable words :—' I take pleasure in hoping that we may never again be subjected to the same trial, and that, in any case, we may bear it in a more dignified fashion.' How Paris bore it, when the terrible event again occurred, is too well known to be retold ; but the incident of ' La Pie Voleuse ' is perhaps the most eccentric of the examples of dramatic and popular eccentricity to be found in the annals of the French stage.

# NORTHUMBERLAND HOUSE AND THE PERCYS.

WHEN Hotspur treads the stage with passionate grace, the spectator hardly dreams of the fact that the princely original lived, paid taxes, and was an active man of his parish, in Aldersgate Street. *There*, however, stood the first Northumberland House. By the ill-fortune of Percy it fell to the conquering side in the serious conflict in which Hotspur was engaged ; and Henry IV. made a present of it to his queen, Jane. Thence it got the name of the Queen's Wardrobe. Subsequently it was converted into a printing office ; and in the course of time, the first Northumberland House disappeared altogether.

In Fenchurch Street, not now a place wherein to look for nobles, the great Earls of Northumberland were grandly housed in the time of Henry VI. ; but vulgar citizenship elbowed the earls too closely, and they ultimately withdrew from the City. The deserted mansion and grounds were taken possession of by the roysterers. Dice were for ever rattling in the stately saloons. Winners shouted for joy, and blasphemy was considered a virtue by the losers. As for the once exquisite gardens, they were converted into bowling-greens, titanic billiards, at which sport the gayer City sparks breathed themselves for hours in the summer time. There was no place of entertainment so fashionably frequented as this second Northumberland House ; but dice and bowls were at length to be enjoyed in more vulgar places, and ' the old seat of the Percys was deserted by fashion.' On the site of mansion and gardens, houses and cottages were erected, and the place knew its old glory no more. So ended the second Northumberland House.

While the above mansions or palaces were the pride of all Londoners and the envy of many, there stood on the strand of the Thames, at the bend of the river, near Charing Cross, a hospital and chapel, whose founder, William Marshal, Earl of Pembroke, had dedicated it to St. Mary, and made it an appanage to the Priory of Roncesvalle, in Navarre. Hence the hospital on our river strand was known by the name of ' St. Mary Rouncivall.' The estate went the way of such property at the dissolution of the monasteries ; and the first lay proprietor of the forfeited property was a Sir Thomas Cawarden. It was soon after acquired by Henry Howard, Earl of Northampton, son of the first Earl of Surrey. Howard, early in the reign of James I., erected on the site of St. Mary's Hospital a brick mansion which, under various names, has developed into that third and present Northumberland House which is about to fall under pressure of circumstances, the great need of London, and the argument of half a million of money.

Thus the last nobleman who clung to the Strand, which, on its south side, was once a line of palaces, has left it for ever. The bishops were the first to reside on that river-bank outside the City walls. Nine episcopal palaces were once mirrored in the then clear waters of the Thames. The lay nobles followed, when they felt themselves as safe in that fresh and healthy air as the prelates. The chapel of the Savoy is still a royal chapel, and the memories of time-honoured Lancaster and of John, the honest King of France, still dignify the place. But the last nobleman who resided so far from the now recognised quarters of fashion has left what has been the seat of the Howards and Percys for nearly three centuries, and the Strand will be able no longer to boast of a duke. It also recently possessed an English earl; but *he* was only a modest lodger in Norfolk Street.

When the Duke of Northumberland went from the Strand, there went with him a shield with very nearly nine hundred quarterings; and among them are the arms of Henry VII., of the sovereign houses of France, Castile, Leon, and Scotland, and of the ducal houses of Normandy and Brittany! *Nunquam minus solus quam cum solus*, might be a fitting

motto for a nobleman who, when he stands before
a glass, may see therein, not only the Duke, but
also the Earl of Northumberland, Earl Percy, Earl
of Beverley, Baron Lovaine of Alnwick, Sir Algernon
Percy, Bart., two doctors (LL.D. and D.C.L.), a
colonel, several presidents, and the patron of two-
and-twenty livings.

As a man who deals with the merits of a book
is little or nothing concerned with the binding
thereof, with the water-marks, or with the printing,
but is altogether concerned with the life that is
within, that is, with the author, his thoughts, and
his expression of them, so, in treating of Northumberland House, we care much less for notices of the
building than of its inhabitants—less for the outward aspect than for what has been said or done
beneath its roof. If we look with interest at a
mere wall which screens from sight the stage
of some glorious or some terrible act, it is not
for the sake of the wall or its builders: our
interest is in the drama and its actors. Who
cares, in speaking of Shakespeare and Hamlet, to
know the name of the stage carpenter at the Globe
or the Blackfriars? Suffice it to say, that Lord
Howard, who was an amateur architect of some
merit, is supposed to have had a hand in designing
the old house in the Strand, and that Gerard
Christmas and Bernard Jansen are said to have been
his ' builders.' Between that brick house and the

present there is as much sameness as in the legendary knife which, after having had a new handle, subsequently received in addition a new blade. The old house occupied three sides of a square. The fourth side, towards the river, was completed in the middle of the seventeenth century. The portal retains something of the old work, but so little as to be scarcely recognisable, except to professional eyes.

From the date of its erection till 1614 it bore the name of Northampton House. In that year it passed by will from Henry Howard, Lord Northampton, to his nephew, Thomas Howard, Earl of Suffolk, from whom it was called Suffolk House. In 1642, Elizabeth, daughter of Theophilus, second Earl of Suffolk, married Algernon Percy, tenth Earl of Northumberland, and the new master gave his name to the old mansion. The above-named Lord Northampton was the man who has been described as foolish when young, infamous when old, an encourager, at threescore years and ten, of his niece, the infamous Countess of Essex; and who, had he lived a few months longer, would probably have been hanged for his share, with that niece and others, in the mysterious murder of Sir Thomas Overbury. Thus, the founder of the house was noble only in name; his successor and nephew has not left a much more brilliant reputation. He was connected, with his wife, in frauds upon the King, and was fined heavily. The heiress of Northumberland, who married his son, came of a noble but ill-fated race, especially after the thirteenth Baron Percy was created Earl of Northumberland in 1377. Indeed, the latter title had been borne by eleven persons before it was given to a Percy, and by far the greater proportion of the whole of them came to grief. Of one of them it is stated that he (Alberic) was appointed Earl in 1080, but that, *proving unfit for the dignity*, he was displaced, and a Norman bishop named in his stead! The idea of turning out from high estate those who were unworthy or incapable is one that might suggest many reflections, if it were not *scandalum magnatum* to make them.

In the chapel at Alnwick Castle there is displayed a genealogical tree. At the root of the Percy branches is ' Charlemagne ;' and there is a sermon in the whole, much more likely to scourge pride than to stimulate it, if the thing be rightly considered. However this may be, the Percys find their root in Karloman, the Emperor, through Joscelin of Louvain, in this way : Agnes de Percy was, in the twelfth century, the sole heiress of her house. Immensely rich, she had many suitors. Among these was Joscelin, brother of Godfrey, sovereign Duke of Brabant, and of Adelicia, Queen Consort of Henry the First of England. Joscelin held that estate at Petworth which has not since gone out of

the hands of his descendants. This princely suitor
of the heiress Agnes was only accepted by her as
husband on condition of his assuming the Percy
name. Joscelin consented; but he added the arms
of Brabant and Louvain to the Percy shield, in
order that, if succession to those titles and possessions should ever be stopped for want of an heir,
his claim might be kept in remembrance. Now,
this Joscelin was lineally descended from ‘ Charlemagne,’ and, *therefore*, that greater name lies at the
root of the Percy pedigree, which glitters in gold
on the walls of the ducal chapel in the castle at
Alnwick.

Very rarely indeed did the Percys, who were
the earlier Earls of Northumberland, die in their
beds. The first of them, Henry, was slain (1407)
in the fight on Bramham Moor. The second, another Henry (whose father, Hotspur, was killed in
the hot affair near Shrewsbury), lies within St.
Alban's Abbey Church, having poured out his life-
blood in another Battle of the Roses, fought near
that town named after the saint. The blood of the
third Earl helped to colour the roses, which are
said to have grown redder from the gore of the
slain on Towton's hard-fought field. The forfeited
title was transferred, in 1465, to Lord John Nevill
Montagu, great Warwick's brother; but Montagu
soon lay among the dead in the battle near Barnet.
The title was restored to another Henry Percy,

and that unhappy Earl was murdered, in 1489, at his house, Cucklodge, near Thirsk. In that fifteenth century there was not a single Earl of Northumberland who died a peaceful and natural death.

In the succeeding century the first line of Earls, consisting of six Henry Percys, came to an end in that childless noble whom Anne Boleyn called 'the Thriftless Lord.' He died childless in 1537. He had, indeed, two brothers, the elder of whom might have succeeded to the title and estates; but both brothers, Sir Thomas and Sir Ingram, had taken up arms in the 'Pilgrimage of Grace.' Attainder and forfeiture were the consequences; and in 1551 Northumberland was the title of the dukedom conferred on John Dudley, Earl of Warwick, who lost the dignity when his head was struck off at the block, two years later.

Then the old title, Earl of Northumberland, was restored in 1557, to Thomas, eldest son of that attainted Thomas who had joined the 'Pilgrimage of Grace.' Ill-luck still followed these Percys. Thomas was beheaded—the last of his house who fell by the hands of the executioner—in 1572. His brother and heir died in the Tower in 1585.

None of these Percys had yet come into the Strand. The brick house there, which was to be their own through marriage with an heiress, was built in the lifetime of the Earl, whose father, as just mentioned, died in the Tower in 1585. The son, too, was long a prisoner in that gloomy palace and prison.   While Lord Northampton was laying the foundations of the future London house of the Percys in 1605, Henry Percy, Earl of Northumberland, was being carried into durance.   There was a Percy, kinsman to the Earl, who was mixed up with the Gunpowder Plot.   For no other reason than relationship with the conspiring Percy, the Earl was shut up in the Tower for life, as his sentence ran, and he was condemned to pay a fine of thirty thousand pounds.   The Earl ultimately got off with fifteen years' imprisonment and a fine of twenty thousand pounds.   He was popularly known as the Wizard Earl, because he was a studious recluse, companying only with grave scholars (of whom there were three, known as ' Percy's Magi ') and finding relaxation in writing rhymed satires against the Scots.

There was a stone walk in the Tower which, having been paved by the Earl, was known during many years as 'My Lord of Northumberland's Walk.'   At one end was an iron shield of his arms ; and holes in which he put a peg at every turn he made in his dreary exercise.

One would suppose that the Wizard Earl would have been very grateful to the man who restored him to liberty.   Lord Hayes (Viscount Doncaster) was the man.   He had married Northumberland's daughter, Lucy.   The marriage had excited the

Earl's anger, as a *low match*, and the proud captive could not 'stomach' a benefit for which he was indebted to a son-in-law on whom he looked down. This proud Earl died in 1632. Just ten years after, his son, Algernon Percy, went a-wooing at Suffolk House, in the Strand. It was then inhabited by Elizabeth, the daughter and heiress of Theophilus, Earl of Suffolk, who had died two years previously, in 1640. Algernon Percy and Elizabeth Howard made a merry and magnificent wedding of it, and from the time they were joined together the house of the bride has been known by the bridegroom's territorial title of Northumberland.

The street close to the house of the Percys, which we now know as Northumberland Street, was then a road leading down to the Thames, and called Hartshorn Lane. Its earlier name was Christopher Alley. At the bottom of the lane the luckless Sir Edmundsbury Godfrey had a stately house, from which he walked many a time and oft to his great wood wharf on the river. But the glory of Hartshorn Lane was and is Ben Jonson. No one can say where rare Ben was born, save that the posthumous child first saw the light in Westminster. 'Though,' says Fuller, 'I cannot, with all my industrious inquiry, find him in his cradle, I can fetch him from his long coats. When a little child he lived in Hartshorn Lane, Charing Cross, where his mother married a bricklayer for her second husband.'　Mr. Fowler was a master bricklayer, and did well with his clever stepson.　We can in imagination see that sturdy boy crossing the Strand to go to his school within the old church of St. Martin (then still) in the Fields.　It is as easy to picture him hastening of a morning early to Westminster, where Camden was second master, and had a keen sense of the stuff that was in the scholar from Hartshorn Lane.　Of all the figures that flit about the locality, none attracts our sympathies so warmly as that of the boy who developed into the second dramatic poet of England.

Of the countesses and duchesses of this family, the most singular was the widow of Algernon, the tenth Earl.　In her widowhood she removed from the house in the Strand (where she had given a home not only to her husband, but to a brother) to one which occupied the site on which White's Club now stands.　It was called Suffolk House, and the proud lady thereof maintained a semi-regal state beneath the roof and when she went abroad.　On such an occasion as paying a visit, her footmen walked bareheaded on either side of her coach, which was followed by a second, in which her women were seated, like so many ladies in waiting!　Her state solemnity went so far that she never allowed her son Joscelin's wife (daughter of an Earl) to be seated in her presence—at least till she had obtained permission to do so.

Joscelin's wife was, according to Pepys, ' a beautiful lady indeed.' They had but one child, the
famous heiress, **Elizabeth** Percy, who at four years
of age was left **to** the guardianship of her proud
and wicked old **grandmother.** Joscelin was dead,
and his widow married Ralph, afterwards Duke of
Montague. The **old** Dowager Countess was **a**
matchmaker, and she contracted her granddaughter,
at the age of twelve, to Cavendish, Earl of Ogle.
Before this couple were of age to live together, Ogle
died. In a year **or two after, the** old matchmaker
engaged **her victim to Mr.** Thomas Thynne, of
Longleat ; **but the young lady had** no mind to him.
In the **Hatton collection of** manuscripts there are
three letters **addressed by** a lady of the Brunswick
family to Lord and Lady Hatton. They are
undated, but they contain a curious reference to
part of the present subject, and are thus noticed in
the first report of the Royal Commission on Historical Manuscripts : ' Mr. Thinn has proved his
marriage with Lady Ogle, but she will not live
with him, for **fear** of being " rotten before she **is**
ripe." Lord **Suffolk,** since he lost his wife and
daughter, lives with his sister, Northumberland.
They have **here** strange ambassadors—one from the
King **of** Fez, **the other from** Muscovett. All the
town has seen the last ; he goes to the play, and
stinks so that the ladies are not able to take their
muffs from their noses all the play-time. The lam-

poons that are made of most of the town ladies are so nasty that no woman would read them, else she would have got them for her.'

'Tom of Ten Thousand,' as Thynne was called, was murdered (shot dead in his carriage) in Pall Mall (1682) by Königsmark and accomplices, two or three of whom suffered death on the scaffold. Immediately afterwards, the maiden wife of two husbands *really* married Charles, the proud Duke of Somerset.   In the same year, Banks dedicated to her (*Illustrious Princess*, he calls her) his 'Anna Bullen,' a tragedy.   He says: 'You have submitted to take a noble partner, as angels have delighted to converse with men;' and 'there is so much of divinity and wisdom in your choice, that none but the Almighty ever did the like' (giving Eve to Adam) 'with the world and Eden for a dower.'   Then, after more blasphemy, and very free allusions to her condition as a bride, and fulsomeness beyond conception, he scouts the idea of supposing that she ever should die.  'You look,' he says, 'as if you had nothing mortal in you.  Your guardian angel scarcely is more a deity than you;' and so on, in increase of bombast, crowned by the mock humility of 'my muse still has no other ornament than truth.'

The Duke and Duchess of Somerset lived in the house in the Strand, which continued to be called Northumberland House, as there had long been a

*Somerset* House a little more to the east. Anthony Henley once annoyed the above duke and showed his own ill-manners by addressing a letter ' to the Duke of Somerset, over against the trunk-shop at Charing Cross.' The duchess was hardly more respectful when speaking of her suburban mansion, Sion House, Brentford. ' It's a hobbledehoy place,' she said ; ' neither town nor country.' Of this union came a son, Algernon Seymour, who in 1748 succeeded his father as Duke of Somerset, and in 1749 was created Earl of Northumberland, for a particular reason. He had no sons. His daughter Elizabeth had encouraged the homage of a handsome young fellow of that day, named Smithson. She was told Hugh Smithson had spoken in terms of admiration of her beauty, and she laughingly asked why he did not say as much to herself. Smithson was the son of ' an apothecary,' according to the envious, but, in truth, the father had been a physician, and earned a baronetcy, and was of the good old nobility, the landowners, with an estate, still possessed by the family, at Stanwick, in Yorkshire. Hugh Smithson married this Elizabeth Percy, and the earldom of Northumberland, conferred on her father, was to go to her husband, and afterwards to the eldest male heir of this marriage, failing which the dignity was to remain with Elizabeth and her heirs male by any other marriage.

It is at this point that the present line of Smithson-Percys begins. Of the couple who may be called its founders so many severe things have been said, that we may infer that their exalted fortunes and best qualities gave umbrage to persons of small minds or strong prejudices. Walpole's remark, that in the earl's lord-lieutenancy in Ireland ' their vice-majesties scattered pearls and diamonds about the streets,' is good testimony to their royal liberality. Their taste may not have been unexceptionable, but there was no touch of meanness in it. In 1758 they gave a supper at Northumberland House to Lady Yarmouth, George II.'s old mistress. The chief ornamental piece on the supper table represented a grand *chasse* at Herrenhausen, at which there was a carriage drawn by six horses, in which was seated an august person wearing a blue ribbon, with a lady at his side. This was not unaptly called ' the apotheosis of concubinage.' Of the celebrated countess notices vary. Her delicacy, elegance, and refinement are vouched for by some ; her coarseness and vulgarity are asserted by others. When Queen Charlotte came to England, Lady Northumberland was made one of the ladies of the queen's bed-chamber. Lady Townshend justified it to people who felt or feigned surprise, by remarking, ' Surely nothing could be more proper. The queen does not understand English, and can anything be more necessary than that she should learn the vulgar tongue ? ' One of the countess's familiar terms for conviviality was 'junkitaceous,' but ladies of equal **rank** had also little slang words of their own, called things by the very plainest names, and spelt *physician* with an ' f.'

There is ample testimony on record that the great countess never hesitated at a jest on the score of its coarseness. The earl was distinguished rather for his pomposity than vulgarity, though a vulgar sentiment marked some **of** both his sayings **and** doings. For example, when Lord March visited him at Alnwick Castle, the **Earl of** Northumberland received him **at the gates with** this queer sort **of** welcome : ' **I believe, my lord, this is** the first time **that ever a Douglas and a Percy met here** in friend-**ship.'** The **censor who said, '** Think **of this** from **a Smithson to a true Douglas,'** had ample ground **for** the exclamation. George III. raised the earl and countess to the **rank** of duke and duchess in 1766. All the earls of older creation were ruffled and angry **at** the advancement; but the honour had its drawback. The King would not allow **the title** to descend to an heir by any other **wife** but the one then alive, who was the true representative **of the Percy line.**

**The old Northumberland** House festivals were right royal things in their way. There was, on the other hand, many a snug, or unceremonious, or ec-centric party given there. Perhaps the most splendid **was** that given in honour of the King of Denmark

in 1768.   His majesty was fairly bewildered with
the splendour.   There was in the court what was
called ' a pantheon,' illuminated by 4,000 lamps.
The King, as he sat down to supper, at the table to
which he had expressly invited twenty guests out
of the hundreds assembled, said to the duke, ' How
did you contrive to light it all in time?'   ' I had
two hundred lamplighters,' replied the duke.   ' That
was a stretch,' wrote candid Mrs. Delany ; ' a dozen
could have done the business ;' which was true.

The duchess, who in early life was, in delicacy
of form, like one of the Graces, became, in her more
mature years, fatter than if the whole three had
been rolled into one in her person.   With obesity
came ' an exposition to sleep,' as Bottom has it.
At ' drawing-rooms ' she no sooner sank on a sofa
than she was deep in slumber ; but while she was
awake she would make jokes that were laughed
at and censured the next day all over London.   Her
Grace would sit at a window in Covent Garden,
and be *hail fellow well met* with every one of a mob
of tipsy and not too cleanly-spoken electors.   On
these occasions it was said she ' signalised herself
with intrepidity.'   She could bend, too, with cleverness to the humours of more hostile mobs ; and
when the Wilkes rioters besieged the ducal mansion,
she and the duke appeared at a window, did salu-
tation to their masters, and performed homage to
the demagogue by drinking his health in ale.

Horace Walpole affected to ridicule the ability of the duchess as a verse writer. At Lady Miller's at Batheaston some rhyming words were given out to the company, and anyone who could, was required to add lines to them so as to make sense with the rhymes furnished for the end of each line. This sort of dancing in fetters was called *bouts rimés*. 'On my faith,' cried Walpole, in 1775, 'there are *bouts rimés* on a buttered muffin by her Grace the Duchess of Northumberland.' It may be questioned whether anybody could have surmounted the difficulty more cleverly than her Grace. For example :

| | |
|---|---|
| The pen which I now take and | brandish, |
| Has long lain useless in my | standish. |
| Know, every maid, from her own | patten |
| To her who shines in glossy | satin, |
| That could they now prepare an | oglio |
| From best receipt of book in | folio, |
| Ever so fine, for all their | puffing, |
| I should prefer a butter'd | muffin ; |
| A muffin, Jove himself might | feast on, |
| If eaten with Miller, at | Batheaston. |

To return to the house itself. There is no doubt that no mansion of such pretensions and containing such treasures has been so thoroughly kept from the vulgar eye. There is one exception, however, to this remark. The Duke (Algernon) who was alive at the period of the first Exhibition

threw open the house in the Strand to the public
without reserve.  The public, without being ungrateful, thought it rather a gloomy residence.
Shut in and darkened as it now is by surrounding
buildings—canopied as it now is by clouds of
London smoke—it is less cheerful and airy than
the Tower, where the Wizard Earl studied in his
prison room, or counted the turns he made when
pacing his prison yard.  The Duke last referred to
was in his youth at Algiers under Exmouth, and in
his later years a Lord of the Admiralty.  As Lord
Prudhoe, he was a traveller in far-away countries,
and he had the faculty of seeing what he saw, for
which many travellers, though they have eyes, are
not qualified.  At the pleasant Smithsonian house
at Stanwick, when he was a bachelor, his household was rather remarkable for the plainness of
the female servants.  Satirical people used to say
the youngest of them was a grandmother.  Others,
more charitable or scandalous, asserted that Lord
Prudhoe was looked upon as a father by many in
the country round, who would have been puzzled
where else to look for one.  It was his elder brother Hugh (whom Lord Prudhoe succeeded) who
represented England as Ambassador Extraordinary
at the coronation of Charles X. at Rheims.
Paris was lost in admiration at the splendour of
this embassy, and never since has the *hôtel* in the
Rue de Bac possessed such a gathering of royal

and noble personages as at the *fêtes* given there
by the Duke of Northumberland.  His sister, Lady
Glenlyon, then resided in a portion of the fine
house in the Rue de Bourbon, owned and in part
occupied by the rough but cheery old warrior, the
Comte de Lobau.  When that lady was Lady
Emily Percy, **she was married** to the eccentric
Lord James Murray, afterwards Lord Glenlyon.
The bridegroom was rather of an oblivious turn of
mind, and it is said that when the wedding morn
arrived, his servant had some difficulty in per-
suading **him that** it was the day on which he had
**to get up and be married.**

**There remains only to** be remarked, that as the
Percy line **has been** often represented only by an
heiress, there have not been wanting individuals
who boasted of male heirship.

Two years after the death of Joscelin Percy in
1670, who died the last male heir of the line,
leaving an only child, a daughter, who married
the Duke of Somerset, there appeared, supported
by the Earl of Anglesea, a most impudent claimant
(as next male heir) in the person **of James** Percy,
an Irish trunkmaker.  This individual professed to
be a descendant of Sir Ingram Percy, who was in
the 'Pilgrimage **of Grace,'** and was brother of
the sixth earl.  The claim **was** proved to be unfounded ; but it may have rested on an *illegitimate* foundation.  As **the** pretender continued to

call himself Earl of Northumberland, Elizabeth, daughter of Joscelin, 'took the law' of him. Ultimately he was condemned to be taken into the four law courts in Westminster Hall, with a paper pinned to his breast, bearing these words: 'The foolish and impudent pretender to the earldom of Northumberland.'

In the succeeding century, the well-known Dr. Percy, Bishop of Dromore, believed himself to be the true male representative of the ancient line of Percy. He built no claims on such belief; but the belief was not only confirmed by genealogists, it was admitted by the second heiress Elizabeth, who married Hugh Smithson. Dr. Percy so far asserted his blood as to let it boil over in wrath against Pennant when the latter described Alnwick Castle in these disparaging words: 'At Alnwick no remains of chivalry are perceptible; no respectable train of attendants; the furniture and gardens are inconsistent; and nothing, except the numbers of unindustrious poor at the castle gate, excited any one idea of its former circumstances.'

'Duke and Duchess of Charing Cross,' or 'their majesties of Middlesex,' were the mock titles which Horace Walpole flung at the ducal couple of his day who resided at Northumberland House, London, or at Sion House, Brentford. Walpole accepted and satirised the hospitality of the London house, and he almost hated the ducal host and hostess at Sion, because they seemed to over-shadow his mimic feudal state at Strawberry! After all, neither early nor late circumstance connected with Northumberland House is confined to memories of the inmates. Ben Jonson comes out upon us from Hartshorn Lane with more majesty than any of the earls; and greatness has sprung from neighbouring shops, and has flourished as gloriously as any of which Percy can boast. Half a century ago, there was a long low house, a single storey high, the ground floor of which was a saddler's shop. It was on the west side of the old Golden Cross, and nearly opposite Northumberland House. The worthy saddler founded a noble line. Of four sons, three were distinguished as Sir David, Sir Frederick, and Sir George. Two of the workmen became Lord Mayors of London; and an attorney's clerk, who used to go in at night and chat with the men, married the granddaughter of a king and became Lord Chancellor.

## LEICESTER FIELDS.

In the reign of James I. there was an open space of ground north of what is now called Leicester Square (which by some old persons is still called Leicester Fields), and which was to the London soldiers and civilians of that day very much what Wormwood Scrubs is to the military and their admirers of the present time. Prince Henry exercised his artillery there, and it continued to be a general military exercise-ground far into the reign of Charles I. People trooped joyfully over the lammas land paths to witness the favourite spectacle. The greatest delight was excited by charges of cavalry against lines or masses of dummies, through which the gallant warriors and steeds plunged and battled—thus teaching them not to stop short at an impediment, but to dash right through it.

In 1631 there were unmistakable signs that this land was going to be built over, and people were aghast at the pace at which London was growing. Business-like men were measuring and staking; the report was that the land had been given to Sydney, Earl of Leicester. Too soon the builders got possession, and **the** holiday folk with military proclivities no longer enjoyed their old ecstasy **of** accompanying the soldiery to Paggington's tune of

My masters and friends and good people, draw near.

Why Sydney was allowed to establish himself **on** the lammas land **no one can tell.** All that we know is, that Lord Carlisle wrote from Nonsuch, in August 1631, to Attorney-General Heath, informing him that it was the king's pleasure that Mr. Attorney should prepare **a licence** to the Earl of Leicester to build upon **a** piece of ground called Swan Close, in St. Martin's-in-the-Fields, a house convenient for his habitation.'

The popular idea of Earl of Leicester is Elizabeth's Robert Dudley. Well, that earl had a sister, Mary, who married Sir Henry Sydney, of Penshurst. This couple had a son, whom they called Robert, and whom King James created at successive periods Baron Sydney, Viscount Lisle, and Earl of Leicester. And this Earl Robert had a son who, in 1626, succeeded to the earldom, and to him **King Charles, in 1631,** gave **Swan Close** and some other part of **the** lammas land, whereon he erected **the** once famous Leicester House.

This last **Robert was the** father of the famous and rather shabby patriot, Algernon Sydney, also of the handsome Henry. He is still more famous as having for daughter Dorothy, the ' Sacharissa ' with whom Waller pretended to be in love, and he gave his family name to Sydney Alley. When, some few years later, the Earl of Salisbury (Viscount Cranbourn) built a house in the neighbourhood, he partly copied the other earl's example, and called the road which led to his mansion Cranbourn Alley.

The lammas land thus given away was land which was open to the poor after Lammastide. Peter Cunningham quotes two entries from the St. Martin's rate-books to this effect : ' To received of the Honble. Earle of Leicester for ye Lamas of the ground that adjoins the Military Wall, 3*l*.' The ' military wall ' was the boundary of the Wormwood Scrubs of that day. The Earl also had to pay ' for the lamas of the ground whereon his house and garden are, and the field that is before his house, near to Swan Close.' The field before his house is now Leicester Square, ' but Swan Close,' says Peter, ' is quite unknown.' Lord Carlisle's letter in the State Paper Office states that the house was to be built ' *upon* Swan Close.'

It was a palatial mansion, that old Leicester House. It half filled the northern side of the present square, on the eastern half of that side. Its noble gardens extended beyond the present Lisle Street. At first that street reached only to the garden wall of Leicester House. When the garden itself disappeared the street was lengthened. It

was a street full of ' quality,' and foreign ambassadors thought themselves lodged in a way not to
dishonour their masters if they could only secure
a mansion in Lisle Street.

Noble as the mansion was, Robert Sydney Earl
of Leicester is the only earl of his line who lived in
it, and his absences were many and of long con-
tinuance.  He was a thrifty man, and long before
he died, in 1677, he let the house to very responsible tenants.  One of these was Colbert.  If the
ordinary run of ambassadors were proud to be
quartered in Lisle Street, the proper place for the
representative of ' *L'Etat c'est moi,*' and for the
leader of civilisation, was the palace in Leicester
Fields ; and there France established herself, and
there and in the neighbourhood, in hotels, cafés,
restaurants, *charcutiers, commissionnaires,* refugees,
and highly-coloured ladies, she has been ever
since.

Colbert probably the more highly approved of
the house as it had been dwelt in already by a
queen.  On February 7, 1662, the only queen that
ever lived in Drury Lane—the Queen of Bohemia
(daughter of James I.)—removed from Drury House
and its pleasant gardens, now occupied by houses
and streets, at the side of the Olympic Theatre, to
Leicester House.  Drury House was the residence
of Lord Craven, to whom it was popularly said
that the widowed queen had been privately married.

                                  R

Her occupancy of Leicester House was not a long one, for the queen died there on the 12th of the same month.

Six years later, in 1668, the French ambassador, Colbert, occupied Leicester House. Pepys relates how he left a joyous dinner early, on October 21, to join Lord Brouncker, the president, and other members of the Royal Society, in paying a formal return visit to Colbert; but the party had started before Pepys arrived at the Society's rooms. The little man hastened after them; but they were 'gone in' and 'up,' and Pepys was too late to be admitted. His wife, perhaps, was not sorry, for he took her to Cow Lane; 'and there,' he says, 'I showed her the coach which I pitch on, and she is out of herself for joy almost.'

It is easy to guess why the Royal Society honoured themselves by honouring Colbert. The great Frenchman was something more than a mere Marquis de Segnelai. Who remembers M. le Marquis? Who does not know Colbert—the pupil of Mazarin, the astute politician, the sharp finance-minister, the patron—nay, the pilot—of the arts and sciences in France? The builder of the French Royal Observatory, and the founder of the Academies of Painting and Sculpture and of the Sciences in France, was just the man to pay the first visit to the Royal Society. Leicester House was nobly tenanted by Colbert, and nobly frequented by the men **of taste and of** talent whom he gathered about him beneath its **splendid roof.**

**The house fell** into other hands, and men who were extremely opposite to philosophers were admitted within its walls *with* philosophers, who were expected to admire their handiwork. In October 1672, the grave Evelyn called at Leicester House to take leave of Lady Sunderland, who was about to set out for Paris, where Lord **Sunderland was the** English ambassador. **My lady made** Evelyn stay to dinner, **and afterwards sent** for Richardson, the **famous fire-eater. A few years ago a** company of Orientals, **black and white,** exhibited certain feats, but they **were too repulsive** (generally) **to attract. What the members of this** company did **was done two** hundred years **ago** in Leicester Square by Richardson alone. ' He devoured,' says Evelyn, ' brimstone on glowing coals before us, chewing and swallowing them ; he melted a large glass and eat it quite up ; then, taking a live coal on his tongue, he put on it a raw oyster, the coal was blowed on with bellows till it **flamed** and sparkled in his mouth, and so remained till the oyster gaped and was quite boiled. Then he melted pitch and wax with sulphur, which he drank down as it flamed. I saw it flaming in his mouth a good while. He also took up a thick piece of iron, such **as** laundresses use to put in their smoothing-boxes, when it was fiery hot, held it between his teeth, then in his hands, and threw it about like a stone; but this I observed, that he cared not to hold very long. Then he stood on a small pot, and bending his body, took a glowing iron in his mouth from between his feet, without touching the pot or ground with his hands; with divers other prodigious feats.' Such was the singular sort of entertainment provided by a lady for a gentleman after dinner in the seventeenth century and beneath the roof of Leicester House.

Meanwhile Little France increased and flourished in and about the neighbourhood, and 'foreigners of distinction' were to be found airing their nobility in Leicester Square and the Haymarket—almost country places both.

Behind Leicester House, and on part of the ground which once formed Prince Henry Stuart's military parade ground, there was a riding academy, kept by Major Foubert. In 1682, among the major's resident pupils and boarders, was a handsome dare-devil young fellow, who was said to be destined for the Church, but who subsequently met his own destiny in quite another direction. His name was Philip Christopher Königsmark (Count, by title), and his furious yet graceful riding must have scared the quieter folks pacing the high road of the fields. He had with him, or rather *he* was with an elder brother, Count Charles John. This elder Count walked Leicester Fields in somewhat strange company—a German Captain Vratz, Borosky, a Pole, and Lieutenant Stern, a third foreigner. To what purpose they associated was seen after that Sunday evening in February 1682, when three mounted men shot Mr. Thomas Thynne (Tom of Ten Thousand) in his coach, at the bottom of the Haymarket. Tom died of his wounds. Thynne had been shot because he had just married the wealthy child-heiress, Lady Ogle. Count Charles John thought *he* might obtain the lady if her husband were disposed of. The necessary disposal of him was made by the three men named above, after which they repaired to the Count's lodgings and then scattered; but they were much wanted by the police, and so was the Count; when it was discovered that he had suddenly disappeared from the neighbourhood of the 'Fields,' and had gone down the river. He was headed, and taken at Gravesend. The subordinates were also captured. For some time indeed Vratz could not be netted. One morning, however, an armed force broke into a Swedish doctor's house in Leicester Fields, and soon after they brought out Vratz in custody, to the great delight of the assembled mob. At the trial, the Count was acquitted. His younger brother, Philip, swore to an *alibi*, which proved nothing, and the King influenced the judges! The three hired murderers went to the gallows, and thought little of it. Vratz excused the deed, on

the ground of murder not having been intended ;
' besides,' said this sample of the Leicester Fields
foreigner of the seventeenth century, 'I am a
gentleman, and God will deal with me accordingly.'
The two counts left England, and made their
names notorious in Continental annals. The French
riding-master shut up his school behind Leicester
House, and removed to a spot where his name still
lives : Foubert's Passage, in Regent Street, opposite
Conduit Street, is the site of the academy where
that celebrated teacher once instructed young
ladies and gentlemen how to ' witch the world with
noble horsemanship.'

We have spoken of the square being almost in
the country. It was not the only one which was
considered in the same light. In 1698 the author
of a book called ' Mémoires et Observations faites
par un Voyageur en Angleterre,' printed at the
Hague in the above year, thus enumerates the
London squares or *places* : ' Les places qui sont
dans Londres, ou pour mieux dire, dans les fau-
bourgs, occupent des espaces qui, joints ensemble,
en fourniraient un suffisant pour bâtir une grande
ville. Ces places sont toutes environnées de
balustrades, qui empêchant que les carrosses n'y
passant. Les principales sont celles de Lincoln's
Inn Fields, de Moor Fields, de Southampton ou
Blumsbury, de St. James, &c., Covent Garden ; de
Sohoe, ou Place Royale, du Lion rouge (Red Lyon),

du Quarré d'Or (Golden Square), et de Leicester Fields.'

All these are said to be in the *suburbs*. Soho Square was called by fashionable people, King Square. It was only vulgar folk who used the prevailing name of Soho.

From early in Queen Anne's days till late in those of George I., the representative of the Emperor of Germany resided in Leicester House. It was said that Jacobites found admittance there, for plotting or for refuge. It is certain that the imperial residence was never so tumultuously and joyously **surrounded as** when Prince Eugene arrived **in Leicester Square,** in the above Queen's reign, on a mission from the Emperor, to induce England to join with him in carrying on the war. During his brief stay Leicester Fields was thronged with a cheering mobility and a bowing nobility and gentry, hastening to ' put a distinguished respect ' on Marlborough's great comrade, who was almost too modest to support the popular honours put on himself. Bishop Burnet and the Prince gossiping **together at their** frequent interviews at Leicester **House have quite** a picturesque aspect.

The imperial chaplain there was often as busy as his master. Here is a sample of one turn of his office :

One evening a man, in apparent hurry, knocked at the door of Leicester House, the imperial ambassador's residence. He was bent on being married, and he accomplished that on which he was bent. This person was the son of a cavalier squire; he was also a Templar, for a time; but he hated law and Fleet Street, and he set up as near to being a courtier as could be expressed by taking lodgings in Scotland Yard, which was next door to the court then rioting at Whitehall. His name was Fielding, and his business was to drink wine, make love, and live upon pensions from female purses. Three kings honoured the rascal: Charles, James, and William; and one queen did him a good turn. For a long time Beau Fielding was the handsomest ass on the Mall. Ladies looked admiringly and languishingly at him, and the cruel beau murmured, ' Let them look and die.' Maidens spoke of him as 'Adonis!' and joyous widows hailed him 'Handsome as Hercules!' It was a mystery how he lived; how he maintained horses, chariot, and a brace of fellows in bright yellow coats and black sarcenet sashes. They were the Austrian colours; for Fielding thought he was cousin to the House of Hapsburg.

Supercilious as he was, he had an eye to the widows. His literature was in Doctors' Commons, where he studied the various instances of marital affection manifested by the late husbands of living widows. One day he rose from the perusal of a will with great apparent satisfaction. He had just

read how Mr. Deleau had left his relict a town
house in Copthall Court, a Surrey mansion at
Waddon, and sixty thousand pounds at her own
disposal. The handsome Hercules resolved to add
himself to the other valuables of which widow
Deleau could dispose.

Fielding knew nothing whatever of the widow
he so ardently coveted; but he, like love, could
find out the way. There was a Mrs. Villars, who
had dressed the widow's hair, and she undertook,
for a valuable consideration, to bring the pair
gradually together. Fielding was allowed to see
the grounds at Waddon. As he passed along, he
observed a lady at a window. He put his hand on
the left side of his waistcoat, and bowed a superlative beau's superlative bow; and he was at the
high top-gallant of his joy when he saw the
graceful lady graciously smile in return for his
homage. This little drama was repeated; and at
last Mrs. Villars induced the lady to yield so very
much all at once as to call with her on Fielding at
his lodgings. Three such visits were made, and
ardent love was made also on each occasion. On
the third coming of Hero to Leander, there was a
delicious little banquet, stimulating to generous
impulses. The impulses so overcame the lady that
she yielded to the urgent appeals of Mrs. Villars
and the wooer, and consented to a private marriage
in her lover's chambers. The ecstatic Fielding

leapt up from her feet, where he had been kneeling, clapt on his jaunty hat with a slap, buckled his bodkin sword to his side with a hilarious snap, swore there was no time like the present, and that he would himself fetch a priest and be back with him on the very swiftest of the wings of love.

That was the occasion on which, at a rather late hour, Fielding was to be seen knocking at the front door of Leicester House. When the door was opened his first inquiry was after the imperial ambassador's chaplain. The beau had, in James II.'s days, turned Papist; and when Popery had gone out as William came in, he had not thought it worth while to turn back again, and was nominally a Papist still. When the Roman Catholic chaplain in Leicester House became aware of what his visitor required, he readily assented, and the worthy pair might be seen hastily crossing the square to that bower of love where the bride was waiting. The chaplain satisfied her scruples as to the genuineness of his priestly character, and in a twinkling he buckled beau and belle together in a manner which, as he said, defied all un-doing.

'Undoing?' exclaimed the lover. 'I marry my angel with all my heart, soul, body, and every-thing else!'—and he put a ring on her finger bearing the poesy *Tibi soli*—the sun of his life.

In a few days the bubble burst. The lady

turned out to be no rich widow, but a Mrs. Wadsworth, **who was given to** frolicking, **and** who thought this the merriest frolic of her light-o'-love life. Fielding, who had passed himself off as a count, had not much to say in his own behalf, and he turned the 'sun of his life' out of doors. Whither he could turn he knew right well. He had long served all the purposes of the Duchess of Cleveland, the degraded old mistress of Charles II.; and within three weeks of his being buckled to Mrs. Wadsworth by the Leicester Square priest he married Duchess Barbara. Soon after he thrashed **Mrs. Wadsworth in the street for** claiming him as **her lawful** husband, **and he beat the Duchess** at **home for** asserting that Mrs. Wadsworth was right. **Old** Barbara did more. She **put two** hundred pounds into that lady's hand, to prosecute Fielding for bigamy, and the Duchess promised her a hundred pounds a year for fifteen years if she succeeded in getting him convicted. And the handsome **Hercules was** convicted accordingly, at the **Old Bailey, and was** sentenced to **be burnt in the hand;** but the rascal produced Queen **Anne's warrant to stay** execution. And **so ended** the Leicester Square wedding.

**As long as** the Emperor's envoy lived in Leicester Fields he **was the** leader of fashion. Crowds assembled to see his 'turn out.' Sir Francis Gripe, in **the** 'Busy-body,' tempts Miranda by saying, 'Thou shalt be the envy of the Ring, for I will carry thee to Hyde Park, and thy equipage shall surpass the what-d'ye-call-'em ambassador's.'

Leicester House was, luckily, to let when the Prince of Wales quarrelled with his father, George I. In that house the Prince set up a rival court, against attending which the 'London Gazette' thundered dreadful prohibitions. But St. James's was dull; Leicester House was 'jolly'; and the fields were 'all alive' with spectators 'hooraying' the arrivals. Within, the stately Princess towered among her graceful maids. With regard to her diminutive husband it was said of his visitors,

> In his embroidered coat they found him,
> With all his strutting dwarfs around him.

Most celebrated among the Leicester House maids of honour was the young, bright, silvery-laughing, witty, well-bred girl, who could not only spell, but could construe Cæsar—the maid of whom Chesterfield wrote—

> Should the Pope himself go roaming,
> He would follow dear Molly Lepell.

And there rattled that other Mary—Mary Bellenden, laughing at all her lovers, the little, faithless Prince himself at the head of them. She would mock him and them with wit of the most audacious sort, and tell stories to the Princess, at which that august lady **would laugh** behind her **fan,** while the wildest, and **not the least** beautiful **of** the maids would throw **back her** handsome head, burst into uncontrollable laughter, **and then run across to** shock prim Miss Meadows, 'the prude,' with the same galliard story. Perhaps the most frolicksome **nights at Leicester** House were when **the Princess of Wales was in** the card-room, where a **dozen** tables were occupied by players, while **the** Prince, in another room, **gave** topazes and amethysts to **be raffled for** by the maids **of** honour, **amid fun and laughter, and little** astonishment **when the** prizes **were found to be more or** less **damaged.**

It **was a sight for a** painter **to see** these, with other **beauties, leaving Leicester** Fields of a morning **to** hunt **with the Prince near** Hampton. Crowds waited **to see** them return in the evening; and, when they were fairly housed again and dressed for the evening, lovers flocked around the young huntresses. **Then** Mary Bellenden snubbed her **Prince** and master, **and walked, whispering, with** handsome **Jack** Campbell; **and Molly Lepell** blushed and laughed encouragingly **at the pleasant phrases poured** into her ear by John, Lord **Hervey.** There Sophy Bellenden telegraphed with her **fan to** Nanty Lowther; and of *their* love-making came mischief, sorrow, despair, **and death.** And there were dark-looking Lord

Lumley and his Orestes, Philip Dormer Stanhope ;
and dark Lumley is not stirred to laugh—as the
maids of honour do, silently—as Stanhope follows
the Princess to the card-room, imitating her walk
and even her voice. This was the ' Chesterfield '
who thought himself a ' gentleman.' The Princess
leans on Lady Cowper's shoulder and affects to
admire what she really scorns—the rich dress of
the beautiful Mary Wortley Montague. On one
of the gay nights in Leicester House, when the
Princess appeared in a dress of Irish silk—a
present from ' the Irish parson, Swift '—the Prince
spoke in such terms of the giver as to induce Lord
Peterborough to remark, ' Swift has now only to
chalk his pumps and learn to dance on the tight-
rope, to be yet a bishop.'

The above are a few samples of life in the
royal household in Leicester Square. There, were
born, in **1721**, the Duke of Cumberland, who was
so unjustly called ' Butcher '; in 1723, Mary, who
married the ' brute ' Prince of Hesse-Cassel ; and
in 1724, Louisa, who died—one of the unhappy
English Queens of Denmark.

After the father of these children had become
George II., his eldest son, Frederick, Prince of
Wales, established enmity with his sire, and an
opposition court at Leicester House, at Carlton
House (which he occupied at the same time), and
at Kew.

Frederick, Prince of Wales, has been the object of heavy censure, and some of it, no doubt, was well-deserved. But he had good impulses and good tastes. He loved music, and was no mean instrumentalist. He manifested his respect for Shakespeare by proposing that the managers of the two theatres should produce all the great poet's plays in chronological order, each play to run for a week. The Prince had some feeling for art, and was willing to have his judgment regulated by those competent to subject it to rule.

In June 1749, some tapestry that had belonged to Charles I. was offered to the Prince for sale. He was then at Carlton House, and he forthwith sent for Vertue. The engraver obeyed the summons, and on being ushered into the presence he found a group that might serve for a picture of *genre* at any time. The Prince and Princess were at table waiting for dessert. Their two eldest sons, George and Edward, then handsome children, stood in waiting, or feigned the service, each with a napkin on his arm. After they had stood awhile in silence, the Prince said to them, ' This is Mr. Vertue. I have many curious works of his, which you shall see after dinner.' Carlton House was a store of art treasures. The Prince, with Luke Schaub in attendance and Vertue accompanying, went through them all. He spoke much and listened readily, and parted only to have another art-conference in the following month.

The illustrious couple were then seated in a pavilion, in Carlton House garden. The Prince showed both knowledge and curiosity with respect to art ; and the party adjourned to Leicester House (Leicester Square), where Mr. Vertue was shown all the masterpieces, with great affability on the part of Frederick and his consort. The royal couple soon after exhibited themselves to the admiring people, through whom they were carried in two chairs over Leicester Fields back to Carlton House. Thence the party repaired to Kew, and the engraver, after examining the pictures, dined at the palace, ' though,' he says, ' being entertained there at dinner was not customary to any person that came from London.'

During the tenancy of Frederick, Prince of Wales, Leicester House was the scene of political intrigues and of ordinary private life occurrences : Carlton House was more for state and entertainment. Leicester House and Savile House, which had been added to the former, had their joyous scenes also. The story of the private theatricals carried on in either mansion has been often told. The actors were, for the most part, the Prince's children. He who was afterwards George III. was among the best of the players, but he had a good master. After his first public address as king, Quin, proud of his pupil, exclaimed, 'I taught the boy to speak.' Some contemporary letter-writers could scarcely find lofty phrases enough wherewith to praise these little amateurs. Bubb Doddington, who served the Prince of Wales and lost his money at play to him ('I've nicked Bubb!' was the cry of the royal gambler, when he rose from the Leicester House card-tables with Bubb's money in his pocket), Bubb, I say, was not so impressed by the acting of these boys and girls. He rather endured than enjoyed it. On January 11, 1750, all that he records in his diary is, 'Went to Leicester House to see " Jane Grey " acted by the Prince's children.' In the following May, Prince Frederick William was born in Leicester House, ' the midwife on the bed with the Princess, and Dr. Wilmot standing by,' and a group of ladies at a short distance. The time was half an hour after midnight. 'Then the Prince, the ladies, and some of us,' says Doddington, ' sat down to breakfast in the next room—then went to prayers, downstairs.' In June the christening took place, in Leicester House, the Bishop of Oxford officiating. 'Nobody of either sex was admitted into the room but the actual servants' (that is, the ladies and gentlemen of the household) ' except Chief Justice Willes and Sir Luke Schaub.' Very curious were some of the holiday rejoicings on this occasion. For example, here is a ' setting out' from

Leicester House to make a day of it, on June 28 :
'Lady Middlesex' (the Prince's favourite), 'Lord
Bathurst, Mr. Breton, and I' (writes Bubb)
'waited on their Royal Highnesses to Spitalfields,
to see the manufactory of silk, and to Mr. Carr's
shop, in the morning. In the afternoon the same
company, with Lady Torrington in waiting, went
in private coaches to Norwood Forest, to see a
settlement of Gipsies. We returned and went to
Bettesworth, the conjurer, in hackney coaches.
. . . . Not finding him we went in search of the
little Dutchman, but were disappointed ; and concluded the particularities of this day by supping
with Mrs. Cannon, the Princess's midwife.' Such
was the condescension of royalty and royalty's
servants in the last century !

In March, of the following year, Bubb Doddington went to Leicester House. The Prince told
him he 'had catched cold' and 'had been blooded.'
It was the beginning of the end. Alternately a
little better and much worse, and then greatly
improved, &c., till the night of the 20th. 'For
half an hour before he was very cheerful, asked to
see some of his friends, ate some bread-and-butter
and drank coffee.' He was 'suffocated' in a fit of
coughing ; 'the breaking of an abscess in his side
destroyed him. His physicians, Wilmot and Lee,
knew nothing of his distemper. . . . Their ignorance, or their knowledge, of his disorder, renders

them equally inexcusable for not calling in other assistance.' **How** meanly **this** prince was buried, how shabbily everyone, officially in attendance, was treated, are well known. The only rag of state ceremony allowed this poor Royal Highness was, that his body went in one conveyance and his bowels in another—which was a compliment, no doubt, but hardly one to be thankful for.

The widowed Princess remained in occupation of the mansion in which her husband had died. One of the **pleasantest domestic** pictures **of Leicester House is given by** Bubb Doddington, under date November 17, 1753 :—

**The Princess sent for me to** attend her between eight and nine o'clock.   **I went to** Leicester House, expecting a **small company and a little musick, but found** nobody but **her Royal** Highness.   **She made** me draw a **stool** and sit **by the fireside.   Soon** after came in the Prince of Wales **and Prince** Edward, and **then the** Lady Augusta, all in an undress, and took their stools and sat round the fire with **us.   We continued** talking of familiar occurrences till between **ten and** eleven, with the ease and unreservedness and unconstraint, as if one had dropped **into a sister's** house that had a family, to pass the evening.   **It is** much to be wished that **the Princes conversed** familiarly with more people of a certain knowledge **of the** world.

**The Princess, however,** did not want for worldly knowledge.   About this time the Princess Dowager of Wales was sitting pensive and melancholy, in a room in Leicester House, while the two Princes were playing about her. Edward then said aloud to George, 'Brother, when we are men, you shall marry, and I will keep a mistress.' 'Be quiet, Eddy,' said his elder brother, ' we shall have anger presently for your nonsense. There must be no mistresses at all.' Their mother thereon bade them, somewhat sharply, learn their nouns and pronouns. 'Can you tell me,' she asked Prince Edward, ' what a pronoun is?' 'Of course I can,' replied the ingenuous youth; ' a pronoun is to a noun what a mistress is to a wife—a substitute and a representative.'

The Princess of Wales continued to maintain a sober and dignified court at Leicester House, and at Carlton House also. She was by no means forgotten. Young and old rendered her full respect. One of the most singular processions crossed the Fields in January 1756. Its object was to pay the homage of a first visit to the court of the Dowager Princess of Wales at Leicester House—the visitors being a newly-married young couple, the Hon. Mr. Spencer and the ex-Miss Poyntz (later Earl and Countess of Spencer). The whole party were contained in two carriages and a ' sedan chair.' Inside the first were Earl Cowper and the bridegroom. Hanging on from behind were three footmen in state liveries. In the second carriage were the mother and sister of the bride, with similar human adornments on the outside as with the first carriage. Last, and alone, of course, as became her state, in a new sedan, came the bride, in white and silver, as fine as brocade and trimming could make it. The chair itself was lined with white satin, was preceded by a black page, and was followed by three gorgeous lackeys. Nothing ever was more brilliant than the hundred thousand pounds' worth of diamonds worn by the bride except her own tears in her beautiful eyes when she first saw them and the begging letter of the lover which accompanied them. As he handed her from the chair, the bridegroom seemed scarcely less be-diamonded than the bride. His shoe-buckles alone had those precious stones in them to the value of thirty thousand pounds. They were decidedly a brilliant pair. Public homage never failed to be paid to the Princess. In June 1763, Mrs. Harris writes to her son (afterwards first Lord Malmesbury) at Oxford: I was yesterday at Leicester House, where there were more people than I thought had been in town.' In 1766 Leicester House was occupied by William Henry, Duke of Cumberland, the last royal resident of that historical mansion, which was ultimately demolished in the year 1806.

But there were as remarkable inhabitants of other houses as of Leicester House. In 1733 there came into the square a man about whom the world more concerns itself than it does about William Henry, and that man is William Hogarth.

There is no one whom we more readily or more completely identify with Leicester Square than Hogarth. He was born in the Old Bailey in 1697, close to old Leicester House, which, in Pennant's days, was turned into a coach factory. His father was a schoolmaster, who is, perhaps, to be recognised in the following curious advertisement of the reign of Queen Anne; 'At Hogarth's Coffee House, in St. John's Gate, the midway between Smithfield Bars and Clerkenwell, there will meet daily some learned gentlemen who speak Latin readily, where any gentleman that is either skilled in the language, or desirous to perfect himself in speaking thereof, will be welcome. The Master of the House, in the absence of others, being always ready to entertain gentlemen in that language.' It was in the above Queen's reign that Hogarth went, bundle in hand, hope in his heart, and a good deal of sense and nonsense in his head, to Cranbourne Alley, Leicester Fields, where he was 'prentice bound to Ellis Gamble, the silver-plate engraver. There, among other and nobler works, Hogarth engraved the metal die for the first newspaper stamp (' one half-penny ') ever known in England. It was in Little Cranbourne Alley that Hogarth first set up for himself for a brief time, and left his sisters (it is supposed) to succeed him there as keepers of a 'frock shop.' Hogarth studied in the street, as Garrick did, and there was no lack of masks and faces in the little France and royal England of the Leicester Fields vicinity. Much **as** Sir James Thornhill disliked his daughter's marriage with Hogarth, he helped the young couple to **set** up house on the east side of Leicester Fields. Thornhill did not, at first, account his son-in-law a painter. 'They say he can't paint,' said Mrs. Hogarth once. 'It's a lie. Look at that!' as she **pointed to one of his great** works. Another day, **as Garrick was leaving the** house in the Fields, Ben **Ives, Hogarth's servant, asked him to** step into the **parlour. Ben showed David** a head of Diana, done **in chalks.** The player and Hogarth's man knew **the model.** 'There, Mr. Garrick!' exclaimed Ives, 'there's a head! and yet they say my master can't paint a portrait.' Garrick thought Hogarth had not succeeded in painting the player's, whereupon the limner dashed a brush across the face and turned it against the wall. It never left Leicester **Square till widow** Hogarth gave it to widow **Garrick.**

**It was towards** the close of Hogarth's career **that James Barry,** from Cork—destined to make his mark in art—caught **sight of** a bustling, active, stout little man, dressed **in a** sky-blue coat, in Cranbourne Alley, and recognising in him the Hogarth whom he almost worshipped, followed

him down the east side of the square towards
Hogarth's house.  The latter, however, the owner
did not enter, for a fight between two boys was
going on at the corner of Castle Street, and
Hogarth, who, like the statesman Windham, loved
to see such encounters, whether the combatants
were boys or men, had joined in the fray.  When
Barry came up Hogarth was acting 'second' to
one of the young pugilists, patting him on the
back, and giving such questionable aid in height-
ening the fray as he could furnish in such a
phrase as, 'Damn him if I would take it of him!
At him again!'  There is another version, which
says that it was Nollekens who pointed out to
Northcote the little man in the sky-blue coat, with
the remark, 'Look! that's Hogarth?'

Hogarth seems to have been one of the first to
set his face against the fashion of giving vails to
servants by forbidding his own to take them from
guests.  In those days, not only guests but those
who came to a house to spend money, were expected to help to pay the wages of the servants for
the performance of a duty which they owed to
their master.  It was otherwise with Hogarth in
Leicester Square.  'When I sat to Hogarth' (Cole's
MSS. collections, quoted in Cunningham's 'London')
'the custom of giving vails to servants was not
discontinued.  On taking leave of the painter at
the door I offered the servant a small gratuity, but

the man very politely refused it, telling me it would be as much **as the loss** of his place **if** his master **knew it. This was so** uncommon, and so liberal in **a man of** Hogarth's profession at **that** time of day, that it much struck me, as nothing of the kind had happened to **me before.'**

Leicester Square will ever be connected with **Hogarth at** the *Golden Head.* **It was not,** at his going there, **in a** flourishing condition, but it improved. In the year 1735, in Seymour's ' **Survey,'** Leicester Fields are described as ' a very handsome **open square, railed about and gravelled** within. **The buildings are very good and well** inhabited, **and frequented by the gentry.** The north and **west rows of buildings, which are in St.** Anne's parish, **are the best** (and may **be said** to be so still), **especially the** north, where is Leicester **House,** the seat of the Earl of Leicester ; being a large building with **a** fair court before it for the reception of coaches, and a fine garden behind it ; the south and east sides being in the **parish of St. Martin's.'**

Next **to this** house is another **large** house, **built by Portman Seymour, Esq.,** which ' being laid **into Leicester House, was** inhabited by their present Majesties ' (George **II.** and Queen Caroline) ' when Prince and Princess **of Wales.'** It was then **that it was** called ' the pouting place of princes.' Lisle Street **is then** described as coming out of

Prince's Street, and runs up to Leicester Garden wall. Both Lisle and Leicester Streets are 'large and well-built, and inhabited by gentry.'

In 1737 the 'Country Journal, or Craftsman,' for April 16, contained the following acceptable announcement: 'Leicester Fields is going to be fitted up in a very elegant manner, a new wall and rails to be erected all round, and a basin in the middle, after the manner of Lincoln's Inn Fields, and to be done by a voluntary subscription of the inhabitants.'

It was to Hogarth's house Walpole went, in 1761, to see Hogarth's picture of Fox. Hogarth said he had promised Fox, if he would only sit as the painter liked, 'to make as good a picture as Vandyck or Rubens could.' Walpole was silent. 'Why, now,' said the painter, 'you think this very vain. Why should not a man tell the truth?' Walpole thought him mad, but Hogarth was sincere. When, after ridiculing the opinions of Freke, the anatomist, some one said, 'But Freke holds you for as good a portrait-painter as Vandyck,' 'There he's right!' cried Hogarth. 'And so, by G——, I am—give me my time, and let me choose my subject.'

If one great object of art be to afford pleasure, Hogarth has attained it, for he has pleased successive generations. If one great end of art be to afford instruction, Hogarth has shown himself well qualified, for he has reached that end ; he taught his contemporaries, and he continues teaching, and will continue to teach, through his **works**. But is the instruction worth having ?  Is the pleasure legitimate, wholesome, healthy pleasure ?  Without disparagement to a genius for all that was great in him and his productions, the reply to these questions may sometimes be in the negative.  The impulses of the painter were not invariably of noble origin.  It is said that the first undoubted sign he gave of having a master-hand **arose from** his poor landlady asking **him for** a miserable sum which **he owed her for rent.**  In his wrath he drew her portrait *in caricatura*. **Men saw that it was** clever, **but vindictive.**

There is no foundation for the story which asserts of **George II.** that he professed no love for poetry or painting.  This **king** has been pilloried and pelted, so to speak, with the public contempt for having an independent, and not unjustifiable, opinion of the celebrated picture, the 'March **to** Finchley.'  Hogarth had the impertinence to **ask** permission **that he** might dedicate the work to the King, and **the** latter observed, with some reason, **that the fellow deserved to** be picketed for his insolence.  **When this picture was** presented as worthy of royal patronage, rebellion **was** afoot and active **in the north (1745).** The Guards were sent thither, and Hogarth's work describes them setting out on their first stage to Finchley. The whole description or representation is a gross caricature of the brave men (though they may have sworn as terribly then as they did in Flanders) whose task was to save the kingdom from a great impending calamity. All that is noble is kept out of sight, all that is degrading to the subject, with some slight exceptions, is forced on the view and memory of the spectator. It has been urged by way of apology for this clever but censurable work, that it was not painted at the moment of great popular excitement, but subsequently. This is nothing to the purpose. What is to the purpose is, that Hogarth represented British soldiers as a drunken, skulking, thieving, cowardly horde of ruffians, who must be, to employ an oft-used phrase, more terrible to their friends than their enemies. The painter may have been as good a Whig as the King himself, but he manifested bad taste in asking George II. to show favour to such a subject ; and he exhibited worse taste still in dedicating it to the king of Prussia, as a patron of the arts. Hogarth was not disloyal, perhaps, as Wilkes charged him with being, for issuing the print of this picture, but it is a work that, however far removed from the political element now, could not have afforded much gratification to the loyal when it was first exhibited.

Hogarth died in Leicester Square in 1764, and

was buried at Chiswick. There was an artist on the opposite side of the square who saw the funeral from his window, and who had higher views of art than Hogarth.

Towards the close of Hogarth's career Joshua Reynolds took possession of a house on the west side of Leicester Square. In the year in which George III. ascended the throne (1760) Reynolds set up his famous chair of state for his patrons in this historical square.

It has been said that Reynolds, in the days of his progressive triumphs in Leicester Square, thought continually of the glory of his being one day placed by the side of Vandyck and Rubens, and that he entertained no envious idea of being better than Hogarth, Gainsborough, and his old master, Hudson. Reynolds, nevertheless, served all three in much the same way that Dryden served Shakespeare; namely, he disparaged quite as extensively as he praised them. Hogarth, on the east side of Leicester Square, felt no local accession of honour when Reynolds set up his easel on the western side. The new comer was social; the old settler ' kept himself to himself,' as the wise saw has it. ' Study the works of the great masters for ever,' was, we are told, the utterance of Sir Oracle on the west side. From the east came Hogarth's utterance, in the assertion, ' There is only one school, and Nature is the mistress of it.'

For Reynolds's judgment Hogarth had a certain contempt. 'The most ignorant people about painting,' he said to Walpole, 'are the painters themselves. There's Reynolds, who certainly has genius; why, but t'other day, he offered a hundred pounds for a picture that I would not hang in my cellar.' Hogarth undoubtedly qualified his sense with some nonsense: 'Talk of sense, and study, and all that; why, it is owing to the good sense of the English that they have not painted better.'

It was at one of Reynolds's suppers in the square that an incident took place which aroused the wit-power of Johnson. The rather plain sister of the artist had been called upon by the company, after supper, as the custom was, to give a toast. She hesitated, and was accordingly required, again according to custom, to give the ugliest man she knew. In a moment the name of Oliver Goldsmith dropped from her lips, and immediately a sympathising lady on the opposite side of the table rose and shook hands with Miss Reynolds across the table. Johnson had heard the expression, and had also marked the pantomimic performance of sympathy, and he capped both by a remark which set the table in a roar, and which was to an effect which cut smartly in three ways. 'Thus,' said he, ' the ancients, on the commencements of their friendships, used to sacrifice a beast betwixt them.' The affair ends prettily. A few days after the

' Traveller ' was published Johnson **read it** aloud
from beginning to end to delighted hearers, of
whom Miss Reynolds was one.   As Johnson closed
the book she emphatically remarked, ' Well, I never
more shall think Dr. Goldsmith ugly.'   Miss Reynolds, however, did not get over her idea.   Her
brother painted the portrait of the new poet, in
the Octagon Room in the Square ; the mezzotinto
engraving of it was speedily all over the town.   Miss
Reynolds (who, it has been said, used herself to
paint portraits with **such** exact imitation of her
brother's defects and avoidance **of his** beauties, that
everybody but **himself** laughed **at** them) thought
it marvellous that so much dignity could have been
given to the poet's face and yet so strong a likeness be conveyed ;  for ' Dr. Goldsmith's cast of
countenance,' she proceeds to inform us, ' and indeed
his whole figure from head to foot, impressed every
one at first sight with **the idea** of his being a low
mechanic ; particularly, I believe, a journeyman
tailor.'   This belief was founded on what Goldsmith
had himself once said.   Coming ruffled into Reynolds's drawing-room, Goldsmith angrily referred
to an insult which his sensitive nature fancied had
been put upon him at a neighbouring coffee-house,
by ' a fellow who,' said Goldsmith, ' took me, I believe, for a tailor.'   The company laughed more or
less demonstratively, **and** rather confirmed than
dispelled the supposition.

Poor Goldsmith's weaknesses were a good deal played upon by that not too polite company. One afternoon, Burke and a young Irish officer, O'Moore, were crossing the square to Reynolds's house to dinner. They passed a group who were gaping at, and making admiring remarks upon, some samples of beautiful foreign husseydom, who were looking out of the windows of one of the hotels. Goldsmith was at the skirt of the group, looking on. Burke said to O'Moore, as they passed him unseen, ' Look at Goldsmith ; by-and-by, at Reynolds's you will see what I make of this.' At the dinner, Burke treated Goldsmith with such coolness, that Oliver at last asked for an explanation. Burke readily replied that his manner was owing to the monstrous indiscretion on Goldsmith's part, in the square, of which Burke and Mr. O'Moore had been the witnesses. Poor Goldsmith asked in what way he had been so indiscreet?

' Why,' answered Burke, ' did you not exclaim, on looking up at those women, what stupid beasts the crowd must be for staring with such admiration at those *painted Jezebels*, while a man of your talent passed by unnoticed ? '—' Surely, my dear friend,' cried Goldsmith, horror-struck, ' I did not say so ! '—' If you had not said so,' retorted Burke, ' how should I have known it ? '—' That's true,' answered Goldsmith, with great humility ; ' I am very sorry; it was very foolish ! I do recollect that

something of the kind passed through my mind, but
I did not think I had uttered it.'

It is a pity that Sir Joshua never records the
names of his own guests; but his parties were so
much swelled by invitations given on the spur of
the moment, that it would have been impossible
for him to set down beforehand more than the
nucleus of his scrambling and unceremonious, but
most enjoyable, dinners. Whether the famous
Leicester Square dinners deserved to be called enjoyable, is a question which anyone may decide for
himself, after reading the accounts given of them at
a period when the supervision of Reynolds's sister,
Frances, could no longer be given to them. The
table, made to hold seven or eight, was often made
to hold twice the number. When the guests were
at last packed, the deficiency of knives, forks, plates,
and glasses made itself felt. Everyone called, as
he wanted, for bread, wine, or beer, and lustily, or
there was little chance of being served.

There had once, Courtenay says, been sets of
decanters and glasses provided to furnish the table
and enable the guests to help themselves. These
had gone the way of all glass, and had not been
replaced; but though the dinner might be careless
and inelegant, and the servants awkward and too
few, Courtenay admits that their shortcomings only
enhanced the singular pleasure of the entertainment.
The wine, cookery, and dishes were but little at-

tended to ; nor was the fish or venison ever talked of or recommended. Amidst the convivial, animated bustle of his guests, Sir Joshua sat perfectly composed ; protected partly by his deafness, partly by his equanimity ; always attentive, by help of his trumpet, to what was said, never minding what was eaten or drunk, but leaving everyone to scramble for himself. Peers, temporal and spiritual, statesmen, physicians, lawyers, actors, men of letters, painters, musicians, made up the motley group, ' and played their parts,' says Courtenay, ' without dissonance or discord.' Dinner was served precisely at five, whether all the company had arrived or not. Sir Joshua never kept many guests waiting for one, whatever his rank or consequence. ' His friends and intimate acquaintance,' concludes Courtenay, ' will ever love his memory, and will ever regret those social hours and the cheerfulness of that irregular, convivial table, which no one has attempted to revive or imitate, or was indeed qualified to supply.'

Reynolds had a room in which his copyists, his pupils, and his drapery-men worked. Among them was one of the cleverest and most unfortunate of artists. Seldom is the name of Peter Toms now heard, but he once sat in Hudson's studio with young Reynolds, and in the studio of Sir Joshua, as the better artist's obedient humble servant ; that is to say, he painted his employer's draperies, and probably a good deal more, for Toms **was** a very fair portrait-painter. Peter worked too for various other great artists, and a purchaser of any picture of that time cannot be certain whether much of it is not from Toms's imitative hand. Peter's lack of original power did not keep him out of the Royal Academy, though in his day he was but a second-class artist. He belonged, too, to the Herald's Office, as the painters of the Tudor period often did, and after filling in the canvasses of his masters in England, he went to Ireland on his own account and in reliance on the patronage **of** the Lord-Lieutenant, the Duke of Northumberland. Toms, however, found that the Irish refused to submit their physiognomies to his limning, and he waited for them to change their opinion of him in vain. Finally, he lost heart and hope. His vocation was gone; but in the London garret within which he took refuge he seems to have given himself a chance for life or death. Pencil in one hand and razor in the other, he made an effort to paint a picture, **and** apparently failed in accomplishing it, for he swept the razor across his throat, and was found the next morning stark dead by the side of the work which seems to have smitten him with despair.

Reynolds saw the ceremony of proclaiming George III. king in front of Savile House, where **the monarch** had **resided** while he was Prince of **Wales.** Into his own house came and went, for

years, all the lofty virtues, vices, and rich nothing-
nesses of Reynolds's time, to be painted. From his
window he looked with pride on his gaudy carriage
(the Seasons, limned on the panels, were by his own
drapery man, Catton), in which he used to send
his sister out for a daily drive. From the same
window he saw Savile House gutted by the 'No
Popery' rioters of 1780; fire has since swept all
that was left of Page's house on the north side of
the Square; and in 1787 Reynolds looked on a new-
comer to the Fields, Lawrence, afterwards Sir
Thomas, who set up his easel against Sir Joshua's,
but who was not then strong enough to make such
pretence. Some of the most characteristic groups
of those days were to be seen clustered round the
itinerant quack doctors—fellows who lied with a
power that Orton, Luie, and even the 'coachers'
of Luie, might envy. Leicester Square, in Reynolds's
days alone, would furnish matter for two or three
volumes. We have only space to say further of Sir
Joshua, that he died here in 1792, lay in state in
Somerset House, and that as the funeral procession
was on its way to St. Paul's (with its first part in
the Cathedral before the last part was clear of
Somerset House) one of the occupants in one of
the many mourning coaches said to a companion,
'There is now, sir, a fine opening for a portrait-
painter.'

While Reynolds was 'glorifying' the Fields,

that is to say, about the year 1783, John Hunter, the great anatomist, enthroned science in Leicester Square. His house, nearly opposite Reynolds's, was next door to that once occupied by Hogarth, on the east side, but north of the painter's dwelling. Hunter was then fifty-five years old. Like his eminent brother, William, John Hunter had a very respectable amount of self-appreciation, quite justifiably.

The governing body of St. Bartholomew's Hospital had failed, through ignorance or favouritism, to recognise his ability and to reward his assiduity. But John Hunter was of too noble a spirit to be daunted or even depressed ; and St. George's Hospital honoured itself by bestowing on him the modest office of house-surgeon. It was thirty years after this that John Hunter settled himself in Leicester Square. There he spent three thousand pounds in the erection of a building in the rear of his house for the reception of a collection in comparative anatomy. Before this was completed he spent upon it many thousands of pounds,—it is said ninety thousand guineas ! With him to work was to live. Dr. Garthshore entered the museum in the Square early one morning, and found Hunter already busily occupied. ' Why, John,' said the physician, ' you are always at work !' ' I am,' replied the surgeon ; ' and when I am dead you will not meet very soon with another John Hunter !' He accused his great brother William of claiming the merit of surgical discoveries which John had made ; and when a friend, talking to him, at his door in the Square, on his ' Treatise on the Teeth,' remarked that it would be answered by medical men simply to make their names known, Hunter rather unhandsomely observed : ' Aye, we have all of us vermin that live upon us.' Lavater took correct measure of the famous surgeon when he remarked, on seeing the portrait of Hunter : ' That is the portrait of a man who thinks for himself!'

After John Hunter's death his collection was purchased by Government for fifteen thousand pounds. It was removed from Leicester Square to Lincoln's Inn Fields, to the College of Surgeons, where it still forms a chief portion of the anatomical and pathological museum in that institution. The site of the Hunterian Museum in Leicester Square has been swallowed up by the Alhambra, where less profitable study of comparative anatomy may now be made by all who are interested in such pursuit. A similar destiny followed the other Hunterian Museum—that established by William Hunter, in Great Windmill Street, at the top of the Haymarket, where he built an amphitheatre and museum, with a spacious dwelling-house attached. In the dwelling-house Joanna Baillie passed some of her holiday and early days in London. She came from her native

Scottish heath, and the only open moor like unto
it where she could snatch a semblance of fresh air
was the neighbouring inclosure of Leicester Square!
William Hunter left his gigantic and valuable
collection to his nephew, Dr. Baillie, for thirty
years, to pass then to the University of Glasgow,
where William himself had studied divinity, before
the results of freedom of thought (both the
Hunters *would* think for themselves) induced him
to turn to the study of medicine. The Hunterian
Museum in Windmill Street, after serving various
purposes, became **known** as the Argyll Rooms,
where human anatomy (it **is** believed) was liberally
**exhibited under** magisterial license and the super-
**vision of a** severely moral police.

Leicester Square has been remarkable for its
exhibitions. Richardson, the fire-eater, exhibited
privately at Leicester House in 1672. A century
later there was a public exhibition on that spot of
quite another quality. The proprietor was Sir
**Ashton Lever,** a Lancashire gentleman, educated
at Oxford. **As** a country squire he formed and
possessed the most extensive and beautiful aviary
**in the kingdom.** Therewith, Sir Ashton collected
animals and curiosities **from** all quarters of the
world. This was the nucleus of the 'museum'
subsequently brought to Leicester Fields. Among
the curiosities was a striking likeness of George
III. 'cut in cannel coal;' also Indian-ink drawings

and portraits ; baskets of flowers cut in paper, and
wonderful for their accuracy ; costumes of all ages
and nations, and a collection of warlike weapons
which disgusted a timid beholder, who describes
them in the 'Gentleman's Magazine' (May 1773)
as 'desperate, diabolical instruments of destruction,
invented, no doubt, by the devil himself.'  Soon
after this, this wonderful collection was exhibited
in Leicester House.  There was a burst of wonder,
as Pennant calls it, for a little while after the
opening ; but the ill-cultivated world soon grew
indifferent to being instructed ; and Sir Ashton got
permission, with some difficulty, from Parliament,
to dispose of the whole collection by lottery.  Sir
William Hamilton, Baron Dimsdale, and Mr.
Pennant stated to the Committee of the House of
Commons that they had never seen a collection
of such inestimable value.  'Sir Ashton Lever's
lottery tickets,' says an advertisement of January
28, 1785, 'are now on sale at Leicester House
every day (Sundays excepted), from Nine in the
morning till Six in the evening, at One Guinea
each ; and as each ticket will admit four persons,
either together or separately, to view the Museum,
no one will hereafter be admitted but by the
Lottery Tickets, excepting those who have already
annual admission.'  It is added that the whole was
to be disposed of owing ' to the very large sum
expended in making it, and not from the deficiency

of the daily receipts (as is generally imagined), which **have** annually increased ; the average **amount** for the last three years being 1833*l.* per annum.'  It sounds odd that a ' concern ' is got rid **of** because it was yearly growing more profitable !

Thirty-six thousand guinea-tickets were offered for sale.  Only eight thousand were sold.  **Of** these Mr. Parkinson purchased two, and with one **of those two** acquired the whole collection, against the other purchasers and **the** twenty-two thousand chances held by Sir **Ashton**.  Mr. Parkinson built an edifice for **his valuable** prize in Blackfriars Road, and **for years, one of the** things **to be** done **was ' to go to the Rotunda.'**  In 1806, the famous museum **was** dispersed **by** auction.  The Surrey Institution next occupied the premises, which subsequently became public drinking-rooms and meeting **place** for tippling patriots, who would fain destroy the Constitution of England as well as their own.

But ' man or woman, good my lord,' let whosoever may **be named** in connection with Leicester Square, **there is** one who must **not be** omitted, namely, **Miss** Linwood.  Penelope worked at her needle to no valuable purpose.  Miss Linwood was more like Arachne in **her work,** and something better in her fortune.  **The** dyer's daughter of **Colophon chose** for her subjects the various loves **of Jupiter** with various ladies whom poets and painters have immortalised ; and grew so proud of her work that, for challenging Minerva to do better, the goddess changed her into a spider. The Birmingham lady plied her needle from the time she could hold one till the time her ancient hand lost its cunning. At thirteen she worked pictures in worsted better than some artists could paint them. No needlework, ancient or modern, ever equalled (if experts may be trusted) the work of this lady, who found time to do as much as if she had not to fulfil, as she did faithfully, the duties of a boarding-school mistress. King, Queen, Court, and 'Quality' generally visited Savile House, Leicester Fields, where Miss Linwood's works were exhibited, and were profitable to the exhibitor to the very last. They were, for the most part, copies of great pictures by great masters, modern as well as ancient. Among them was a Carlo Dolci, valued at three thousand guineas. Miss Linwood, in her later days, retired to Leicester, but she used to come up annually to look at her own Exhibition. It had been open about half a century when the lady, in her ninetieth year, caught cold on her journey, and died of it at Leicester in 1844. She left her Carlo Dolci to Queen Victoria. Her other works, sold by auction, barely realised a thousand pounds ; but the art of selling art by auction was not then discovered.

In 1788, a middle-aged Irishman from county

Meath, named Robert Barker, got admission to Reynolds, to show him a half-circle view from the Calton Hill, near Edinburgh, which Barker had painted in water-colours on the spot. The poor but accomplished artist had been unsuccessful as a portrait-painter in Dublin and Edinburgh. But he had studied perspective closely, an idea had struck him, and he came with it to Reynolds. The latter admired, but thought it impracticable. The Irishman thought otherwise. Barker exhibited circular views from nature, in London and also in the provinces, with indifferent success. At last, in 1793, on part of the old site of Leicester House, a building arose which was called the Panorama, and in which was exhibited a view of the Russian fleet at Spithead. The spectator was on board a ship in the midst of the scene and the view was all around him. King George and Queen Charlotte led the fashionable world to this most original exhibition. For many years there was a succession of magnificent views of foreign capitals, tracts of country, ancient cities, polar regions, battles, &c., exhibited ; and 'Have you been to the new panorama?' was as naturally a spring question as 'Have you been to the Academy?' or the Opera? The exhibition of the 'Stern Realities of Waterloo' alone realised a little fortune, and 'Pandemonium,' painted by Mr. Henry Selous, was one of the latest of the great successes.

At the north-east corner of Leicester Square, the Barkers, father and son, achieved what is called ' a handsome competency.'  At the death of the latter, Robert Burford succeeded him, and, for a time, did well; but ' Fashion ' wanted a new sensation.  The panoramas in Leicester Square and the Strand, admirable as they were, ceased to draw the public ; and courteous, lady-like, little Miss Burford, the proprietress, was compelled to withdraw, utterly shipwrecked. .She used to receive her visitors like a true lady welcoming thorough ladies and gentlemen.  The end was sad indeed, for the last heard of this aged gentlewoman was that she was enduring life by needle-work, rarely got and scantily paid, in a lodging, the modest rent of which, duly paid, kept her short of necessary food.  An attempt was made to obtain her election to the ' United Kingdom Beneficent Association,' but with what result we are unable to record.

Shadows of old Leicester Square figures come up in crowds, demanding recognition.  They must be allowed to pass —to make a ' march past,' as it were ; as they glide by we take note of Mirabeau and Marat, Holcroft, Opie, Edmund Kean, and Mulready, with countless others, to indite the roll of whose names only would alone require a volume.

## *A HUNDRED YEARS AGO.*

PERUSING records that are a century old is something better than listening to a centenarian, even if his memory could go back so far. The records are as fresh as first impressions, and they bring before us men and things as they were, not as after-historians supposed them to be.

The story which 1773 has left of itself is full of variety and of interest. Fashion fluttered the propriety of Scotland when the old Dowager Countess of Fife gave the first masquerade that ever took place in that country, at Duff House. In England, people and papers could talk or write of nothing so frequently as masquerades. 'One hears so much of them,' remarked that lively old lady, Mrs. Delany, 'that I suppose the only method not to be tired of them is to frequent them.' Old-fashioned loyalty in England was still more shocked when the Lord Mayor of London declined to go to St. Paul's on the 30th of January to profess himself sad and sorry at the martyrdom of Charles I. In the minds of certain religious people there was satisfaction felt at the course taken by the Uni-

versity of Oxford, which refused to modify the
Thirty-nine Articles, as more liberal Cambridge
had done. Indeed, such Liberalism as that of the
latter, prepared ultra-serious people for awful
consequences ; and when they heard that Moel-
fammo, an extinct volcano in Flintshire, had resumed business, and was beginning to pelt the air
with red-hot stones, they naturally thought that
the end of a wicked world was at hand. They
took courage again when the Commons refused to
dispense with subscription to the Thirty-nine
Articles, by a vote of 159 to 64. But no sooner
was joy descending on the one hand than terror
advanced on the other. Quid-nuncs asked whither
the world was driving, when the London livery
proclaimed the reasonableness of annual parlia-
ments. Common-sense people also were perplexed
at the famous parliamentary resolution that Lord
Clive had wrongfully taken to himself above a
quarter of a million of money, and had rendered
signal services to his country !

Again, a hundred years ago our ancestors were
as glad to hear that Bruce had got safely back into
Egypt from his attempt to reach the Nile sources,
as we were to know that Livingstone was alive
and well and in search of those still undiscovered
head-waters. A century ago, too, crowds of well-
wishers bade God speed to the gallant Captain
Phipps, as he sailed from the Nore on his way to

that North-west Passage which he did not find, and which, at the close of a hundred years, is as impracticable as ever. And, though history may or may not repeat itself, events of to-day at least remind us of those a hundred years old. The Protestant Emperor William, in politely squeezing the Jesuits out of his dominions, only modestly follows the example of Pope Clement XIV., who, in 1773, let loose a bull for the entire suppression of the order in every part of the world. Let us not forget too, that if orthodox ruffians burnt Priestley's house over **his** head, and would have **smashed all power** of thought out of that head **itself, the Royal** Society conferred on the great philosopher **who** was the brutally treated pioneer of modern science, the Copley Medal, for his admirable treatise on different kinds of air.

But there was a little incident of the year 1773, which has had more stupendous consequences than any other with which England has been connected. England, through some of her statesmen, asserted her right to tax her colonists, without asking their consent or allowing them to be represented in the home legislature. In illustration of such right and her determination to maintain it, England sent **out** certain ships with cargoes of tea, on which a small duty was imposed, to be paid by the colonists. The latter declined to have the wholesome herb at such terms, but England forced it upon them.

Three ships, so freighted, entered Boston Harbour.
They were boarded by a mob disguised as Mohawk
Indians, who tossed the tea into the river and then
quietly dispersed. A similar cargo was safely
landed at New York, but it was under the guns of
a convoying man-of-war. When landed it could
not be disposed of, except by keeping it under
lock-and-key, with a strong guard over it, to
preserve it from the patriots who scorned the cups
that cheer, if they were unduly taxed for the
luxury. That was the little seed out of which has
grown that Union whose President now is more
absolute and despotic than poor George III. ever
was or cared to be; little seed, which is losing its
first wholesomeness, and, if we may trust transatlantic papers, is grown to a baleful tree, corrupt
to the core and corrupting all around it. Such at
least is the American view—the view of good and
patriotic Americans, who would fain work sound
reform in this condition of things at the end of an
eventful century, when John Bull is made to feel,
by Geneva and San Juan, that he will never have
any chance of having the best argument in an
arbitration case, where he is opposed by a system
which looks on sharpness as a virtue, and holds
that nothing succeeds like success.

Let us get back from this subject to the
English court of a century since. A new year's
day at court was in the last century a gala day,

which made **London** tradesmen rejoice. There
were some extraordinary figures at that **of 1773,** at
**St.** James's, **but no one** looked so much out of
ordinary **fashion as** Lord Villiers. His coat **was**
of pale purple velvet turned up with lemon colour,
‘ **and** embroidered all **over** ’ (says Mrs. Delany)
‘ with **SSes of** pearl as **big as peas,** and in all the
**spaces** little medallions **in beaten** gold—*real* **solid** !
in various **figures** of **Cupids** *and the like* ! ”

The **court** troubles **of the year were** not insignificant ; **but the good** people below **stairs had**
their share **of them.** If the King continued **to be**
vexed **at the marriages of** his brothers Gloucester
and **Cumberland with** English ladies, the King's
servants had **sorrows of their own. The** newspapers stated **that ‘ the wages of** his Majesty's
servants were miserably **in arrear ;** that their
families were consequently distressed, and that
there was great clamour **for** payment.’ The court
was never more bitterly satirised than in some
lines put in circulation (as Colley Cibber's) **soon**
after Lord Chesterfield's death, to whom **they were**
generally ascribed. They were **written before** the
decease **of** Frederick, Prince **of Wales.** The
laureate was **made to say—**

> Colley **Cibber,** right **or wrong,**
> Must celebrate this **day,**
> And tune once more his tuneless song
> And strum the venal lay.

> Heav'n spread through all the family
>   That broad, illustrious glare,
> That shines so flat in every eye
>   And makes them all so stare!
>
> Heav'n send the Prince of royal race
>   A little coach and horse,
> A little meaning in his face,
>   And money in his purse.
>
> And, as I have a son like yours,
>   May he Parnassus rule.
> So shall the crown and laurel too
>   Descend from fool to fool.

Satire was, indeed, quite as rough in prose as it was sharp in song. One of the boldest paragraphs ever penned by paragraph writers of the time appeared in the 'Public Advertiser' in the summer of 1773. A statue of the King had been erected in Berkeley Square. The discovery was soon made that the King himself had paid for it. Accordingly, the 'Public Advertiser' audaciously informed him that he had paid for his statue, because he well knew that none would ever be spontaneously erected in his honour by posterity. The 'Advertiser' further advised George III. to build his own mausoleum for the same reason.

And what were 'the quality' about in 1773? There was Lord Hertford exclaiming, 'By Jove!' because he objected to swearing. Ladies were dancing 'Cossack' dances, and gentlemen figured

at balls in black coats, red waistcoats, and red
sashes, or quadrilled with nymphs in white satin—
themselves radiant in brown silk coat, with cherry-
coloured waistcoat and breeches. Beaux who
could not dance took to cards, and the Duke of
Northumberland lost two thousand pounds at
quince before half a dancing night had come to an
end. There was Sir John Dalrymple winning
money more disastrously than the duke lost it.
He was a man who inveighed against corruption,
and who took bribes from brewers. Costume balls
were in favour at court, Chesterfield was making
jokes to the very door of his coffin ; and he was
not the only patron of the arts who bought a
Claude Lorraine painted within the preceding half-
year. The macaronies, having left off gaming—
they had lost all their money—astonished the town
by their new dresses and the size of their nosegays.
Poor George III. could not look admiringly at the
beautiful Miss Linley at an oratorio, without being
accused of ogling her. It was at one of the King's
balls that Mrs. Hobart figured, 'all gauze and
spangles, like a spangle pudding.' This was the
expensive year when noblemen are said to have
made romances instead of giving balls. The in-
teriors of their mansions were transformed, walls
were cast down, new rooms were built, the decora-
tions were superb (three hundred pounds was the
sum asked only for the loan of mirrors for a single

night), and not only were the dancers in the most gorgeous of historical or fancy costumes, but the musicians wore scarlet robes, and looked like Venetian senators on the stage. It was at one of these balls that Harry Conway was so astonished at the agility of Mrs. Hobart's bulk that he said he was sure she must be hollow.

She would not have been more effeminate than some of our young legislators in the Commons, who, one night in May, 'because the House was very hot, and the young members thought it would melt their rouge and wither their nosegays,' as Walpole says, all of a sudden voted against their own previously formed opinions. India and Lord Clive were the subjects, and the letter-writer remarks that the Commons 'being so fickle, Lord Clive has reason to hope that after they have voted his head off they will vote it on again the day after he has lost it.'

When there were members in the Commons who rouged like pert girls or old women, and carried nosegays as huge as a lady mayoress's at a City ball, we are not surprised to hear of macaronies in Kensington Gardens. There they ran races on every Sunday evening, 'to the high amusement and contempt of the mob,' says Walpole. The mob had to look at the runners from outside the gardens. 'They will be ambitious of being fashionable, and will run races too.' Neither mob nor macaronies had the swiftness of foot or the lasting powers of some of the running footmen attached to noble houses. Dukes would run matches of their footmen from London to York, and a fellow has been known to die rather than that 'his grace' who owned him should lose the match. Talking of 'graces,' an incident is told by Walpole of the cost of a bed for a night's sleep for a duchess, which may well excite a little wonder now. The king and court were at Portsmouth to review the fleet. The town held so many more visitors than it could accommodate that the richest of course secured the accommodation. 'The Duchess of Northumberland gives forty guineas for a bed, and must take her chambermaid into it.' Walpole, who is writing to the Countess of Ossory, adds: ' I did not think she would pay so dear for *such* company.' The people who were unable to pay ran recklessly into debt, and no more thought of the sufferings of those to whom they owed the money than that modern rascalry in clean linen, who compound with their creditors and scarcely think of paying their ' composition.' A great deal of nonsense has been talked about the virtues of Charles James Fox, who had none but such as may be found in easy temper and self-indulgence. He was now in debt to the tune of a hundred thousand pounds. But so once was Julius Cæsar, with whom Walpole satirically compared him. He let his

securities, his bondsmen, pay the money which
they had warranted would be forthcoming from
him, 'while he, as like Brutus as Cæsar, is indifferent about such paltry counters.' When one
sees the vulgar people who by some means or
other, and generally by any means, accumulate
fortunes the sum total of which would once have
seemed fabulous, and when we see fortunes of old
aristocratic families squandered away among the
villains of the most villainous 'turf,' there is
nothing strange in what we read in a letter of a
hundred years ago, namely : 'What is England
now ?  A sink of Indian wealth ! filled by nabobs
and emptied by macaronies; a country over-run
by horse-races.' So London at the end of July
now is not unlike to London of 1773 ; but we
could not match the latter with such a street
picture as the following : 'There is scarce a soul
in London but macaronies lolling out of windows
at Almack's, like carpets to be dusted.' With the
more modern parts of material London Walpole
was ill satisfied.  *We* look upon Adam's work
with some complacency, but Walpole exclaims,
'What are the Adelphi buildings?' and he replies,
'Warehouses laced down the seams, like a soldier's
trull in a regimental old coat !' Mason could not
bear the building brothers.  'Was there ever such
a brace,' he asks, 'of self-puffing Scotch cox-
combs?'  The coxcombical vein was, nevertheless,

rather the fashionable one. Fancy a nobleman's postillions in white jackets trimmed with muslin, and clean ones every other **day !** In **such** guise **were Lord** Egmont's postillions to be seen.

The chronicle of fashion is dazzling with the record of the doings **of** the celebrated Mrs. Elizabeth Montagu. At **her** house in Hill Street, Berkeley Square, were held the assemblies which were scornfully called ' blue-stocking ' by **those** who were not invited, or who affected **not to care** for them if they *were*. Mrs. Delany, who certainly **had a great regard for** this ' lady of the last century,' **has a sly hit at** Mrs. Montagu in **a** letter **of May 1773.** ' **If,**' she writes, ' I had paper and time, **I could entertain** you with Mrs. Montagu's room of Cupidons, which **was** opened with an assembly **for all the** foreigners, the literati, and the macaronies of the present age. Many and sly are the observations how such a *genius*, at her age and **so** circumstanced, could think of painting the walls of her dressing-room with bowers **of** roses and jessamine, entirely inhabited by little Cupids in all their little wanton **ways.** It **is** astonishing, unless she looks **upon** herself **as the wife of** old Vulcan, **and mother** to all those little **Loves !**' This is a **sister** woman's testimony of a **friend !** The *genius* **of Mrs.** Montagu was of a higher class than that **of** dull but good **Mrs.** Delany. **The** *age* **of** the same lady **was** a little over fifty, when she might fittingly queen it, as she did, in her splendid mansion in Hill Street, the scene of the glories of her best days. The 'circumstances' and the 'Vulcan' were allusions to her being the wife of a noble owner of collieries and a celebrated mathematician, who suffered from continued ill-health, and who considerately went to bed at *five* o'clock P.M. daily!

The great subject of the year, after all, was the duping of Charles Fox, by the impostor who called herself the Hon. Mrs. Grieve. She had been transported, and after her return had set up as 'a sensible woman,' giving advice to fools, ' for a consideration.' A silly Quaker brought her before Justice Fielding for having defrauded him. He had paid her money, for which she had undertaken to get him a place under government; but she had kept the money, and had not procured for him the coveted place. Her impudent defence was that the Quaker's immorality stood in the way of otherwise certain success. The Honourable lady's dupes believed in her, because they saw the style in which she lived, and often beheld her descend from her chariot and enter the houses of ministers and other great personages; but it came out that she only spoke to the porters or to other servants, who entertained her idle questions, for a gratuity, while Mrs. Grieve's carriage, and various dupes, waited for her in the street. When these dupes, however, saw Charles Fox's chariot at Mrs. Grieve's door, and that gentleman himself entering the house—not issuing therefrom till a considerable period had elapsed—they were confirmed in their credulity. But the clever hussey was deluding the popular tribune in the house, and keeping his chariot at her door, to further delude the idiots who were taken in by it. The patriot was in a rather common condition of patriots; he was over head and ears in debt. The lady had undertaken to procure for him the hand of a West Indian heiress, a Miss Phipps, with 80,000*l.*, a sum that might soften the hearts of his creditors for a while. The young lady (whom ' the Hon.' never saw) was described as a little capricious. She could not abide dark men, and the swart democratic leader powdered his eyebrows that he might look fairer in the eyes of the lady of his hopes. An interview between them was always on the point of happening, but was always being deferred. Miss Phipps was ill, was coy, was not ' i' the vein'; finally she had the smallpox, which was as imaginary as the other grounds of excuse. Meanwhile Mrs. Grieve lent the impecunious legislator money, 300*l.* or thereabouts. She was well paid, not by Fox, of course, but by the more vulgar dupes who came to false conclusions when they beheld his carriage, day after day, at the Hon. Mrs. Grieve's door. The late Lord Holland expressed his belief that the loan from Mrs. Grieve was a foolish and improbable story. 'I have heard Fox say,' Lord Holland remarks in the 'Memorials and Correspondence of Fox,' edited by Lord John (afterwards Earl) Russell, 'she never got or asked any money from him.' She probably knew very well that Fox had none to lend. That he should have accepted any from such a woman is disgraceful enough: but there may be exaggeration in the matter.

Fox—it is due to him to note the fact here—had yet hardly begun seriously and earnestly his career as a public man. At the close of 1773 he was sowing his wild oats. He ended the year with the study of two widely different dramatic parts, which he was to act on a private stage. Those parts were Lothario, in 'The Fair Penitent,' and Sir Harry's servant, in 'High Life below Stairs.' The stage on which the two pieces were acted, by men scarcely inferior to Fox himself in rank and ability, was at Winterslow House, near Salisbury, the seat of the Hon. Stephen Fox. The night of representation closed the Christmas holidays of 1773-4. It was Saturday, January 8, 1774. Fox played the gallant gay Lothario brilliantly; the livery servant in the kitchen, aping his master's manners, was acted with abundant low humour, free from vulgarity. But, whether there was incautious management during the piece, or incautious revelry after it, the fine old house was burned to the ground **before** the morning. It was then that Fox turned more than before **to** public **business ;** but without giving up any of his private enjoyments, except those he did not care for.

The duels **of** this year which gave rise to the most gossip **were,** first, that between Lord Bellamont **and** Lord Townshend, and next the one **between Messrs.** Temple and Whately. The two lords fought (after some shifting on Townshend's side) on a quarrel arising from a refusal **of** Lord Townshend, in **Dublin, to** receive Bellamont. The offended **lord was badly shot** in the stomach, and a **wit (so called) penned** this epigram **on** the luckier adversary :—

Says Bell'mont to Townshend, ' You turned on your heel,
    And that gave your honour a check.'
" 'Tis my way,' replied Townshend. 'To the world I appeal,
    If I didn't the same at Quebec.'

Townshend, at Quebec, had succeeded to the command after Monckton was wounded, and **he** declined to renew the conflict with De Bougainville. The duel **between** Temple and Whately arose out of extraordinary circumstances. There were in the British **Foreign Office letters** from English and also **from** American **officials** in the transatlantic colony, which advised coercion **on** the part of our government as the proper course to be pursued for the successful administration of that colony. Benjamin

Franklin was then in England, and hearing of these letters, had a strong desire to procure them, in order to publish them in America, to the confusion of the writers. The papers were the property of the British Government, from whom it is hardly too much to say that they must have been stolen. At all events, an agent of Franklin's, named Hugh Williamson, is described as having got them for Franklin ' by an ingenious device,' which seems to be a very euphemistic phrase. The letters had been originally addressed to Whately, secretary to the Treasury, who, in 1773, was dead. The ingenious device by which they were abstracted was reported to have been made with the knowledge of Temple, who had been lieutenant-governor of New Hampshire. The excitement caused by their publication led to a duel between Temple and a brother of Whately, in whose hands the letters had never been, and poor Whately was dangerously wounded, to save the honour of the ex-lieutenant-governor. The publication of these letters was as unjustifiable as the ingenious device by which they were conveyed from their rightful owners. It caused as painful a sensation as any one of the many painful incidents in the Geneva Arbitration affair, namely, when—it being a point of honour that neither party should publish a statement of their case till a judgment had been pronounced—the case made out by the United States counsel was to be bought, before the tribunal was opened, as easily as if it had been a ' last dying speech and confession ! '

In literature Andrew Stewart's promised ' Letters to Lord Mansfield ' excited universal curiosity. In that work Stewart treated the chief justice as those Chinese executioners do their patients whose skin they politely and tenderly brush away with wire brushes till nothing is left of the victim but a skeleton. It was a luxury to Walpole to see a Scot dissect a Scot. ' They know each other's sore places better than we do.' The work, however, was not published. Referring to Macpherson's ' Ossian,' Walpole remarked, ' The Scotch seem to be proving that they are really descended from the Irish.' On the other hand, the ' Heroic Epistle to Sir William Chambers ' was being relished by satirical minds, and men were attributing it to Anstey and Soame Jenyns, and to Temple, Luttrell, and Horace Walpole, and pronouncing it wittier than the ' Dunciad,' and did not know that it was Mason's, and that it would not outlive Pope. Sir William Chambers found consolation in the fact that the satire, instead of damaging the volume it condemned, increased the sale of the book by full three hundred volumes. Walpole, of course, knew from the first that Mason was the author ; he worked hard in promoting its circulation, and gloried in its success. ' Whenever I was asked,' he writes, ' have you read " Sir John

Dalrymple ? " I replied, " Have *you* read the ' Heroic Epistle ' ? " The *Elephant* and *Ass* have become constellations, and ' *He has stolen the Earl of Denbigh's handkerchief,*' is the proverb in fashion. It is something surprising to find, at a time when authors are supposed to have been ill paid, Dr. Hawkesworth receiving, for putting together the narrative of Mr. Banks's voyage, one thousand pounds in advance from the traveller, and six thousand from the publishers, Strahan & Co. It really seems incredible, but this is stated to have been the fact.

Then, the drama of 1773 ! There was Home's ' Alonzo,' which, said Walpole, ' seems to be the story of David and Goliath, worse told than it would have been if Sternhold and Hopkins had put it to music ! ' But the town really awoke to a new sensation when Goldsmith's ' She Stoops to Conquer ' was produced on the stage, beginning a course in which it runs as freshly now as ever. Yet the hyper-fine people of a hundred years ago thought it rather vulgar. This was as absurd as the then existing prejudice in France, that it was vulgar and altogether wrong for a nobleman to write a book, or rather, to publish one ! There is nothing more curious than Walpole's drawing-room criticism of this exquisite and natural comedy. He calls it ' the lowest of all farces.' He condemns the execution of the subject, rather than the ' very

vulgar' subject itself. He could see in it neither
moral nor edification. He allows that the situations
are well managed, and make one laugh, in spite of
the alleged grossness of the dialogue, the forced
witticisms, and improbability of the whole plan and
conduct. But, he adds, ' what disgusts one most
is, that though the characters are very low, and
aim at low humour, not one of them says a sentence
that is natural, or that marks any character at all.
It is set up in opposition to sentimental comedy,
and is as bad as the worst of them.' Walpole's
supercilious censure reminds one of the company
and of the dancing bear, alluded to in the scene
over which Tony Lumpkin presides at the village
alehouse. ' I loves to hear the squire' (Lumpkin)
' sing, says one fellow, ' bekase he never gives us
anything that's low!' To which expression of
good taste, an equally *nice* fellow responds ; ' Oh,
damn anything that's low ! I can't bear it !' Whereupon, the philosophical Mister Muggins very truly
remarks : ' The genteel thing is the genteel thing
at any time, if so be that a gentleman bees in a
concatenation accordingly.' The humour cul-
minates in the rejoinder of the bear-ward : ' I like
the maxim of it, Master Muggins. What though
I'm obligated to dance a bear ? A man may be a
gentleman for all that. May this be my poison
if my bear ever dances but to the very genteelest
of tunes—" Water parted," or the minuet in

" Ariadne " ' All this is low, in one sense, but it is far more full of humour than of vulgarity. The comedy of nature killed the sentimental comedies, which, for the most part, were as good (or as bad) as sermons. They strutted or staggered with sentiments on stilts, and were duller than tables of uninteresting statistics.

Garrick, who would have nothing to do with Goldsmith's comedy except giving it a prologue, was ' in shadow ' this year. He improved ' Hamlet,' by leaving out the gravediggers ; and he swamped the theatre with the ' Portsmouth Review.' He went so far as to rewrite ' The Fair Quaker of Deal,' to the tune of ' Portsmouth and King George for ever ! ' not to mention a preface, in which the Earl of Sandwich, by name, is preferred to Drake, Blake, and all the admirals that ever existed ! If Walpole's criticisms are not always just, they are occasionally admirable for terseness and correctness alike. London, in 1773, was in raptures with the singing of Cecilia Davies. Walpole quaintly said that he did not love the perfection of what anybody can do, and he wished ' she had less top to her voice and more bottom.' How good too is his sketch of a male singer, who ' sprains his mouth with smiling on himself ! ' But to return to Garrick, and an illustration of social manners a century ago, we must not omit to mention that, at a private party at Beauclerk's, Garrick played the ' short-armed orator ' with Goldsmith ! The latter sat in Garrick's lap, concealing him, but with Garrick's arms advanced under Goldsmith's shoulders; the arms of the latter being held behind his back. Goldsmith then spoke a speech from 'Cato,' while Garrick's shortened arms supplied the action. The effect, of course, was ridiculous enough to excite laughter, as the action was often in absurd diversity from the utterance.

In the present newspaper record of births a man's wife is no longer called his ' lady ; ' a hundred years ago there was plentiful variety of epithet. ' The **Princess of** Mecklenburg-Strelitz, spouse to the Prince of that name, of a Princess,' is one form. ' **Earl Tyrconnel's lady of** a child,' is another. ' **Wife** ' was seldom used. One birth is announced in the following words: ' **The** Duchess of Chartres, **at Paris, of a Prince who has the** title of Duke of **Valois.'** Duke of **Valois? ay,** and subsequently Duke **of** Chartres, Duke of Orléans, finally, Louis Philippe, King **of the** French !

The chronicle of the marriages of the year seems to have been loosely kept, unless indeed parties announced themselves by being **married** twice over. There is, for example, a double chronicling of the marriage of the following personages: ' July 31st. The Right Hon. the Lady Amelia D'Arcy, daughter of the Earl of Holdernesse, to the Marquis of Carmarthen, son of his **Grace** the Duke of Leeds.'

Lady Amelia having thus married my Lord in July, we find, four months later, my Lord marrying Lady Amelia. 'Nov. 29th. The Marquis of Carmarthen to Lady Amelia D'Arcy, daughter of the Earl of Holdernesse.' This union, with its double chronology, was one of several which was followed by great scandal, and dissolved under circumstances of great disgrace. But the utmost scandal and disgrace attended the breaking up of the married life of Lord and Lady Carmarthen. This dismal domestic romance is told in contemporary pamphlets with a dramatic completeness of detail which is absolutely startling. Those who are fond of such details may consult these liberal authorities : we will only add that the above Lady Amelia D'Arcy, Marchioness of Carmarthen, became the wife of Captain Byron ; the daughter of that marriage was Augusta, now better known to us as Mrs. Leigh. Captain Byron's second wife was Miss Gordon, of Gight, and the son of that marriage was the poet Byron. How the names of the half-brother and half-sister have been cruelly conjoined, there is here no necessity of narrating. Let us turn to smaller people. Thus, we read of a curious way of endowing a bride, in the following marriage announcement : 'April 13th. Rev. Mr. Morgan, Rector of Alphamstow, York, to Miss Tindall, daughter of Mr. Tindall, late rector, who resigned in favour of his son-in-law.' In the same month, we meet with a better known couple

—'Mr. **Sheridan, of** the Temple, to the celebrated Miss Linley, of Bath.'

The deaths of the year included, of course, men of very opposite qualities. The man **of finest quality who went** the inevitable way was he whom **some** call the *good*, and some the *great* Lord Lyttel**ton.** When a man's designation rests on two such **distinctions, we** may take it for granted that he **was not** a common-place **man.** And yet how little remains of him in the **public** memory. His literary works are fossils; **but,** like fossils, **they** are not without **considerable value.** Good **as he** was, there **are not a few** people who jumble together **his and his son's** identity The latter was un**worthy of his sire.** He was a disreputable person **altogether.**

**Lord Chesterfield** was another of the individuals of note whose **glass ran out** during this year. He was always protesting that he cared nothing for death. Such persistence of protest generally arises from a feeling contrary to that which is made the sub**ject** of protest. **This lord** (as we have said) jested to **the** very **door of** his **tomb.** That must have reminded **his friends** during those Tyburn days, how **convicts on their** way **up** Holborn Hill to the gallows used **to veil their terror** by cutting jokes **with** the crowd. **It was the** very Chesterfield of highwaymen, who, going up the Hill in the fatal **cart,** and observing **the** mob to be hastening

onwards, cried out, ‘It’s no use your being in such
a hurry; there’ll be no fun till I get there!’  This
was the Chesterfield style, and its spirit also.  But
behind it all was the feeling and conviction of Marmontel’s philosopher, who having railed through a
long holiday excursion, till he was thoroughly tired,
was of opinion, as he tucked himself up in a feather-
bed at night, that life and luxury were, after all,
rather pretty things.

Chesterfield was, nevertheless, much more of a
man than his fellow peer who crossed the Stygian
ferry in the same year, namely, the Duke of
Kingston.  The duke had been one of the handsomest men of his time, and, like a good many
handsome men, was a considerable fool.  He
allowed himself, at all events, to be made the fool,
and to become the slave, of the famous Miss
Chudleigh—as audacious as she was beautiful.
The lady, whom the law took it into its head to
look upon as *not* the duke’s duchess—that is, not
his wife—was resigned to her great loss by the
feeling of her great gain.  She was familiar with
her lord’s last will and testament, and went into
hysterics to conceal her satisfaction.  She saw his
grace out of the world with infinite ceremony.  To
be sure, it was nothing else.  The physicians whom
she called together in consultation *consulted*, no
doubt, and then whispered to their lady friends,
while holding their delicate pulses, ‘Mere cere-

mony, upon my honour!' The widow kept the display of grief up to the last. When she brought the ducal corpse up from Bath to London, she rested often by the way. If she could have carried out her caprices, she would have had as many crosses to mark the ducal stations of death as were erected to commemorate the passing of Queen Eleanor. As this could not be, the widow took to screaming at every turn of the road, and at night was carried into her inn kicking her heels and screaming at the top of her voice.

Among the other deaths of the year 1773, the following are noteworthy. At Vienna, of a broken heart, from the miseries of his country, the brave Prince Poniatowski, brother to the King of Poland, and a general in the Austrian service, in which he had been greatly distinguished during the last war. The partition of Poland was then only a year old, and the echoes of the assertions of the lying Czar, Emperor, and King, that they never intended to lay a finger on that ancient kingdom, had hardly died out of the hearing of the astounded world. England is always trusting the words of Czars and their Khiva protestations, always learning and never coming to the knowledge of the truth. A name less known than Poniatowski may be cited for the singularity attached to it. 'Hale Hartson, Esq., the author of the "Countess of Salisbury" and other ingenious pieces—a young gentleman of fine parts, and who, though very young, had made the tour of Europe three times.' An indication of what a fashionable quarter Soho, with its neighbourhood, was in 1773, is furnished by the following announcement: 'Suddenly, at her house in Lisle Street, Leicester Fields, Lady Sophia Thomas, sister of the late Earl of Albemarle, and aunt of the present.' Foreign ambassadors then dwelt in Lisle Street. Even dukes had their houses in the same district; and baronets lived and died in Red Lion Square and in Cornhill. Among those baronets an eccentric individual turned up now and then. In the obituary is the name of Sir Robert Price, of whom it is added that 'he left his fortune to seven old bachelors in indigent circumstances.' The death of one individual is very curtly recorded; all the virtues under heaven would have been assigned to her, had she not belonged to a vanquished party. In that case she would have been a high and mighty princess; as it was, we only read, 'Lately, Lady Annabella Stuart, a relation of the late royal family, aged ninety-one years, at St.-Omer.' A few of us are better acquainted with the poet, John Cunningham, whose decease is thus quaintly chronicled: 'At Newcastle, the ingenious Mr. John Cunningham. A man little known, but that will be always much admired for his plaintive, tender, and natural pastoral poetry.' Some of the departed personages seem to have held strange appointments. Thus we find Alexander, Earl of Galloway, described as 'one of the lords of police;' and Willes, Bishop of Bath and Wells, who died in Hill Street when Mrs. Montague and her blue stockings were in their greatest brilliancy, is described as 'joint Decypherer (with his son, Edward Willes, Esq.) to the king.' We believe that the duty of decypherer consisted in reading letters that were opened, on suspicion, in their passage through the post-office. Occasionally a little page of family history is opened to us in a few words, as, for instance, in the account of Sir Robert Ladbroke, a rich City knight, whose name is attached to streets, roads, groves, and terraces in Notting Hill. After narrating his disposal of his wealth among his children and charities, the chronicler states that 'To his son George, who sailed a short time since to the West Indies, he has bequeathed three guineas a week during life, to be paid only to his own receipt.' One would like to know if this all but disinherited young fellow took heart of grace, and, after all, made his way creditably in the world. Such sons often succeed in life better than their brothers. Look around you *now*. See the sons born to inherit the colossal fortune which their father has built up. What brainless asses the most of them become! Had they been born to little instead of to over-much, their wits would

perhaps have been equal to their wants, and
they would have been as good men as their
fathers.

It was a son of misfortune, who, on a July
night of 1773, entered the *King's Head* at Enfield,
weary, hungry, penniless, and wearing the garb of
a clergyman. He was taken in, poor guest as he
was, and in the hospitable inn he died within a few
days. It was then discovered that he was the Rev
Samuel Bickley. In his pockets were found three
manuscript sermons, and an extraordinary petition
to the Archbishop of Canterbury, dated the previous February. The prayer of the petition was
to this effect : 'Your petitioner, therefore, most
humbly prays, that if an audience from your
Grace should be deemed too great a favour, you
will at least grant him some relief, though it be
only a temporary one, in our deplorable necessity
and distress ; and,' said the petitioner with a simplicity or an impudence which may have accounted
for his condition, 'let your Grace's charity cover
the multitude of his sins.' He then continues :
'There never yet was anyone in England doomed
to starve ; but I am nearly, if not altogether so ;
denied to exercise the sacred functions wherein I
was educated, driven from the doors of the rich
laymen to the clergy for relief; by the clergy,
denied ; so that I may justly take up the speech of
the Gospel Prodigal, and say : ' How many hired

servants of my father have bread enough and to spare, while I perish with hunger!' Here was, possibly, an heir of great expectations, who, scholar as he was, had come to grief, while, only a little while before him, there died a fortunate impostor, as appears from this record : 'Mr. Colvill, in Old Street, aged 83. He was much resorted to as a fortune-teller, by which he acquired upwards of 4,000*l*. ; ' at the same time, a man in London was quintupling that sum by the invention and sale of peppermint lozenges.

Let us look into the newspapers for January 1773, that our readers may compare the events of that month with January 1873, a hundred years later. We find the laureate Whitehead's official New Year Ode sung at court to Boyce's music, while king, queen, courtiers and guests yawned at the vocal dulness, and were glad when it was all over. We enter a church and listen to a clergyman preaching a sermon ; on the following day we see the reverend gentleman drilling with other recruits belonging to a regiment of the Guards, into which he had enlisted. The vice of gambling was ruining hundreds in London, the suburbs of which were infested by highwaymen, who made a very pretty living of it—staking only their lives. We go to the fashionable noon-day walk in the Temple Gardens, and encounter an eccentric promenader who is thus described : ' He

wore an old black waistcoat which was quite
threadbare, breeches of the same colour and com-
plexion; a black stocking on one leg, a whitish
one on the other; a little hat with a large gold
button and loop, and a tail, or rather club, as thick
as a lusty man's arm, powdered almost an inch
thick, and under the club a quantity of hair re-
sembling a horse's tail. In this dress he walked
and mixed with the company there for a considerable time, and occasioned no little diversion.' The
style of head-decoration then patronised by the
ladies was quite as nasty and offensive as that
which was in vogue about ten years ago. It was
ridiculed in the popular pantomime 'Harlequin
Sorcerer.' Columbine was to be seen in her dressing-room attended by her lover, a macaroni, and a
hairdresser. On her head was a very high tower
of hair, to get at which was impossible for the
*friseur* till Harlequin's wand caused a ladder to
rise, on the top rung of which the *coiffeur* was
raised to the top surface of Columbine's chignon;
having dressed which they all set off for the
Pantheon. While pantomime was thus triumphant
at Covent Garden there was something like cavalry
battles close to London; that is to say, engage-
ments between mounted smugglers and troops of
Scots Greys. The village Tooting in this month
was a scene of a fight, in which both parties shot
and cut down antagonists with as much alacrity as

if they were foreign invaders, where blood, and a good deal of it, was lavishly spilt. Sussex was a favourite battle-field; a vast quantity of tea and brandy, and other contraband, was drunk in Middlesex and neighbouring counties where there was sympathy for smugglers, who set their lives on a venture and enabled people to purchase articles duty free.

At this time the union of Ireland with the other portions of the British kingdom was being actively agitated. The project was that each of the thirty-two Irish counties should send one representative to the British Parliament. Forty-eight Irish Peers were to be transferred to the English Upper House. One very remarkable feature in the supposed government project was, that Ireland should retain the shadow of a parliament, to be called 'The Great Council of the Nation.' The Great Council was to consist of members sent by the Irish boroughs, each borough to send one representative, 'their power not to apply further than the interior policy of the kingdom.' The courts of law were to remain undisturbed. It will be remembered that something like the above council is now asked for by those who advocate Home Rule; but as some of those advocates only wish to have the council as the means to a further end, the Irish professional patriot now, as ever, stands in the way to the real improvement and the permanent prosperity of that part of the kingdom.

In many other respects the incidents of to-day are like the echoes of the events a hundred years old. We find human nature much the same, but a trifle coarser in expression. The struggle to live, then as now, took the guise of the struggle of a beaten army, retreating over a narrow and dangerous bridge, where each thought only of himself, and the stronger trampled down the weaker or pushed him over into the raging flood. With all this, blessed charity was not altogether wanting. Then, as in the present day, charity appeared on the track of the struggle, and helped many a fainting heart to achieve a success, the idea of which they had given up in despair.

END OF VOL. I.

LONDON: PRINTED BY
SPOTTISWOODE AND CO., NEW-STREET SQUARE
AND PARLIAMENT STREET

S.

9 783337 250744